The Author of Dead Men

THE
AUTHOR OF
DEAD MEN

DENNIS M. BANAHAN

Memorial Park Publishing, LLC

Dedicated to my sister, my dadisto,

Alice White

January 29, 1934 – July 17, 2012

ACKNOWLEDGMENTS

I would like to thank several of my friends for allowing me to use their names, and assisting me with the research for this book, although the characterizations and situations are purely fictional.

Father Thomas Nangle, retired Chicago Police Department Catholic chaplain, not only for his friendship, but also for his lifelong dedication to the men and women of the Chicago Police Department, and their families in time of tragedy.

My friend and internationally acclaimed author, Charlie Newton, for not only allowing me to use his name in this book but for his constant guidance along the way.

Dina Bernichio – My friend of some forty-five years is in the medical field, not the legal profession, but I'm sure if she were she would have made a great prosecutor.

Donna Adams – retired CPD officer and owner of Donna's CafeChicago. Ranger up!

Sgt. Bill Peak -retired from the job with the same enthusiasm he came on with.

Sgt. Ken Abels – retired CPD, and my lifelong friend.

Curt Scherr – retired CPD Bomb and Arson specialist.

Sgt. Tom Martin – retired CPD and the most dedicated policeman whoever wore a badge.

Jimmie Daniels – Retired SAC Norfolk & Southern Railway Police.

A special shout-out to my nephew, Barney Brannigan, his beautiful wife, Kim, and Freddie Brannigan, the Morkie from hell. Barney provided me with the theme for the book and all research on the Mercantile Exchange.

Though, not mentioned by name in the book, I would like to thank my friend and author, James D. Keating, for his inspiration, advice, and being my most loyal supporter.

And, I would be remiss if I didn't seize this opportunity to thank my editor, Laura Stoffel, for her outstanding editorial skills, and my publisher, Memorial Park Publishing LLC

CHAPTER 1

Lifeless forms on gurneys, strewn about haphazardly in the deserted basement of the old Cook County Morgue on Polk Street, stare up at me imploringly with dead, leaden eyes at half-mast. Pools of blood coagulate under misshapen heads like spilled jelly; human bodies ripped open like mini-boxes of Post-Toasties; mutilations, eviscerations, gunshot wounds, mechanical strangulations—they're all here; all so different yet all the same. They come to me at night—they always come to me at night. Like a voyeur, I pick through the labyrinth of cold steel beds and gawk into empty body cavities, the unmistakable, rancid stench of putrefying flesh gags me. I light up a cigar, cup it in my hands, and suck the pungent smoke through my nostrils to mask the odor. It's eerily quiet. My footsteps reverberate in the hollow chamber. So many people I have to talk to, or should have talked to, but I can't remember any of their names now for some reason; they're all jumbled up in my brain. Undistinguishable faces, cloaked in a thick veil of fog, peep out at me from darkened doorways. Am I in

1

London? I'm confused. A voice from the Rose Room, the meat locker where bodies in advanced stages of decomposition are kept, whispers my name. I want to investigate, but my feet refuse to move in that direction. I'm ashamed anyone will find out I'm afraid. I must maintain my game face. I try to draw my gun but it weighs in my holster like a ship's anchor. At long last, I find my legs and the courage to move forward. I inch toward the entrance of the Rose Room with great trepidation. I'm trembling, inside and out. I need Father Nangle, the department chaplain, but I'm uncertain why; is it to absolve me of all my sins or to give me the last rites? I try my gun again, but the goddamn thing won't come out of my holster. Be a man, I tell myself. You can't be a gunfighter if you're afraid to die. Taking a deep breath, I pivot empty-handed into the doorway of the Rose Room to confront the destiny that awaits me. Someone, or something, with a foul smell whirs past me, and the hairs on my neck bristle. It's Michael Jackson! It's Michael fucking Jackson! He begins singing, "Thriller," and all of the corpses, even the infants, leap off of their gurneys and start dancing grotesquely like wooden puppets out of sync. I'm in a video! Thank you, Jesus, I cry, this is only a video! None of it is real! The elation lasts but a moment, and then an onslaught of tears begins running down my face as I stare into the vacuum of cold, vacant eyes and gray waxen faces, and I realize I know all the dancers. Sweet Mother of Jesus, I know all of the dancers.

• • •

My Blackberry vibrated and skittered across the lamp table next to my bed. The perspiration-soaked bed-sheet felt like a handkerchief from an Irish funeral. I groped in the dark, knocking an ashtray with a half-dozen panetela butts onto the salmon-colored carpeting.

Propping myself up onto one elbow, I growled into the phone, "Whoever this is, it better be good."

"Lieutenant, this is Sergeant Peak. I'm sorry to call so late but we had a triple in Avalon Trails a few hours ago. Possibly drug related."

"So what?" I moaned, "Aren't they still going to be dead when I get into the office in the morning, Bill?"

"Yes, sir, I'm sure they will be, but I thought you'd want to be notified on this one right away. We recovered a rental car on the scene. A guy named Charlie Newton rented it. Isn't that your writer-friend?"

That got my attention. I bolted upright, swung my legs out of the bed, and ground the panetelas into the carpeting. "Charlie Newton?"

"Yes, sir. We lifted one set of prints from the inside of a Corvette parked in the driveway and one set of prints from inside the house. They both belong to him."

"Are you sure it's *my* Charlie Newton?" I asked, "That's not too uncommon a name."

"Rental agency said the renter gave a home address in South Africa. Isn't that where your friend lives?"

"That would be Charlie's white ass, the *Afrikan* American. And he's not there?"

"No, he's in the wind."

"I'm going to throw some clothes on and I'll be in the Area in a half hour or so."

"Lieutenant, one other thing. We got Newton's rap

sheet back. Did you know he was arrested for a felony possession of marijuana in the early 80s?"

"No, Bill, I didn't. What is that supposed to mean?"

"Nothing, just that this might be drug related."

"I don't routinely run background checks on my friends. Charlie may have failed to mention it to me because it was thirty years ago. You were running name checks on Burt and Ernie around then, weren't you?"

I hung up before he could answer. Blurry eyes glanced at the clock: 0345 hours! Stumbling to my feet, I muttered, "Oh, my achin' ass!" I stepped on the fallen ashtray, punted it across the room, almost breaking two of my toes, and fired up the first of many panetelas.

I gimped hurriedly to the bathroom and braced for a cold shower. While showering, my thoughts went back a dozen years to when I first met Charlie. A retired copper-turned-writer friend of mine asked me if I could give Charlie technical advice on murder investigations for a police novel he was writing, his first. I would have said no because I'm famous for not getting along well with non-police persons, but the retired copper was a good friend of mine so I consented. Right then, I wished I hadn't.

Charlie sent me an email later that night and told me he'd be taking the Metra from Rosemont into Union Station the next morning. It was scheduled to arrive at noon and asked where he should meet me. I told him I'd pick him up at the train station and he provided me with a vague description of himself. The next day at noon, I parked in the tow zone at Jackson and Canal across the street from the Chicago River and entered the vast, cavernous twentieth-century architectural wonder of Daniel Burnham through an ornate entrance off of Canal Street. A confluence of the world's ethnicities scurried about, babbling and bumping into each other, reminding me of cockroaches when the lights go on. Some looked lost, others in awe of the grandiose structure. Shuffling feet and disjointed, muffled conversations made a constant humming sound, like a drone of bees. Refracted rays shone through the vaulted skylight and illuminated a character right off of the pages of an Elmore Leonard novel, languidly propped up against an immense white support column in front of one of the two grand staircases. He was near 6'4", raw-boned, and wore a felt pea-green porkpie hat, which lent another four inches to his height. A brown suede bomber jacket was draped across a long, sinewy left arm and a pair of Ben Franklins rested on the tip of his nose. He was reading a scratch sheet.

I made him for a track rat; that was my first impression, a guy that hangs around the two-dollar window and tells you out of the corner of his mouth he's got a tip on a horse in the fifth. Maybe even an ex-pug, but a novelist, no.

As I approached, arctic-blue eyes narrowed speculatively over the top of his cheaters. He shot me an obligatory smile and ambled toward me.

"Lt. Cahill, I presume?" he asked, extending a large, banged-up right hand, which enveloped mine.

"That would be me," I responded.

Charlie smiled. "I appreciate your assistance on this manuscript. I hope it won't be too much of an inconvenience, but I am metempirical in the field of homicide investigations."

A cultured, well-educated voice belied the tough-guy

outer shell he projected. I would be more likely to run into this guy giving a lecture at Northwestern than at Arlington's two-dollar window.

"Metempirical?" I repeated, "I'll have to get back to you later on that one when I figure out what the fuck you said."

Charlie blinked, stroked his grizzled goatee, and drilled me with those deliberate blue eyes. A pervasive, pregnant pause hung in the air. He didn't know how to take the gibe. Worse yet, I didn't know how to take him. I tucked my chin into my shoulder in the event he decided I wasn't as cute as I thought I was, and responded with a left hook to the jaw. He looked big enough and strong enough to cause some damage. At last, a wicked grin crossed his face and he asked, "You must be from the Southside?"

A fellow ball-buster. I retorted, "Yeah, and judging from your vocabulary, you must be one of those anal retentive assholes from the Northside?"

Charlie caught on quick, and his grin stretched into a smile. He enjoyed the repartee, not a response I get often. Most people don't understand, or appreciate, my wry sense of humor; in fact, almost nobody does.

"I'm staying at the Marriott downtown," Charlie said as we threaded our way through the crowd toward the exit. "Can we meet for dinner or drinks later?" he asked.

"It depends on what's going on at work. I don't work for the FBI; this isn't a nine to five job," I said. "I'll give you a call at the Marriott when I'm free, and we'll set something up."

"Great. Where can I catch a cab?" Charlie asked.

"I'll give you a ride to the Marriott."

When we exited on Canal Street, Gorilla Mae in a meter maid's uniform was issuing a parking ticket on my squad car.

I trotted toward her and hollered, "Hey, that's a police car." She continued writing the citation.

I was out of breath when I reached her, and repeated, "That's a Chicago Police Department squad car."

"I don't give a fuck. You above all people should know better than to park illegally." She handed me the citation and I watched as the wildebeest waddled down the street to the next car. I was still watching when Charlie caught up to me.

"If that ass-teroid hits Lake Michigan we'll have to cancel the St. Patrick's Day Parade because of the ensuing tsunami," I said as I turned to Charlie. "You see the police are held in high esteem in this city?"

Charlie laughed. "I see that."

We got into the squad car, I tossed the ticket on the dashboard as Charlie fumbled with his seat belt, and we pulled away.

"Do you want to play with the siren?" I asked.

Charlie disregarded the taunt and laid a copy of his manuscript on the front seat between us.

"Perhaps when you have time, you could read this. Any suggestions or criticisms are welcome," he said.

Fifteen minutes later, I dropped him off in front of the Marriott.

Charlie stepped out of the car on Michigan Avenue and snatched his porkpie hat with catlike reflexes, as a gust of wind off of Lake Michigan tried to relocate it somewhere along the Magnificent Mile.

I shouted out the door, "You should have let it go."

Charlie bent over and leaned back into the car, still smashing his hat to his head. "You don't like my hat?" he asked.

"I love it. I wish you had two of them. One to shit in and one to cover it up with."

• • •

Madison Avenue, Shitcago's Mason-Dixon Line, which separated the Northside from the Southside, soon faded, and Charlie and I became fast friends. I taught him all the four-letter words I know and he taught me all the words he knows with five-letters or more, or at least some of them. I soon learned Charlie was a quick study. He absorbed information like a sanitary napkin, committed it to memory, and never forgot it again. He wanted to know the minutia of all things police: What color of ink do police use in their pens? Was the floor tile the same color in all police Area headquarters? He pounded me with thousands of questions on police nuances, jargon and forensics. He was sucking my brain dry, not that it was overflowing with knowledge to begin with. By the time Charlie finished his fourth manuscript, he knew more about police policies and procedures than the superintendent.

Charlie's research, I learned around his fourth novel, took him to places I wouldn't care to travel without the security of my Browning and a back-up unit. While researching book #2, for instance, Charlie hired a speedboat in Key West, Florida; under the cover of darkness, he took a seven-hour boat ride across the shark-infested Straits of Florida into Havana, Cuba. Who in their right mind would want to do that? I asked him if he didn't become wary when he noticed all the other boats were going the other way! But Charlie didn't want to be a voyeur; if he was going to write about it, he wanted to see it, hear it, taste it, smell it, and feel it before he wrote it. He'd eat shit if you told him it was the local cuisine.

• • •

I felt like I was living in a dome home in Nome, an igloo, when I stepped out of the shower. The house was cold. Shivering uncontrollably and clenching my teeth, I wrapped a white monogrammed towel around my waist, and hot-trotted to the automatic thermostat on the wall off of my bedroom, dripping water like a duck all the way. The thermostat is programmed to lower the heat four degrees between the hours of 10:00 PM and 6:00 AM, the comfort range when you're snuggled under the covers in a nice warm bed, but not so comfortable if you're taking a shower. When I read the outside temperature, I tapped a few times on the thermostat, hoping it was stuck. It said the outside temperature was −16°. I kicked the thermostat up to 80°. My teeth stopped chattering about five minutes after I dried off, and I once again had feeling in my scrotum. I hung the wet "His" monogrammed towel back on the rack, next to where the towel that read "Hers" used to be, but it had been gone for eighteen months. I snatched a blue pinstripe suit off the hanger and grabbed a pair of black Florsheims from the floor of the closet. I would forego the camel hair overcoat this morning in lieu of my bright-orange North Face parka with the coyote-trimmed hood and a neon-orange woolen watch cap. Not conservative business attire, but certainly more practical, and if somebody shot me he couldn't later claim he thought I was a deer. Fumbling with the laces on my shoes, I cursed under my breath and started over. I don't do mornings well even under the best of circumstances, in the nicest weather, and this was neither of them. I wrapped a Windsor on a silk red, white, and blue regimental-striped tie and hurried for the garage. A blast of frigid air hit me in the face when I opened the door, and I pulled the watch cap lower over my ears.

In spite of Charlie's Northside eccentricities, idiosyncrasies, and out-and-out quirks, he wasn't a murderer. I was sure of that. The gravity of the situation suddenly hit me in the head like a wrecking ball; Charlie was either an offender, or Charlie was a victim, one or the other, but no matter how you tossed the coin, Charlie was in deep shit.

CHAPTER 2

January 6, 2014
Monday
0445 hours

I entered Area South Headquarters at 0445 hours. A uniformed officer was holding three reporters at bay by the stairway leading up to the homicide offices.

In general, I don't like the media. I knew one of the three reporters, and I didn't like him in particular. He was a douche bag. Last year, he crashed my office, waving a Xerox copy of a Department General Order in my face, which mandates police cooperate with the media. It seemed two detectives had refused to give him information on an ongoing homicide investigation. Without further ado, I grabbed him by the scruff of his neck and the ass of his pants and launched him down the stairs. I said something cute as he took flight like, "The public washrooms are on the first floor, and you can wipe your fat ass with the General Order."

When I read about it the next morning in the Scum-Times, it didn't seem nearly as funny. The big brass didn't think so either. They weren't happy, but they weren't surprised. I'm asshole intolerant. They know that and they forgave me—in time. I hadn't seen the reporter since that incident. I don't know what prompted him to return, especially on such a frigid night. Maybe he saw the error of his ways, or maybe he thought I forgot him. But I never forget a douche bag. I'll bet he doesn't crash my office this morning, though, and jam a directive in my face.

"Lieutenant, is there anything you can give us on the triple homicide investigation from Avalon Trails?" the youngest of the three reporters asked. He looked to be about twelve years old, and his voice sounded as if his gonads have not yet activated. I must be getting old. I asked him if he was wearing a varsity sweater under his coat, and he puffed up like a rooster but didn't respond.

"Gentlemen, as you can see, I'm just walking in the door. As soon as I'm brought up to date on the investigation, I'll give you what I can"—looking over at douche bag, I continued—"that doesn't impede a murder investigation." Douche sneered.

To the uninitiated or the unfamiliar, they might expect the homicide offices to be abuzz with activity, a maelstrom of chaos with a triple homicide investigation and two unrelated shooting investigations being juggled simultaneously; phones ringing, people shouting, detectives cursing, bad guys hooked up to the wall screaming for their lawyers. That's how it always is on TV, but at 0445 hours, there was more noise and activity going on at the Medical Examiner's Office than there was in Area South. Two dicks from the dogwatch sat quietly at their desks, pecking away on supplementary reports. Another detective led a handcuffed punk rocker out of an Interview Room. She had rings in her nose, eyes, ears, and lips, with a Mohawk haircut dyed blue, yellow, and orange. I asked her as she was passing by if her father had fucked a parrot. She was still screaming epithets at me, something about my mother, when I entered the sergeant's office, the anteroom outside of mine. Sgt. Peak was reading a homicide file and sipping coffee. The rest of the floor was unoccupied, and after Polly Parrot's invective outburst subsided, it was library quiet once again.

"I'm sorry I was short with you earlier on the phone. I'm a miserable bitch this time of day," I said.

"With all due respect, Lieutenant, you're a miserable bitch any time of day. If it will ease your conscience any, we're all used to it."

"What do we have on the triple?" I asked.

"Unlikely trio to take a dirt nap together. They each took two shots; one to various parts of the body, and the second shot to each was a coup de grâce to the right temple, stippling on the entrance wounds of all three. Shaughnessy recovered two spent out of the floor; they look like a 9mm, but no casings were found. He doesn't know if they'll be suitable for comparison, but the M.E. should be able to dig a few more out of the victims. The owner of the house, forever more known as victim #1, is Hiram Goldenstein. He was a commodity broker at the Mercantile Exchange and, judging from the house and the new Benz in the garage, did well for himself. Victim #2, Jerry Doherty, looks like a long time heroin user and a burnout. Tracks running up and down both arms like the Norfolk and Southern.

He's the only one with a criminal history. According to his rap sheet, he's been cracked four times for Possession of a Controlled Substance. And Victim #3, Chiang Yu, was Asian from the Province of Yunnan, according to a passport we found on his person, wherever the hell that is. We don't have a connection between any of the three of them yet. Shaughnessy and Zemaitis are still out beating the bush for your friend, Charlie Newton."

"I've known Charlie a long time. He's not our offender", I said.

"If he's not our offender, and he's not wearing a toe tag, where is he?" Sgt. Peak asked.

"If I knew that, I wouldn't be here now."

"Any ideas where he might be if he's not a victim?"

"No. None," I said. "Charlie doesn't even have a permanent address in the U.S. He's a nomad. In the last two years, he's lived in South Africa, Laos, Ireland, Scotland, and, most recently, Germany."

"Any chance he's on his way back to one of those countries, one that doesn't have an extradition treaty with the U.S.?"

"Trust me, Charlie's not a candidate for this year's Darwin awards. If he capped these three dudes, he wouldn't leave his rental car and his fingerprints all over. Besides, he wouldn't leave without calling me to bust my balls."

"Lieutenant, do you think a guy in his right mind who just committed a triple homicide would call the police lieutenant in charge of the investigation?"

"Charlie would," I said, "You'd have to know him to understand. He couldn't resist the opportunity to throw me a parting shot like, 'Ta-ta, Devlin lad, good luck in your pursuit of lawbreakers.'"

I moseyed over to the coffee machine and poured a cup of 10W-30 into my mug.

"How's the coffee?" Peak grinned.

"Just the right viscosity. How long has it been sitting there?" I asked.

"Six hours would be a conservative estimate."

● ● ●

"Lieu, I got Shaughnessy on the line. They're at the Congress Hotel downtown. They said that's where Newton was staying, but there's no sign of him there."

"Tell them to standby. I'm on my way."

CHAPTER 3

January 6, 2014
Monday
0545 hours

I pushed the brass rail on the revolving glass door of the Pick-Congress and entered into the opulence and grandeur of a bygone era. An elderly doorman with a ruddy complexion shrugged his shoulders and quivered under the scarlet-caped, heavy wool overcoat to gather warmth. He doffed the brim of the matching military-style cap, and smiled wide. "Tis a bit brisk out there this morning, sir," he said, blowing hot air into his hands and rubbing them together.

"My nut-sack is frozen to my thighs," I replied, and we both laughed.

· · ·

I stood thirty feet below the high ornamental ceiling and scanned the lobby. A long column of over-stuffed red velvet sofas and occasional chairs were set up into conversational groupings to my right. John Patrick Shaughnessy lounged comfortably on one of the sofas, legs crossed, blowing smoke rings into the air. He spotted me coming and rose to his feet.

• • •

"Working hard?" I asked.

"This job isn't as easy as everybody thinks," he said, and blew two more smoke rings into the air for emphasis.

"Where's Zemaitis?" I asked.

"He's still up in Newton's suite waiting for you and the crime lab to arrive."

"He isn't stealing any of Charlie's shit, is he?"

"Not that I know of. I don't think Newton left much up there to steal."

• • •

Shaughnessy and Zemaitis were the perfect marriage for a homicide team: Shaughnessy, the bloodhound; Zemaitis, the attack dog. We strolled across the plush carpeting to a bank of elevators and I pushed the pearl up-button. A moment later, the elevator doors opened with an almost inaudible swoosh. Shaughnessy informed me on the ride up to the Lakeview Suite that he and Zemaitis had already given the room a thorough toss.

"Who reported the murders?" I asked.

Shaughnessy flipped open his leather pad holder and read from the notes on a sheet of legal-sized yellow paper.

"Brannigan, Bernard. A colleague of Goldenstein's from the Merc. They were planning a golfing trip this weekend in Florida. Brannigan called him four times throughout the evening to firm up their plans and left messages on his answering machine. When Goldenstein didn't respond, he loaded up his dog, Fred, and took a ride over there. Saw Newton's car in the driveway and figured Goldenstein had company. He rang the bell a few times, didn't get any answer, so he looked through the window and there they were."

"Do you think he's legit?" I asked.

"Yeah, he was shaken up. I checked Goldenstein's answering machine and caller ID, too. Four calls on there from Brannigan's home phone, all close together, and he lives in Darien. He wouldn't have had time to drive here, whack them, and drive back home between calls."

"What time did he find the bodies?" I asked.

"About 2330. The call came into 911 at 2333. We got here at midnight, and rigor was already present in the jaws and upper torso of the bodies, so I'm guessing they were dead five or six hours when we got here."

"Brannigan know anything about the other two guys?"

"Nope, said he doesn't know them and never heard of them."

I rapped lightly on the door of Charlie's room. Zemaitis called out from within, "Room service?"

"Yeah, I have something for you to eat. Open the door," I replied.

Nothing was amiss in the room. No blood, no sign of a struggle. Charlie's clothes were hung neatly in the closet. A few baseball caps and a porkpie hat were on the top shelf, and several pairs of shoes were lined up on the floor next to one empty suitcase stowed in the corner of the closet. Charlie's Apple MacBook Pro was charging on a nightstand next to the bed. He wouldn't leave his computer behind even if he were fleeing the country.

Shaughnessy wandered over to the window and peered out. "Did you check out the view? You can see Buckingham Fountain. I'll bet it's beautiful in the summer."

"I'll have to come back in the summer to check it out. When the lab gets here, have them throw some powder around and see if we can lift some prints out of here other than Charlie's. I want the rental car crazy glued for prints, too."

"Ten-fo," Zemaitis replied.

"Take the laptop, let's see what's on there," I said. "Charlie will accuse me of plagiarism when we find him, but I'll cross that bridge later. Check with the hotel staff to see if anybody saw Charlie coming in or going out and if he was with anybody. Also check to see if he had any incoming or outgoing calls."

"With all due respect, Lieutenant, this isn't our first homicide investigation," Zemaitis began. "We already checked with the on-duty staff, including the doorman, the bellboys, and the front desk. Nobody seems to remember him. We checked the hotel phone records, too. No calls, in or out, which isn't surprising if he has a cell phone. We also took it upon ourselves to call for the Crime Lab to come out and process the room, and, believe it or not, I was going to tell them to dust for prints and crazy glue the car."

I realized how my instructions to two veteran homicide detectives could sound demeaning, like Homicide 101, and I apologized. I told them I was, more or less, thinking out loud. John Patrick Shaughnessy had more time in homicide than I had on the job.

"Have a crew from days and a crew from afternoons come back and check with the other respective shifts."

"Sgt. Peak told us that this guy is a friend of your's," Shaughnessy said. "Is it possible his cell phone number is on *your* caller ID?"

"It was until recently. He switched to one of those 4G phones with a new provider and got a new number. He hasn't called me since changing phones."

"I'm sure we'll come up with it," Shaughnessy said.

"It's a new phone, so it probably has a GPS tracking device on it. As soon as you come up with a number, put a track on it; let's see if we can get a location." Zemaitis rolled his eyes.

The Crime Lab showed up a few minutes later, dusted the room and the laptop for prints, and took a few photos. Not much of a scene to process.

I asked one of the techs if they had any computer geeks at the lab that could open up the computer to see what was on there. He said they had a couple of computer wizards and inventoried the laptop.

Zemaitis told the tech, "If you find any photos of our lieutenant engaged in any unnatural sex acts, delete them."

• • •

The two Johns and I walked out of the Pick-Congress together. I stopped outside the revolving door entrance and fumbled around for my Dutch Masters. A whirling mass of arctic air swept across Lake Michigan and whistled through the naked branches of the trees across the street in Grant Park, numbing me to the bone. I turned my back to the wind and cupped purple hands around the Zippo as much for warmth as to light the cigar.

I turned toward Shaughnessy and Zemaitis and shouted over the hiss of tires crawling over wet pavement and the vortex of a howling wind, "I know it's not looking good for my friend Charlie Newton right now, but believe me, he's not our offender."

Shaughnessy and Zemaitis didn't comment. Shaughnessy's eyes watered, and his glasses iced up. Both of their noses glowed bright red and reminded me of big, old-fashioned Christmas tree lights.

Shaughnessy continued to focus on wiping the moisture off his glasses with a handkerchief, avoided eye contact with me, and said, "I hope not, Lieu, but if my mother murdered three people, you know I'd lock her up, right?" He dabbed at his runny nose with the handkerchief and returned it to his back pocket.

"I wouldn't expect any less, John," I assured him. "I ask only that you keep an open mind."

A yellow cab idled in the taxi-parking lane outside the Congress. The Mideastern driver had been eyeballing us hard for the last several minutes, hoping to snag a fare. Finally, leaning across the front seat, he shouted angrily out the window, "You want the cab or no?" Zemaitis hollered back, "Go buy a Dunkin' Donuts, you goat-fucker." The cabbie held up his society finger, and on that note, we left.

CHAPTER 4

January 6, 2014
Monday
0645 hours

I stopped by the crime scene on the way into Area Headquarters. Avalon Trails is a bedroom community nestled within the Hegewisch neighborhood located on Chicago's far southeast side. Most of the residents are white city workers and live in moderately priced brick ranches with well-manicured lawns and detached garages. Other than teens drinking in the park, crime is virtually non-existent. This was the second time I had a case there in fifteen years, and the first one was a suicide so that didn't count.

I pulled up in front of an immense, rustic Tudor mansion with yellow herringbone brickwork and tall, mullioned windows, inconsonant amidst the humble homes of Avalon Trails, and got out. The house sits on the back of what must be three city lots. Crime scene tape was strung across the front doors.

I toddled up the icy walkway, ducked under the yellow tape, and tried the front doors. They were locked. I strolled around the perimeter of the house, peering through windows, but there wasn't much to see other than Mr. Goldenstein's lavish taste in furnishings. I expected no less, given the layout of this joint. I don't know what the hell I expected to see or find there. The dicks were gone, the lab was gone, the bodies were gone, and the house was locked up. Medical Examiner seals were affixed to both the front and rear doors. Maybe I was expecting Charlie to come sliding down one of the seven gables or climb out one of the two tall chimneys. Nothing there for me to search. Confucius said, "The hardest thing of all is to find a black cat in a dark room, especially when there is no black cat."

I returned to the squad car and headed back into the office. Dawn broke and the early morning commuters trickled onto streets and roadways, belching carbon monoxide as they scuttled toward the Dan Ryan Expressway in a race to beat the morning rush hour downtown. In a half hour, the Ryan would be in a state of complete inertia. Shaughnessy and Zemaitis should have been well into their supp by the time I got back to the Area. We'd put our heads together and see what we had so far and where we'd go from there.

• • •

When I got back to Area South Headquarters, the reporters were still waiting. They converged on me like crackheads on a pipe.

Harry Potter chirped first.

"Lieutenant, you said you'd give us something after you were brought up to date?"

"Gentlemen, all I can tell you at this time is that we have three confirmed homicide victims from Avalon Trails. I can tell you the victims were shot and that the motive is unknown at this time."

"Is it true that a rented vehicle from the scene was impounded?" the douche bag asked.

"Yes, that's true. The lab is in the process of examining it as we speak."

"Is it true that the vehicle was registered to crime novelist, Charlie Newton?" asked the douche bag again.

"No, the vehicle is registered to a rental agency, and Charlie Newton leased it."

"Do the police know Charlie Newton's whereabouts?" asked the douche.

"No, not at this time."

The third reporter shouldered his way past the other two and managed to slip in a question.

"Is Charlie Newton a suspect, Lieutenant?"

"Mr. Newton is someone we have to talk to but we have no suspects at this point."

"Is it fair to say Mr. Newton is a person of interest?"

"Yes, that would be fair to say."

The douche bag looked like he rolled out of bed in his rumpled khakis and baggy sweatshirt. He stepped in front of the other two reporters and glared at me.

"Lieutenant, is it true that you and Mr. Newton are friends?"

God, he was an annoying fucker! I didn't know where he got his information from so fast, but I had to give the devil his due; he was good. I don't think it was the question that angered me as much as it was the person who was asking it. I'm sure the other reporters saw it in my face, too. I fought the urge not to reach out, grab the douche bag by the throat, and make him do the chicken, but I managed to maintain my composure.

"Yes, Mr. Newton and I are friends."

I turned to go up the stairs, but the douche bag stepped in front of me, blocking my path. He was now within inches of my grasp and I found myself focused on his throat like a cat on a bird. This must be the temptation Adam felt before he bit into the apple.

"I assume, Lieutenant, you are going to recuse yourself from this investigation?"

"Mr. Douche Bag, you know the old saying, 'When you assume, you make an ass out of "u" and … in this case … just "u."'"

I brushed him aside with a forearm and climbed the stairs to the homicide offices. The veins in my head were pulsating steel cables. I wanted to strangle the plump irritating bastard, but I knew if I did, I'd be reading about it the next day in the paper. I didn't want to give him fodder for his rag. The douche bag was living proof the pen is mightier than the Browning 9mm.

CHAPTER 5

January 6, 2014
Monday
0720 hours

Shaughnessy and Zemaitis were seated at Zemaitis's desk, still on the format of their supp. Zemaitis had an unlit Lucky dangling out the corner of his mouth, hammering away at the keyboard with two lightning-fast index fingers. Despite his speed, he hadn't adapted well to modern technology, punishing the keys with every stroke, like he was still banging away on an old manual Olivetti—old habits die hard. Shaughnessy shouldered up next to him, leaning across the desk with his head cocked back, straining through the half-glasses on the tip of his nose to see the words as they appeared on the monitor. Both men had ties pulled down and shirtsleeves rolled up. Two Styrofoam cups of midnight oil sat on the desk beside them. They had been working since 1700 hours the previous afternoon and were going into their seventeenth hour.

"Anything?" I asked.

Zemaitis continued hammering away at the keys. Shaughnessy responded. "Lab called back. They crazy glued the car. No prints other than Newton's."

Zemaitis stopped typing, removed the unlit Lucky Strike from his mouth, and looked me in the eyes.

"Lieu, you asked us to keep an open mind, but all bullshit aside, are *you* keeping an open mind? It's starting to look more and more like your guy did a no-no. Three times."

"John, I've known Charlie twelve years, longer than I've known most of the dicks up here, and I've spent hundreds of hours with him on a dozen manuscripts. He told me once he wouldn't do anything that landed him in prison or got him killed because either one would seriously infringe upon his writing career, which is his foremost concern in life, and I believe him."

Shaughnessy echoed Sgt. Peak's sentiment. "He's a victim or he's our offender, one of the two, and if he's a victim, I think we'd know by now."

Shaughnessy took a sip of the thick black sludge in the cup. "Any ideas at all on where we might find him? Friends, family?" he asked.

"It didn't occur to me until I was driving back into the office that as long as I've known Charlie, I have no way to reach out to him, other than his phone or email," I said. "I had his cell phone number, but as I told you earlier, he changed numbers. His parents are deceased and he has a brother he doesn't keep in contact with. I don't know his brother's first name or even what state he lives in. We'd have a hard time tracking down a guy with the last name Newton somewhere in America."

"Friends?"

"I met two of his friends, Pete and Beth, but I don't

remember their last name. They live in some ritzy suburb up north, but I don't remember which one. They're the only ones in Chicago I've ever heard Charlie mention. I remember Beth studied art in Paris and speaks fluent French; Pete's an insurance executive who likes his beer. I don't think that wealth of information is going to be of much help tracking them down, though."

Zemaitis reinserted the Lucky in the corner of his mouth and went back to typing.

Shaughnessy quipped, "Sounds like Pete's Irish. I'll start checking the north suburban directories for all O'Briens and O'Malleys with the first name Peter."

Without missing a keystroke, Zemaitis added, "When you get to the S's be sure to check the Shaughnessys, too."

I was glad in their twentieth hour of work they still had a sense of humor. Mine was waning fast.

"I know a few literary associates of Charlie's he talks about all the time: "Easy" Ed Stackler, Simon Lipskar, Jason Kaufman, and Don McGuinn, a former marine. I know a couple of them are editors, and one of them is his agent, but I don't who's who. The bad news is I don't think any of them live in Chicago. Have someone run literary agents and editors on the computer. They probably all know one another, so if we find one of them, we might be able to find all of them. If there's anyone Charlie would contact other than me, or Pete or Beth, it would be one of … " I stopped mid-sentence. "Wait a minute! Book acknowledgements! I'm certain Charlie acknowledged Beth in his first book. It'll have her last name in there."

I stood and threw my suit jacket back on, calling back over my shoulder as I hustled toward the stairway,

"I'm going home to get the book. I'll call you back with the name. If you're done with your supp before I get back, give the info to the day crew and have them locate her."

● ● ●

When I got home, I pulled out my autographed copies of *Calument City* and *Start Shooting*. The latter title was turning out to be prophetic. *Steffen. Beth Steffen.* I called Shaughnessy and Zemaitis from my Blackberry with the information as I trotted back to my car.

● ● ●

They were on the last page of their report when I returned to the office.

"Good news and bad news," Shaughnessy said. "We located and contacted Pete and Beth Steffen, but they haven't heard from Newton in several days. We also located Ed Stackler, Simon Lipskar, and Jason Kaufman. Neither Stackler nor Lipskar have heard from him. Kaufman didn't answer, but we left a message on his voice mail. We're waiting for him to call back. We haven't been able to track down the jarhead yet."

I hadn't expected any of them to have heard from Charlie, but I was disappointed nonetheless. If Kaufman or McGuinn hadn't heard from Charlie, I didn't know where else to begin. Time was our enemy.

Sgt. Abels, the second-watch sergeant, called out from the office. "Shaughnessy, line one."

Shaughnessy picked up the phone and spoke for a brief moment.

"That was Kaufman, Lieu. He hasn't heard from Newton either."

We still have to locate and contact McGuinn, I thought, but our prospects were looking bleak. If McGuinn hadn't heard from Charlie, and I didn't guess he had, all we could do was sit and wait until Charlie surfaced; I could only hope he didn't surface in Lake Michigan.

CHAPTER 6

January 7, 2014
Tuesday
0600 hours

I couldn't sleep that night, so I went into the office before daybreak. I sat at my desk and tried to review other open homicide files, but it was no use. I was too tired, and too preoccupied with Charlie's disappearance to make any sense out of anything. I'd get to the bottom of a page and realize I had no idea what I read.

The black face of my Seiko read 1200 hours, and still no word from, or on, Charlie. White cinderblock walls in my office closed in on me. I felt anxious, like I was having a panic attack, but worse than that, I felt useless. For all I was accomplishing here, I could have stayed at home. I needed to be out on the street doing something, looking someplace, not sitting in here with my thumbs up my ass, but I didn't have a place to begin.

The pax, the interdepartmental phone, rang.

I answered, "Lt. Cahill."

"Devlin, this is the chief. Can you take a run down to my office this afternoon?"

It wasn't a request. Declining the invitation was not an option. It was the chief's way of politely telling me to get my ass down there.

He continued, "I'd like to talk to you in person about the triple in Avalon Trails."

"Yes, sir. I'm on the way as we speak."

• • •

I arrived at Chief W.J. Daniels's office, commonly referred to as Jimmy "D" by the troops, at 1330 hours, not bad timing considering I had to navigate the Dangerous Dan Ryan, also known as the Afro 500, around noon.

Chief Daniels was an affable, big black bear of a man. I had known him for twenty-some years, since we were both patrolmen, and I've always liked and respected him for being a working-policeman. Doughnut-eaters are cute and cuddly, and usually tell good jokes, but other than that, we don't share any common interests. The Chief's feeling for me must have been mutual, evidenced by the fact the he hadn't kicked my ass to the curb by now.

His secretary announced me and told me to go in.

The Chief stood and extended a meaty paw, which could crush someone's skull like an aluminum beer can.

"Hey, Devlin, how's it going?"

"Good, Chief. And yourself?"

"Good. I guess you know why I asked you down here?"

"I have a sneaking suspicion."

"Have you read the late edition of today's paper?"

"Not yet."

"It says you referred to one of the reporter's as Mr. Douche Bag."

I smirked. "I must have mispronounced his name."

The chief laughed.

"Yes, you *must* have. I can understand that though, given the name Schwartzman is so similar sounding to Douche Bag, but I thought you'd have the pronunciation of his name indelibly etched in your brain since you threw him down a flight of stairs last year."

"A snafu," I admitted.

Chief Daniels laughed. "Seriously, Devlin, we have a problem here. Mr. *Douche* makes a good point. If this Charlie Newton character is a friend of yours, I should reassign the investigation to Central. I'm confident you'd conduct an impartial and unbiased investigation, but we don't want the perception of impropriety, for your friend's sake, as well as our own. *Assuming* he is innocent, with the friends you've managed to endear in the media, they could paint another picture. Do you agree?"

"Yes, sir, actually I do. I'd prefer to have the case stay in Area South, of course, but I wouldn't want to see Charlie get tried in the media and railroaded because of our friendship. I only ask that you assign the best dicks available from Central to the investigation and let it be known to them that you have an interest in the case."

"Done deal. If we find Mr. Newton alive, I'll see to it he gets a fair shake."

Chief Daniels stood and crushed my hand goodbye.

"We'll keep you posted," he said as I was turning to leave.

The Chief's words made a resounding thud in my chest as I exited his office.

"If we find Mr. Newton alive."

CHAPTER 7

The next day, a sense of relief washed over me when I learned Chief Daniels had assigned Bill Donovan and Jack Barcomb to the follow-up investigation, two of the best dicks in Central. I'm sure Shaughnessy and Zemaitis found some sense of relief, too, knowing the case had been reassigned to Central and they were off the hook. I believed their police-instincts were telling them Charlie was the culprit, and it would have been awkward for them, at the very least, to proceed with their investigation knowing the boss is just as convinced of Charlie's innocence. Not an envious position for them. I neither resented nor begrudged them their difference of opinions. Police intuition is not inherent. It is developed and honed over years of investigative experience, and though both Shaughnessy and Zemaitis' sixth sense is keener than most, gut instincts are still based on the information available, and I had information they didn't. I know Charlie Newton. I prayed my friendship with Charlie wasn't clouding my judgment, as Zemaitis had suggested, but as the hours rolled by with still no word from Charlie, I must admit, I was beginning to distrust my own inclinations.

Later that afternoon, Sgt. Abels came into my office and tossed a newspaper on my desk.

"You should find this article helpful if you're constipated."

I began reading the article written by Erik Schwartzman.

A nationwide search is underway for famed novelist, Charlie Newton, wanted for questioning in the triple slaying yesterday afternoon in Chicago's Avalon Trails neighborhood. Records indicate Mr. Newton, and at least one of the three victims, has a history of narcotics violations.

Lt. Devlin Cahill, commanding officer of the Area South Violent Crimes Unit is a personal friend of Mr. Newton's and has been removed from the investigation. Due to the fact that Mr. Newton has resided in several countries outside of the United States in the last several years, the FBI has been notified and has issued a UFAP (unlawful flight to avoid prosecution) for Mr. Newton.

Lt. Cahill still remains in charge of the Area South Violent Crimes Unit despite the fact the investigation has been reassigned and that the Chicago Police Department has a strict policy of forbidding police officers to associate with known felons.

• • •

Fat motherfucker! Now I wished he would have landed on his head when I tossed him down the stairs last year.

The pax rang. I hoped it was Donovan or Barcomb with some news, some good news.

It was Chief Daniels.

"Devlin, the Chief again. Did you read Schwartzman's column?"

"Yeah, I read it. That fat bastard is trying my patience!"

"Well, what about Newton's criminal history?"

"Charlie was arrested one time, about thirty years ago when he was twenty years old with about two grams over the misdemeanor limit for marijuana. And he wasn't convicted. He got a couple of months of supervision. I don't think that ranks him up there with Richard Speck or the Son of Sam."

Unaware my voice was reaching a crescendo, the chief chided, "Alright, calm down. I had to ask because you know the big bosses are going to be asking me questions and I have to know how to reply. Don't get mad at me; I don't want to show up at the Area someday and have you pick me up by the seat of my pants and toss me down the stairs."

I drew a visual on that and laughed.

"Chief, I don't think I could lift you up by the seat of your pants with an electric floor winch."

We both laughed. It's the first time I had laughed in two days, and it felt good.

"If you could, it would be the biggest wedgie in the 'anals' of Chicago Police Department history." The Chief found his play on words more humorous than I did, but I figured I'd better laugh because he was the guy that was keeping my head above raw sewerage.

It was time for me to get off of work, and I didn't know what I was going to do or where I was going to go. I was sure if Donovan and Barcomb had anything new, they would have called me. I pondered for a moment whether I should call the Steffens, or Lipskar, or Stackley, but I was sure if they had heard anything from Charlie, they would have called too. I could either go find the douche bag, and make him do the chicken, or take a ride to Darien and re-interview Brannigan. The latter seemed like the better career move, so I gave him a call and made arrangements to interview him.

• • •

Forty-five minutes later, I pulled into the parking lot of an upscale condominium complex in Darien. I rang the bell and faced the closed-circuit camera in the lobby. A moment later I was buzzed in.

An attractive, statuesque blond answered the door and invited me in. She introduced herself as Barney's wife, Kim, and asked me to have a seat. Barney Brannigan raced out from another room with Fred, the Morkie, prancing at his heels before I had the chance to sit. He introduced himself and asked me to be seated. Kim asked if I'd like some coffee, and when I told her I never refused coffee, she retreated to the kitchen.

Barney Brannigan was trim and tanned and looked like he was coming back from Florida instead of planning to leave. Fred, the attack Morkie, was less cordial. He began barking and nipping at my ankles like he was possessed the moment I was seated. Brannigan vaulted from his seat like he was shot out of a cannon and chased Fred away, but Fred returned with a vengeance. Brannigan leaped from his seat again and again, and soon they were doing laps around the sofa.

Brannigan was laughing from his toes until his eyes watered as he continued to chase Fred around the sofa, with the Mork from Ork stopping to bite at me every time he rounded the corner. "I trained him myself," Barney laughed.

"You missed your vocation," I said. "Does he know any other tricks?"

Brannigan laughed harder, "No, this is it."

Kim returned from the kitchen and placed a cup of coffee in front of me on the coffee table. In a thin voice, she said, "Fred, you're being rude." Amazingly, Fred ceased the assault and climbed into an overstuffed dog bed large enough for a St. Bernard. His name was embroidered on the cushion in gold lettering.

Barney was out of breath and perspiring when he returned to the sofa and plopped down, still laughing, "I love that little bastard." A moment later, he sprang up and rushed over to the TV to turn it off. He rushed back to the sofa, sat down, bounced up, and went to adjust the amount of light coming in through the blinds. The man was a ball of nervous energy.

If I could get him to sit still long enough, I could ask him some questions. If not, I'd have to jump up and follow him around the room.

"Fred needs a lot of exercise," he said, still giggling and trying to catch his breath.

"I think Fred needs to be exorcised," I said.

"Can I call you Barney?"

He chuckled, "No matter what you call me, I've been called worse."

"How well did you know Hiram Goldenstein?" I asked.

"Not well at all. We worked together at the Mercantile Exchange for several years, but he dabbled in pork bellies and I'm in the cattle pit, so I only knew him to say hi and bye, until a few weeks ago. He said he was a golfer, and he looked like someone I could beat," he chuckled, "so I suggested we catch a plane down to Florida and get a few rounds in. Outside of that, we never socialized."

"Did he have any enemies at the exchange that you know of?" I asked.

"Lieutenant, from 9:00 AM, when the floor opens, until the bell rings at 1:00 PM, everybody at the Merc is your enemy. Occasionally, fists fly because somebody went through somebody on a trade, but when that one o'clock bell rings, everybody kisses and makes up, then they all go out drinking together and get schnockered."

Brannigan vaulted out of his seat so fast I thought the condo was on fire. He ran into the kitchen and returned a nanosecond later with the coffee pot and refilled my three-quarters-full cup.

"My wife's beautiful, but she's slow with the coffee," he said.

"She'd have to be a track star to beat you," I quipped. "Could Goldenstein have gone through somebody on a trade, and bad blood continued past the one o'clock bell?"

"Not that I'm aware. I've never heard a bad word about the man."

"How about the two men that were murdered with

him?"

"I didn't know them, but if they were his best friends I wouldn't know. I never socialized with Goldenstein outside of the Merc. This golf outing was going to be our first gathering outside of the building."

"How did you know where he lived?" I asked.

"We had exchanged information, but I forgot to get his email address, so I called him."

"Please excuse me for saying, but it seems odd to me that you'd drive all the way from Darien to Hegwisch at 11:30 PM to visit a guy whose house you've never been to before."

Brannigan thought about the statement for a moment before he responded.

"Yes, I can see where it would look odd, but I had to know whether we were still on because I had to make reservations at the country club and book airfares. If Hiram changed his mind about going for some reason, I was going to cancel the whole thing. Besides, Fred likes to go for a ride at night, so I usually take him for a spin even when I don't have anyplace to go."

Shaughnessy was right. Brannigan was legit. Fred may have killed these guys, but not Brannigan. I thanked him for his cooperation, and his beautiful wife for her hospitality, and left for home.

CHAPTER 8

January 9, 2014
Thursday
2300 hours

I zonked out within two minutes of sitting down in the Laz-Z-Boy in front of the big screen. A commercial was being broadcast on erectile dysfunction when I awoke to the phone ringing. I wondered if I had it? I didn't eighteen months ago, of that I was sure, but it was something I should explore. The only problem was, I couldn't bring myself to make love to anyone other than Kerri. I'm not wired that way. There would be an equipment failure, which could prove to be embarrassing.

I didn't know what time I dozed off, or how long I was asleep, but I knew it was well after 0200 hours. My neck and back were crippled and not cooperating with my feet as I hurriedly stumbled toward the phone. Maybe information about Charlie?

"Lieutenant? Bill Peak. You got trouble."

"They found Charlie?"

"No, they found Erik Schwartzman, with two bullet holes in the back of his head."

"You're shittin' me!"

"No, I'm not shitting you. The Deputy called a few minutes ago and wanted to know if, by chance, you were in the office and asked me for your home address. Expect a knock on your door."

I heard several vehicles pull up in front of my house and several car doors being closed softly.

"I think my guests have arrived, Bill. Thanks for the heads up."

I bent the mini blinds and peered out the window. I could make out the scrambled eggs on the visor of the Assistant Deputy Superintendent's cap, and four men in civilian dress with him, coming up my walkway. They rang the doorbell, and I waited a minute or two before answering so it wouldn't look like Sgt. Peak had wired me up.

"Lieutenant, can we come in and speak to you for a few minutes?" the Deputy asked.

"Sure, come in."

The Deputy introduced himself as ADS Carone, and two of the suits with him as detectives from Central Violent Crimes. The third man, also dressed in casual business attire, was a sergeant from the Bureau of Internal Affairs, and the fourth man in civvies was a civilian investigator from the Independent Police Review Authority, the unit that investigates excessive force complaints against police officers, up to and including homicides.

The Deputy began by saying, "Lieutenant, I want to be frank with you. Maybe I can save us all a lot of time here. We had a homicide of a newspaper reporter named Erik Schwartzman earlier this evening. I believe you knew him?"

"You already know I knew the douche bag or you wouldn't be here."

"It doesn't sound like you liked him?" the Deputy asked.

"No, I didn't like him at all. I didn't like him when he was alive, and I don't like him any better now that he's dead."

"Do you own a 9mm?"

"Do I own a 9mm?" I repeated. "Why, do you think I killed the fat fuck?"

"We don't know who killed him, Lieutenant, but people are going to be asking questions given your recent history with the deceased."

"What people are going to be asking questions?" I asked. "This is absurd! Yes, I own a Browning 9mm, and a 357 Colt Python, and a 38 Smith five-shot snub." I paused for dramatic effect and glared at each of them.

"Lieutenant, there's no need to get huffy. It's no secret there was bad blood between you. You allegedly threw the man down a flight of stairs last year and called him a douche bag the other day in the presence of two other reporters. Then, of course, he wrote a less than flattering article about you the next day. Now he's dead."

"*Allegedly* is the key word in that second sentence, Deputy. Defined by Webster as "to assert without proof." And as for the other allegation, I did not call him a douche bag. I called him Mr. Something or Other. I may have mispronounced his name."

"We'd like you to voluntarily come downtown with us so we can officially eliminate you as a suspect," the Deputy said.

"Voluntarily?" I asked. "No. You can either arrest me, or, Deputy, you can give me a direct order to go downtown."

"I'd prefer not to do either, Lieutenant. I was hoping you'd be more cooperative."

"Gentlemen, we all went to the same police academy. I remember on the first or second day of class, the law instructor told us that the smartest thing for a suspect to do when he's the subject of a criminal investigation, whether he's guilty or innocent, is to take the fifth. And, after almost thirty years on the job, I can tell you empirically (a word I learned from Charlie), he was right. So, whether I'm arrested or ordered downtown, the outcome will be the same. I will invoke my right to remain silent, and we've all wasted everybody's time."

The civilian investigator from IPRA said, "We can arrest you, Lieutenant, if necessary."

"*You* can't do shit, jerk balls, so why don't you sit there and keep your mouth shut while I'm talking to policemen."

The civilian-dressed officer the Deputy had introduced as the sergeant from the BIA had a complexion like a sausage pizza. Apparently, he felt obligated to defend his civilian counterpart and said, "Hey, pal, there's no need for name calling; we're not trying to jam you up. We're trying to unravel some of this mess."

"Pal? Listen pee-pee pants, until such time as I am arrested or fired from this fuckin' job, you will address me as Lieutenant or sir, got it?"

The sergeant lowered his gaze to the floor and didn't respond.

"I said, have—you—got— it?"

"Yes, sir."

"And get your ugly ass off of my sofa!"

The Deputy interceded and held up his hands in mock surrender, "Lieutenant, please calm down."

"Calm down my ass. You come into my house at 3:30 in the morning, wake me up, accuse me of murder, and then this insolent cocksucker starts calling me by his dog's name. If he wants to be that informal, maybe he'd like to come out in the alley with me and we'll discuss it informally and unofficially," I shouted, nodded toward the IPRA investigator, and added, "He'd better bring the other peter puffer with him in case the discussion gets heated." I was in the red zone by then, and there wasn't any doubt in my mind my mouth had already overloaded my ass.

The Deputy breathed a sigh of resignation. "We'd like to take your Browning to the lab for examination. It would eliminate you as a suspect and certainly help expedite the investigation."

I was going to tell him to get a warrant if they wanted my 9mm, but there was no sense in being more obstinate than necessary and delaying the inevitable. The ballistics, after all, were going to come back negative, so I went into my bedroom and retrieved the weapon. I jacked the slide, removed the clip, and handed it to the Deputy.

"Take it with my blessing. Do you want my 357 and my snub, too, in case there are any other open homicide investigations matching those calibers, or my nightstick for any uncleared bludgeoning murders?"

They slipped silently out the door and into the ink of night. That went well, I thought. I bent the blinds and peeped out the window as they strolled to their respective vehicles, talking and shaking their heads. I'm sure they were all saying what an asshole I was. They could have been right, too. I'd have to remember to call them later in the day and apologize for my rude behavior. I'd tell the sergeant from the BIA I was sorry and that he and I could now be *pals*.

CHAPTER 9

January 9,2014
Thursday
0600 hours

After the Mickey Mouse Club left, I lay staring at the alarm clock, watching the minutes tick by hour after hour. I wasn't as worried about the Schwartzman homicide as I was pissed off about it. How could any competent police investigator think I would flush a twenty-four year career, and my life, down the tubes because some guy wrote a nasty article about me? If I murdered everybody I called a name, Chicago would have a population of about 50,000. My gun was going to come back clean, so I wasn't worried about that, and of course, they couldn't have anything else on me because there was nothing else. Dumbfucks. I was more concerned about Charlie. He had a much bigger problem. I tried to erase this sickening thought in the back of my mind that told me Charlie was dead, but it kept clawing and scratching its way back to the forefront of my thoughts.

I gave up on the notion of sleep around 6:00 AM. My body ached, and my head felt like somebody hit me with a sewer cover. Sleep had to come soon. I got up and put on a pot of coffee, ripped the cellophane off a half-dozen biscotti, and started dunking. When they were gone, I ate a Hershey's Almond bar and had four panetelas for breakfast. My body was exhausted, but I couldn't shut my mind off, and I couldn't stand being pent up in the house any longer. If the Mickey Mouse Club had thrown me in the Cook County Jail, at least I'd have somebody to talk to. I'd welcome a nice roach-infested mattress if I could only sleep. I showered and shaved, lit up my fifth Dutch Masters, and headed to the office—if I still had an office. Chief Daniels would soon hear about the predawn party at my house with the Street Deputy and his entourage. I guessed he wouldn't be happy. Even Chief Daniels would have to be getting tired of my bullshit soon. I would be if I were him. I wondered if the reporters would be waiting anxiously to interview me about the Schwartzman homicide. I thought not. If they believed I already smoked one reporter, I bet they'd write some nice shit about me.

I entered the Area South parking lot at 0700 hours, half expecting the SWAT team to be there waiting for me. I scanned the rooftop looking for guys in flak jackets with laser scopes, and flitting red dots on my jacket around my heart. No reporters in the lobby waiting to interview me. Imagine that!

Sgt. Peak's tour of duty hadn't ended yet. He was leaned back in a swivel chair with his size twelves propped up on the sergeant's metal desk, bleary-eyed, reading reports and drinking coffee when I entered.

"Hey, Lieu, what happened?"

"What you'd expect. Those incompetent assholes think I smoked Schwartzman and asked me to voluntarily accompany them downtown. I told them I'll be taking the fifth, called the weasel-faced IPRA investigator a peter puffer, and invited the sergeant from the BIA outside."

Peak laughed. "I know I shouldn't be laughing, Lieu, but you are smooth."

"Like the head of a penis."

I nodded at Bill's cup. "How fresh is the coffee?"

"I made it about fifteen minutes ago."

Sgt. Peak and I walked into the sergeant's office and I poured a cup. Two open files lay on his desk with today's date.

"What are these?" I asked.

"Two unrelated gangbanger homicides, one from Kensington and one from the Bush. Nobody in custody on either of them, but will be soon. Facchini said he thinks Tiger Woods murdered the Mexican."

"Tiger Woods?"

"Yeah, he said who else could get two holes in Juan."

We both laughed, and I asked, "I imagine if there was any news on Charlie or the triple you would have told me by now?"

"Yes, sir, I would have. Maybe Area Central will come up with something today."

"Yeah, I hope so. I don't like this feeling of being left out of the loop."

I was on my second or third cup of coffee when the second-watch detectives started drifting in. Sgt Peak was bringing the second-watch sergeant, Ken Abels, up to snuff on the new murders when the phone rang.

Sgt. Abels informed me Chief Daniels was on line one.

"Shit," I mumbled and spear-chucked my coffee into the waste receptacle, the spatter climbing the wall. I went into my office and closed the door behind me, so in the event I had to cry or plead for my job, the troops wouldn't hear me. Here I go again.

"Good morning, boss," I chirped.

"Good morning, my ass! What in the name of Sweet Jesus are you doing, Devlin? Have you lost your friggin' mind? Should I schedule an appointment for you with the fucking department shrink?"

"No, I don't think that would be of any value, Boss. Do you know what Sigmund Freud said about the Irish? 'This is one race of people for whom psychoanalysis is of no use whatsoever.'"

"Goddamn it, Devlin, be serious. You threatened to kick the sergeant from the BIA's ass in front of the Deputy and three other witnesses. Do you want to get dumped from the unit? Or get fired? Or go to prison?"

"If this is a multiple choice quiz, I'll take 'D,' none of the above," I quipped, but the Chief wasn't laughing, so I added, "For the record, I didn't threaten to take the BIA sergeant outside and kick his ass; I invited him outside to discuss in private his being insubordinate. They may have misconstrued my intentions. I'll call him today and apologize for any misunderstanding. I was, and still am, worried about my friend Charlie Newton, and I had been up twenty-four consecutive hours without sleep when they came ringing my doorbell at 3:30 in the morning. I may have overreacted, but you can understand how I could become irritable when the Deputy and a member from the

Bureau of Internal Assholes show up at my door accusing me of murdering some fat prick because he wrote a nasty story about me. Do you know how many other reporters have cast me in a less than flattering light and I didn't give them a double-tap to the head? Even if I did toss the Pillsbury Doughboy down the stairs and mispronounce his name, it's a long stretch from calling somebody a name to putting two in the back of his skull."

"Devlin, do me a favor," the chief sighed. "Call the Deputy, call the sergeant from the BIA, call the IPRA investigator, and apologize to all of them. Don't say anything cute or witty; apologize! Then take the rest of the goddamn day off. Go home and get some sleep. You need it; for your sake as well as ours."

"Thank you, Chief. I'll do that."

"And, Devlin, don't make any more enemies. You're in shit as deep as your friend Charlie Newton, if he's alive."

"Thanks again, Chief. I'm sure with that sobering thought I'll sleep peacefully."

The phone clicked in my ear.

• • •

IPRA and the BIA were going to have to put a lot of dots together before they could hang Schwartzman's murder on me. How could the stumblebums turn calling someone a douche bag into a prosecutable murder charge? They're playing with their ying yangs. I shouldn't even dwell on it. When the ballistics come back on my 9mm, I'll be exonerated. Charlie, on the other hand, still had something to worry about. I had to stay focused on his investigation.

CHAPTER 10

January 13, 2014
Monday
0900 hours

Charlie had been missing for seven days, and I feared the worst. I felt fatigued, beaten. There was a commercial on TV in the wee hours of the morning describing twelve signs of clinical depression. It said if you suffer from two or more of these signs, you could be clinically depressed. I'm fucked; I suffer from all twelve.

Reluctantly, the morning after the mouseketeers' predawn raid at my house, I called everyone to make my apologies. Deputy Carone seemed cool toward me, but understanding. I think Pizza Face, the BIA sergeant, detected a lack of sincerity in my voice, as I detected a lack of sincerity in his voice when he said he accepted my apology. The IPRA investigator didn't even pretend to accept my apology. He hung up on me, the peter puffer. I have to respect the twerp for that, though. That's what I'd do under the same circumstances.

I pulled out my top-left desk drawer. A photograph of Kerri in an oak frame sat on top of my clipboard. I recalled how happy she was the day the photo was taken. She was racing across the white sands of Playa Linda, her iridescent auburn hair glistening in the early morning Cancun sun and her pale blue eyes, the color of the beach water, flickering in the light. The camera picked up a few beads of perspiration over her brow, and a hint of sunburn brought out a few freckles on her nose. That was 2008, a thousand years ago. It didn't seem right for me to keep her picture, she wasn't mine anymore, but I couldn't summon the strength to part with it, either. I took one last, long, hard look at the photo and nudged the drawer close with a sigh.

Sgt. Abels stuck his head in the door. "Lieu, Detective Barcomb on one."

I punched the button for line one. "Lieutenant Cahill", I answered.

"Hi, Lieu. I want to give you an update on the triple. We had Financial Crimes do a history on Charlie Newton. There's been no activity on any of his credit cards since he rented that vehicle. We flagged all his cards; so if anybody tries to use them, we'll be notified immediately. We also got a cell phone number for him. It's a new phone. Dozen or so calls made on it, all made before he went missing. Most of them are to his editor and his agent, one to Peter Steffens, two to the car rental agency and two to the Pick-Congress Hotel. There's only one call we can't account for; it's to one of those throwaway cells. I don't think there's anything we can do with that, but we'll try. We tried to track Newton's cell phone, too. It's either off, broken, or in Lake Michigan. No signal."

We also located Newton's friend, Don McGuinn. He hasn't seen or heard from Newton in two or three weeks. And we had guys from the second and third watches go back to the Pick-Congress and interview staff members from those respective shifts. One desk clerk says he remembers Newton from when he checked in but doesn't recall seeing him after that. Nobody else remembers him."

"Thanks for the update, Jack. That's what I expected at this point."

"If anything else comes up, Lieu, I got your cell. I'll call you right away."

"Thanks, Jack. I appreciate it," I said and hung up the phone.

If I drank, I would've gotten drunk that night. Or traded some mutt a panetela for a blunt. I managed to make it through my teen years without smoking one of those bad boys, but I'm told they work wonders for the overwrought. They make you laugh and they make you sleep, and I was in dire need of both. With my luck, Random Drug would call and ask me to donate a cup of piss first thing the following morning, and my *pal* from the Bureau of Internal Assholes, Pizza Face, would be the guy administering the test. I couldn't risk giving him the satisfaction of firing me, and calling me *pal* again, so I settled for a glass of warm milk and a couple of Unisoms.

CHAPTER 11

I had my entertainment schedule for the evening well planned out. A stack of DVDs, everything written, produced, or starred in by Clint Eastwood, rested next to me on the lamp table.

I watched *Dirty Harry* first and was relieved to find out that after eighteen months of celibacy, I didn't suffer from erectile dysfunction after all. When Harry ground his heel into the child-killer's wounded leg, I got a diamond cutter that would have sliced through a four-inch plate of glass like a chainsaw through balsa wood. I was halfway through *The Unforgiven* when the phone interrupted. I was beginning to feel a sense of dread every time I heard it ring. It was always bad news.

"Devlin?"

I recognized the voice at once, and my heart started fibrillating.

"Who else would you expect?" I snapped.

"Devlin, I've been trying to work up the courage to

call you for several days. I've been reading about you and Charlie in the papers and I wanted to see if there was any news on Charlie and how you're doing," Kerri said with reserve.

"Peachy. How are you and Kermit the Frog doing?"

"His name is Emmett."

"Okay, Emmett the Frog. Couldn't you at least have gotten a guy with more class than a defense attorney; like a child molester or a nice necrophiliac?"

"Please, Devlin, I didn't call to argue with you."

"Why did you call, Kerri?"

"I wanted to know if you're okay."

"If you cared whether I was okay, you wouldn't have left me eighteen months ago."

She started explaining, for the umpteenth time, and I cut her off. I've heard it all before; it wasn't me, it was the job.

"Do you and Kermit have any kids on the way yet?"

She wept openly. "No, we don't have any kids on the way yet."

"What was it that great black barrister said during the O.J. trial?'If the condom doesn't fit, then you must spit.'" The phone went dead in my ear.

I don't know why I do that. Compulsion, I guess. I should join AA (Assholes Anonymous). I had been hoping everyday for months she would call. I rehearsed the conversation in my head a thousand times. I would be civil, tell her I love her and how much I miss her, and make an impassioned plea for her to come back. But when I open my mouth, that's what comes out.

I ejected *The Unforgiven*. Maybe I OD'd on Clint that night. "This is a 44 magnum, the most powerful handgun in the world and can blow your head clean off your shoulders. I am now going to stick the six-inch barrel of it up my ass as far as it will go and pull the trigger." What an unbelievable moron I am at times!

The phone rang again. I wouldn't tell Kerri I was sorry. I'd done enough apologizing that week.

Nevertheless, I answered contritely. "Hello."

"Devlin?"

Again, I recognized the voice and my heart began pounding.

"*Charlie?*"

CHAPTER 12

"Charlie, where in the hell are you?"

"I'm alive and well in beautiful Juarez, Mexico, Lieutenant Devlin. Call off Search and Rescue," Charlie sang in my ear.

"Search and Rescue isn't looking for you, Charlie, but every goddamned federal, state, and local police agency in America is. The FBI has an UFAP out on you. They think you murdered three men in Chicago."

"They think *I* murdered those three guys?" Charlie asked incredulously.

"Of course they do! Your car was left at the scene, your prints are in the house and you're nowhere to be found. For a Mensa guy with an IQ of 145, sometimes you aren't too goddamned smart, Charlie!"

"Hmmm. What an interesting turn of events."

" *Interesting turn of events?* That's all you can say? You're in deep shit!"

Charlie started saying something but I interrupted him and asked, "Are you calling from your cell phone?"

"No, I don't know where it is."

"Good, if you find it, throw it away. The G has cell site simulators called Stingrays, and they'll be slapping the cuffs on you before you can order a taco," I admonished. Don't use your credit cards either, they're flagged. Do you still have them?"

"Yes, I still have them, but not using them may present a problem, Devlin lad. I don't have enough cash on hand to get back to Chicago. Don't you want to know what happened?"

"Oh, you have no idea how badly I want to know what happened, Hemingway, but not over the phone. The BIA may have my home phone tapped, too."

"Why would the BIA have your phone tapped?'

"Long story; I'll explain later."

"How about I call you on your cell phone?" Charlie asked.

"No, they may have that Stingray set up for my cell phone, too. Call me at my brother's house in a half hour," I said and gave him the number.

I heard Mexican music in the background.

"Can we make it an hour?" Charlie asked. "I serendipitously stumbled into a quaint little cantina with the cutest mesera you've ever seen."

"They won't give her conjugal visits in prison, Carlos. Half hour."

• • •

I arrived at my brother Bernie's house in twenty minutes. He warned me if I lit up a cigar in his house his wife would be drawing two chalk outlines on the living room floor. She's Italian, so I agreed. I was giving my brother a brief synopsis of what was going on when his phone rang. He answered and handed it to me.

"Charlie, what the hell is happening?"

"It's a long, mind-boggling chronicle, Devlin lad."

"Boggle me, Charlie."

"A man, who introduced himself as Mario Fontanetta, attended one of my book signings about ten days ago and struck up a conversation. Seemed like a nice enough chap, nothing knavish about him. In the course of the conversation, I happened to mention I was in the midst of writing a novel centering on the Mercantile Exchange, high finances, and murder. He told me he could introduce me to a friend of his who was a commodity broker and could provide me some insight into the inner workings of the exchange. The next day I picked him up in my car and we drove to the southeast side of Chicago. No sooner had we stepped in the door than he produced an automatic handgun and opened fire. I fell to the floor and rolled behind a sofa for cover. Moments later, a second man entered the home. I was certain at that point I had written my last novel, until the second man duct-taped my mouth and eyes and put plastic flex ties on my wrists. They took me from the house and stuffed me into the trunk of a car, and we were off. I'm sure there was a third man in the car, too, but I never saw his face, only heard his voice. We drove for hours and hours. When they removed the tape from my eyes, I was in a private residence. I deduced from the architectural styling and building materials used in the home I was in Mexico, but I wasn't certain until they released me."

"What did this Mario Fontanetta look like?" I asked.

"Male white, thirtyish, 5'11", 190 pounds, short black hair, well coifed, brown eyes, Kirk Douglas chin with a DeNiro mole on his left cheek. Nattily dressed in a tan camel hair jacket and a nice pair of chocolate gabardine slacks."

I rolled my eyes. "You don't happen to remember what color socks the fashion plate was wearing, do you?"

"Brown, naturally," Charlie replied dryly. "What other color socks would you be wearing with tan camel hair and chocolate slacks?"

"Why didn't they kill you?"

"I have no idea why, and I didn't ask. I didn't want to plant the seed, so to speak. Maybe they like my books."

"Did they say or do anything to you?"

"No, they didn't do anything to me. Actually, my captors seemed quite convivial."

"That's commendable, Charlie. Perhaps they can present your sterling approval of their hospitality in mitigation at their trial." I continued, "Given your limited funds, do you think you can get into El Paso?"

"I'm certain I can. I've done it before when I was researching …"

I interrupted him again. "Charlie, this isn't a goddamn novel. You're in real trouble. I believe your story, but I don't think anybody else will."

"Lots of material here for a book," he quipped.

"They don't give you unlimited access to computers in

prison, nor do they give you sharp objects, like pens and pencils. Can you write your next novel in crayon? You'd better take this more seriously, Charlie."

"I *am* taking it seriously, but I am an inveterate optimist, Devlin lad, and I have faith in our criminal justice system. When the smoke clears, I'll be exonerated."

"God bless you—John Wayne—and American juris prudence. Listen, when you get into El Paso, call my brother's house at this number and give him a location where I can pick you up. Don't leave a message on his machine; only talk to him."

"Sounds like a plan. Now, if you don't mind, I'm going to indulge in dos cervezas and try to woo Salma Hayek's enchanting baby sister out of her drawers." I could almost hear him smiling roguishly at her as she picked her way around the tables in the cantina.

"Don't get too involved with Salma and forget to call," I warned him, but I knew he wouldn't. If there's one thing Charlie doesn't do, it's forget.

I hung up and called the office. Sgt. Peak answered, and I asked him to run Mario Fontanetta and provided him with a physical. I didn't expect a hit, but I'd feel stupid if he had used his real name, or the same alias before, and I didn't try. I told Sgt. Peak I wasn't at home and asked him to call me back on my cell phone as soon as he got the results.

I depressed the switch hook and called Midway Airport. Delta had a flight departing for ELP at 0630 hours with a one-hour layover in Minneapolis. I reserved a full-size Chevy at National Car Rental so I wouldn't have to listen to Charlie bitch all the way back to Chicago about his knees being up to his Van Dyke. I used my brother's computer to check for hotels near the Mexican border, and I booked a room at the Hotel El Camino Real in El Paso, six blocks from the Juarez border.

I thanked my brother for his hospitality and his amenities and informed him I didn't have time to chat. I had a plane to catch. Besides, I needed a cigar.

My cell phone rang while I was driving home. It was Sgt. Peak calling to tell me there was no record on file for Mario Fontanetta. Surprise, surprise.

CHAPTER 13

January 14, 2014
Tuesday
1000 hours

After I checked into the El Camino Real, I called my brother from the hotel phone. He told me Charlie called an hour ago and said that he would be at the El Rincon de Cortez Restaurant at noon. Charlie also told him that because I was a trained detective I shouldn't have much difficulty finding him in the restaurant. Everybody would be wearing cowboy hats or sombreros except him. He'd be the guy in the porkpie hat.

If he was wearing that porkpie hat, I didn't want to be seen with him, not in Mexico, not in Texas, and especially not on the Southside of Chicago.

I arrived at the El Rincon de Cortez at precisely 12:00 PM, Pacific Standard Time. From the short time it took me to walk from the air-conditioned car to the entrance of the restaurant, I was soaked with perspiration. My shirt stuck to my skin, and I felt like I pissed in my pants. Was it only a few hours ago I was numb from cold?

I was scanning the roomful of dark, sunburned faces

when a voice called out, "Devlin lad." Charlie was beaming, weaving his way around tables with a catlike grace and outstretched arms. His face was gaunt, accentuating his high cheekbones and square jaw. Everyone was looking at him. I prayed he wouldn't kiss me. Thank God he lied about the porkpie hat or I'd have had to turn and run back out the door into the blistering heat. I must confess, porkpie hat or not, and even though he's a Northsider, I couldn't remember the last time I was ever so happy to see someone. I wouldn't tell him that, though. I was beginning to believe the next time I saw Charlie Newton he would be in a 55-gallon drum.

I ordered coffee and listened in amazement as Charlie went on about the primary ingredients and preparation of Mexican cuisine. Was he shittin' me? He'd been bound, gagged, stuffed in the trunk of a car, and held captive for over a week, and he thinks I'm interested in hearing how to make Alambres de Puerco? The police wouldn't be interested either, and that's why I was glad I found him before they did.

I caught myself staring at him in disbelief. I absorbed the end of his rambling, " … and I think they have a wee bit too much cilantro in here," he opined.

"That's good to know, Charlie. I'll be sure not to order it the next time I'm in El Paso to pick up a fugitive. I rented a room at a nearby hotel. Finish what you're eating and let's get out of here. We have a lot more important things to discuss than tacos."

Charlie held up his hand. "Senorita, traigame la cuenta, por favor."

When the waitress returned with the check, Charlie added, "Gracias, senorita, eso es para usted" and stuffed an extra sawbuck into her apron pocket.

"If you gave her an extra ten for bringing you a burrito, I wonder what you gave Salma's baby sister last night."

He snickered, "My undying gratitude, Devlin lad."

•   •   •

Back at the hotel room, I said, "Okay, Charlie, let's be serious here for awhile. They've reassigned the triple homicide investigation from Area South to Area Central because you and I are friends. That's best for all concerned. The two detectives they assigned to the investigation from Central are Jack Barcomb and Bill Donovan, two of the best dicks in the city. They're both sharp guys and they know bullshit when they hear bullshit, and that's exactly what your story is going to sound like to them: bullshit," I said.

"It's not bullshit," Charlie protested.

"Let me run this by you to see if I have the facts straight. A perfect stranger approaches you at a book signing, introduces himself to you as Mario Fontanetta, who, by the way, doesn't exist, and invites you to meet his commodity-broker friend. The victims apparently knew Mario Fontanetta because they admitted him to the house, and, without warning or a word being spoken, he executes everybody in the joint, except you, leaving you the only witness to a triple homicide. Then an accomplice appears, and together, they bind, gag, and abduct you and hold you captive for a week in an unknown location in Mexico. How I am I doing so far?" I asked.

"Splendid."

"You're not robbed, beaten, battered, boogered or held for ransom. You're treated well and then ... poof ... released. Does that sound about right?

"You're very astute, Devlin lad."

"Why? Why didn't they kill you? Why would they leave a witness to a triple homicide alive? It doesn't make any sense."

"I contemplated those same questions while I was being held, Devlin lad, and I'd be the first guy to agree it defies logic. I realize the story lacks verisimilitude, but that's what happened."

"You and I know that's what happened, but the police and the Assistant State's Attorney won't believe it."

"Que sera, sera," Charlie replied.

"Let's face it, Charlie. You're a novelist, and this sounds like a plot in a dime-store novel. Writers of fiction aren't known for their veracity."

Charlie's face flushed with indignation, and he turned a cold eye to me. "I don't write *dime-store* novels!"

I had rankled his ego. "Easy, Hemingway. Here's what they're going to think: You and the dead guys were engaged in some shady deal, the deal went south—and so did you— to Mexico—leaving three bodies in your wake. You stayed out of the country for a week to give yourself enough time to come up with a plausible story."

"It is my hope that they've read my books and realize that in a week's time I could have come up with a much better story than this. I agree with what you're saying, but what can I say other than the truth?"

"That's why I wanted to talk to you before the authorities. I don't want you to tell them anything. If you tell them *that* story, even though it's the truth, they'll slap the bracelets on you faster than a 47th Street whore can drop her panties. Say nothing. Take the fifth. That will give us breathing room to try to find Fontanetta."

"Okay, when do we start?" Charlie asked.

"We've already started. First, it appears you were not a random fall guy. Fontanetta targeted you specifically. Why?"

"I have no idea. I have no enemies that I'm aware of. No shady business dealings, underworld associates, jealous boyfriends or husbands. Nothing. My books are fiction so I don't think I could have threatened to expose or offend anyone."

"Let's not rule out jealous boyfriends or husbands, just yet," I said. "Here's another question; you said you brought up the subject of writing about a commodity broker; how would this Mario guy know beforehand you were writing a book about a commodity broker?"

"Any number of ways. I've discussed the premise of the novel on several radio talk shows and it's been mentioned in several newspaper and magazine articles, both online and in hard print. It was no secret."

I leaned back in the chair and lit up a panetela. "There has to be a reason they picked Charlie Newton. If we can figure out why, maybe we can figure out who."

Charlie nodded toward my cigar and waved his hand under his nose in an affected manner. "Those things do stink; would you mind blowing the smoke the other way?"

"Listen, you whining Northside bitch, I spent $1,500 getting down here to save your white Afrikaner ass, so suck it up."

"Are you going to smoke them in the car all the way back to Chicago?" he asked.

"I smoke twice as much when I'm driving. Now, what about the third guy in the car?"

"What about him? I never saw him, but I'm sure I heard three distinct voices in the car. I couldn't distinguish what they were saying, and I'd never be able to recognize the third guy's voice again. Acoustics aren't great in the trunk of a car."

"I wouldn't know; I've never ridden in the trunk of a car," I said. "Did it seem as if he was trying to avoid letting you see him?"

"I don't know if he tried to *avoid* letting me see him or not. He didn't come into the house, that's for sure, and when they brought me outside my eyes were taped. Judging from the direction of the voices in relation to the location of the trunk, I believe the third guy was seated in either the front passenger or rear passenger seat, and I don't believe he ever got out of the vehicle. One thing I did forget to mention: he got out of the car shortly after I was put in the trunk. He didn't go to Mexico with us. I could determine by the speed and sounds of outside traffic we were on the interstate for approximately ten or fifteen minutes, exited, and crossed two sets of railroad tracks before he exited the vehicle."

"So, mystery guest #3 was neither the muscle nor the getaway driver. Sounds like he might be the man with the plan. Fontanetta and the other guy are only goons."

"Reasonable assumption, but before we can find him, we have to find Mr. Fontanetta and his associate, yes?"

"You can ID Fontanetta when we find him?"

"I can ID both of the guys that came in the house. What is the probability they'll talk?" Charlie asked.

"Good. These types of guys like me for some inexplicable reason. I'll establish a rapport with them, and they'll want to talk to me."

Charlie checked his Rolex. "Devlin lad, it's 5:00 PM. You know what that means?"

"It's Miller time?" I asked and nodded at his wrist. "Nice watch. Wal-Mart?"

"A celebratory profligacy I indulged myself after *Calumet City* made the bestseller list."

"I don't speak Spanish, remember?" I said.

"I splurged," Charlie explained.

"I'm surprised they didn't take your Rolex."

"They didn't take anything from me."

"How about your phone?" I asked.

"I don't recall them taking it from me. I could have dropped it at the scene of the murders."

"No, it wasn't there or we'd have found it."

"If it wasn't there, perhaps they did confiscate it."

"Let's see if we can **profligate** you a beluga caviar taco and me some peasant food so we can get to bed early. We have a lot of ground to cover in the next two days. When we get to Chicago, I'll surrender you in the morning to Donovan and Barcomb at Area Central. If you're capable of keeping your mouth shut and taking the fifth, we should be out of there within the hour."

Charlie waved his hand in front of his face like the house was on fire. "Are you going to smoke those stinking cigars in the car for twenty-four consecutive hours?" he asked. "I'll be dead from second hand smoke."

"Yes, I am, and you're lucky you're not dead already from first hand smoke … gunsmoke."

CHAPTER 14

I was seriously considering giving Charlie a double-tap to the temporal lobe and leaving his body on the shoulder of the highway not long after leaving El Paso. He was already complaining about his legs being cramped and second hand smoke, and he kept changing radio stations every five seconds like he had Tourette Syndrome in his index finger: financial reports, blues, the weather station, blues, then back to the financial reports.

"Now I know why they released you. The fact that they didn't kill you is a tribute to their self-restraint."

Charlie responded with a smirk. He's mastered the art of pushing my buttons, both figuratively and literally.

After a few miles of silence, I asked, "Hey, did you ever call Fontanetta from your cell phone?"

Charlie pondered the question briefly. "Once. I called him to ask where I should pick him up."

"That would be the call to the throwaway phone on your cell phone records," I said, giving voice to my thoughts. "And where did you pick him up?"

"The train depot at 103rd & Beverly."

"That won't help us. He could have taken the train from anywhere."

"There's one more thing that may be of value. When I called him, he was close to a fire truck. I heard the siren. He asked me to hold on a minute while he stepped away because he couldn't hear me."

"Are you sure it was a fire truck, not a squad car or an ambulance?" I asked.

"No, I'm sure. Too deep and throaty."

"When we get back to Chicago, I'll have Donovan and Barcomb contact the fire department to see if they have any records of fires that coincide with the time on your cell phone records. Since Fontanetta wasn't expecting your call at that exact time, he may have been on his home turf when he answered. That would narrow down the area where we should start looking for him."

"So, if my information results in the arrests and convictions of the perpetrators of this triple homicide, do I get a reward or something?" Charlie asked.

"Why, yes, you do; two rewards, in fact. You get to not spend the rest of your natural life in prison, and," I held an unwrapped cigar to his face, "one of these fine tobacco, machine wrapped, fifty-cent stogies could be yours, but first you have to clear the triple."

Charlie sneered, punched the selector button on the radio, and we were back to Howlin' Wolf. I didn't dare tell him I like the blues, or he'd switch back to the Dow Jones.

"Can we stop, please?" he asked. "I have to get out and stretch my legs; they're cramping."

Double-tap. Badda boom—badda bing. If we do catch the kidnappers, they should be canonized instead of incarcerated. I'll threaten to lock them up in an interrogation room with Charlie for seven days if they don't fess up. They'll be begging for me to come in and beat them with a phone book and a rubber hose after three. On the bright side, they'll have an extensive vocabulary and an outstanding command of the English language when they hit Statesville. The other inmates will be impressed.

• • •

I drove the first six hours, and Charlie took the next six. He exited I-44 in Tulsa, Oklahoma, around 2300 hours, and we dropped $40 at the Motel 6. The last thing I heard Charlie say before I slipped into the arms of Morpheus was, "This isn't the Pick-Congress, is it?"

• • •

I was sleeping soundly, the first time in weeks, when grunting noises woke me at 0700. I jacked one eye open but didn't have enough strength to lift my head off of the pillow. Charlie was in his boxer shorts, lying on the floor with his legs up on the bed doing stomach crunches, which meant he'd already completed his ritual fifty push-ups. I wasn't surprised, nor was I happy. I could have easily slept until ten o'clock. Charlie adheres to a strict daily regimen. He wakes at precisely 0400 hours, writes until 0700, exercises until 0800, showers, and drinks exactly two cups of iced coffee—½ coffee, ½ chocolate milk. He would burn to death in the house if it caught fire between those hours rather than deviate from his schedule. I'd have to remember to ask him when I was fully awake how he survived while being held captive.

We ate a continental breakfast and were back on the road by 9:00 AM. I estimated we should arrive in Chicago around 2000 hours. Charlie didn't realize that if he didn't stop pushing the buttons on the radio he'd never see Chicago again—not alive anyway.

We pulled onto the apron of my garage at 8:30 PM. Charlie was going to crash at my house, and in the morning, he'd surrender to Barcomb and Donovan at Area Central. If he was capable of keeping his mouth shut and invoking the fifth like I told him, he'd walk out of there with me within the hour. If he didn't listen to me, he'd be walking out of there in about eighty years. The State's Attorney had a good circumstantial case against him now, but I was certain it was too early to formally charge him.

CHAPTER 15

I heard the shower running when I woke up. In Charlie-world, that meant it was eight o'clock. I was starting to feel better with a couple of nights of restful sleep under my belt. I dumped a carafe of water into the Bunn and called Area Central while it was brewing. The second-watch sergeant answered, and I asked him to notify Barcomb and Donovan I'd be bringing Charlie Newton in at 1000 hours.

Charlie entered the kitchen looking fresh, showered and clean-shaven.

"Good morning, Devlin lad. Are you ready for the big day?"

"The question is, *are you ready for the big day?* They're looking to put *you* in prison, not me, Hemingway," I responded as I poured him his first of two cups of coffee.

"Do you have chocolate milk?" he asked.

"No, I sent the butler out to get some."

He sipped the black coffee. "Well, what's our game plan?"

"I already called Central. They're waiting for me to surrender you at 1000 hours."

"I find your choice of words, 'surrender me,' distasteful."

"If it makes you feel better, *escorting you* to Central, where I'll tell Barcomb and Donovan the ridiculous truth. They'll be getting the story from me, not you, so it's hearsay and can't be used against you in court … if it ever comes down to that."

"I'd prefer to tell them myself," Charlie said.

"I'm sure you would, but I'd prefer you to keep your mouth shut, if that's possible, and take the fifth," I said. "I'll have them schedule their CGI guy to make a couple of composite sketches of Fontanetta and Asshole #2, though I'd prefer them to use our sketch artist in Englewood."

"Sounds like a plan, Devlin lad."

"Remind me to ask them to check with the fire department to see if we can determine where Fontanetta was when he took your call. It's not much but it's all we have right now. We can start showing the composite sketches around that area."

Charlie got up, refilled our coffee cups, and looked at his Rolex. "Your butler must be a Southsider. Is he looking for a brown cow to give chocolate milk?"

• • •

I had to return the rental car to National after the interview, so we took two cars to Area Central. I was driving the rental with Charlie following close behind me on the Dangerous Dan in my Beamer when he apparently became bored or frustrated with the slow-moving traffic. Abruptly changing lanes, he pulled up in the next lane even with me and, with a wide grin and a cutesy wave goodbye, accelerated, crossed two lanes of traffic, and hit the shoulder of the road doing 95 mph. I was still spewing obscenities when I entered the parking lot of Area Central about ten minutes later. I saw the Beamer parked in the lot and checked to make sure it still had two doors, four fenders, and a rear end. The engine was already cold. It was a few minutes before ten o'clock.

Charlie was standing behind the double glass doors in the vestibule of Area Central, watching me examine my car for damage, which brought a smile to his face.

"Did you stop for coffee and doughnuts, Devlin lad?"

"You Northside, no-driving asshole! You will never drive my car again. Ever."

Charlie sniggered as we climbed the stairs to the second floor.

Barcomb and Donovan were there waiting. Donovan, Barcomb, and I went into Interview Room #1, out of Charlie's earshot, and I ran the story down to them. I told them if it were up to Charlie, he'd talk to them until tomorrow morning, but on my advice, he'd be taking the fifth. Everything he knew or had to say would come through me. I assured them I wasn't trying to derail their investigation and explained I needed to stall for time to find Fontanetta.

Both detectives were amenable, but Barcomb said, "Lieutenant, we want to be up front with you; we're not as convinced as you are of Newton's innocence, neither are the dicks who work for you, but we'll give him every benefit of the doubt. We'll thoroughly investigate everything he gives us until there is no more to investigate, or until such time we prove it's all bullshit. If this thing doesn't turn out the way you'd like, I hope it won't ruin our friendship."

"If Charlie turns out to be our bad guy, I'll apologize to everybody involved in this case, starting with you."

Charlie was subsequently taken into the Interview Room, camera turned on, and given his Miranda Rights. He took five and the interview was officially terminated. Camera off.

I asked Donovan if we could use the police sketch artist from Englewood for the composite drawings instead of the CGI software without raising any eyebrows. He said they often used him for high-profile cases, and called the *Wood* to see if he was working. Good fortune smiled upon us, and a half hour later, Officer Melton, the police artist, arrived at Area Central.

Charlie described in meticulous detail the facial characteristics of both suspects. So exact that the descriptions seemed contrived, even to me. The finished sketches were not of the generic variety. Anyone could pick these two guys out of the upper decks at White Sox Park (Cubs Park for Charlie). I could read the skepticism in the faces of Donovan and Barcomb, and the sketch artist, too.

While Charlie was providing descriptions to the artist, Donovan contacted the fire department and made arrangements to review their records.

Two hours later, Barcomb and Donovan dropped us back off in the parking lot of Area Central.

"Why don't you drop off the rental car and we'll go for

lunch? I discovered a quaint Italian restaurant close to the airport," Charlie suggested.

"I don't want Italian," I said.

"I thought you love Italian?"

"I do; the only bad thing about Italian food is three days later and you're hungry again."

CHAPTER 16

January 18, 2014
Saturday
0700 hours

I arrived at the office an hour early the next morning. Sgt. Peak informed me that the IPRA had called Friday afternoon and wanted to know my work schedule. They left a formal notice for me to report to their office at 1100 hours on today's date.

I called the Area Central detectives to see if there had been any progress on the triple.

"We were going to give you a call, Lieu," Detective Barcomb said. "I think we have something on the fire. Two fires reasonably close together that correspond to Newton's phone records. One of them was in the heart of the ghetto, and the second one was around the corner from the Rosebud Restaurant on Taylor Street. I'm going to go out on a limb here and guess our paisan would be more likely to be on Taylor Street than in the Ida B. Wells projects. We're going to take a run up there and show these sketches around, see if we can come up with something."

"That's great news, Jack. Keep me posted."

I don't know many people from Taylor Street, but I did grow up on 69th Street, a predominantly Italian neighborhood, and *I know a guy who knows a guy who might know our guys.* In verbal camouflage Italiano, that means I'll get you the information, but I won't divulge my sources. I gave my paisan, the "Rat Man", a call and made arrangements to meet him for lunch after my IPRA appointment.

● ● ●

The IPRA investigator asked me to take a seat, and I graciously declined. "No thanks, I'm not going to be here that long."

He presented me with the Notification of Charges and Criminal Rights forms, indicating I was a suspect in the murder of Eric Schwartzman, and asked me to sign both forms. I checked the box indicating I'm exercising my constitutional right to remain silent on the Criminal Rights Form and told him to have a pleasant day.

At 1200 hours, I met the Rat Man at the Balagio Ristorante in Homewood. Despite the unflattering sobriquet, Rat is anything but a rat. It was a moniker we hung on him when we were kids, and it followed him through life. Rat's a legit middle-class, blue-collar worker, and though he's not hooked up to the guys with broken noses and mustaches, he knows the players. I gave him a copy of the composite sketches, and he studied them for a minute. Neither one of the subjects in the drawings looked familiar to him, but he promised to show them around to his guys on Taylor Street. He knows who to talk to and how to talk to them. We talked about the old neighborhood and old friends for a while. Twenty minutes later, we were sopping up olive oil and balsamic vinegar with remnants of a peasant loaf. I reached for the check, and Rat wrapped five fingers the size of Italian sausages around my hand and whispered in an intimidating manner, "Get da fuck oudda here!" He's been doing that to me for thirty years now, and I'd prefer to let him pay the check than fight him. Those are the only two choices you get with the Rat Man.

● ● ●

As I was driving back to Area South, I reflected upon my appointment with the IPRA investigator and the Schwartzman homicide investigation. How in the name of Sweet Jesus could I still be considered the prime suspect? These people must have bubblegum for brains! I thought they would have at least waited until the ballistic results came back on my 9mm before presenting me with a Criminal Rights Form. They're going to look foolish when the results do come back and I'm exonerated. This was insane. I'd like to get a gander at the homicide file, but given I'm the prime suspect, I'm sure the powers that be would frown on that. I hoped some overly zealous young Assistant State's Attorney, fresh out of law school, wasn't looking to put the first notch on his gun. Bagging a copper is like bagging a 16- point white tail, difference being in this case it would be my 16-pound white ass. Rule of thumb: any lawyer can put a guilty man in prison, but it takes a true master of the craft to send an innocent man up the river.

I'd be the first guy in the annals of American Jurisprudence to get life for calling somebody a douche bag.

• • •

I got back to the office at 1345 hours. Sgt. Abels handed me the two gangbanger homicide files from the other day. Turned out Tiger Woods wasn't the offender in Facchini's case after all. The shooter was a seventeen-year-old kid, barely out of diapers. He forfeited his freedom and will most likely spend the rest of his natural life in prison, and for what? Because somebody wore the visor of his baseball cap the wrong way? He was still doing better than the sixteen-year-old kid with the cap, though.

No messages from Chief Daniels, detectives Barcomb or Donovan, IPRA, or the IAD. Some I would like to hear from; others, not so much.

I strolled into my office and closed the door behind me. I hung my jacket, loosened my tie, undid my top shirt button, and then plopped into the desk chair and dropped my head into my hands. I was tired, not so much physically anymore, but mentally. I wanted this triple murder nightmare, and the Schwartzman investigation, to go away. I had to pull Charlie out of the fire, and myself as well, but I wasn't having much success at either.

I opened the desk drawer and took out Kerri's photo again. I wasn't having much luck there, either. She hadn't deserved the salvo of insults I launched at her the other night. This tough guy façade of mine is self-destructive and getting old. Kerri knows it's a veneer, but she didn't have any more luck penetrating it than I do. She would have stayed and tried to make the marriage work if I had been willing to meet her halfway. Get out of Homicide, work straight days in some less dangerous unit, but the enemy within wouldn't allow me to compromise.

I pressed my lips to her photo, crushed the frame against my forehead, and told the photo words Kerri's ears would probably never hear again: I love you. My eyes misted over, and I choked down a growing lump in the back of my throat. I put her photo back in the drawer. She's much better off with Emmett the Frog.

CHAPTER 17

I got home early from work. Didn't seem to be much more I could do on the Schwartzman homicide or the triple for the time being except sit tight and wait until some new developments popped up.

I was preparing peanut butter and jelly sandwiches when I heard a knock on the door.

I opened it, and standing there was a man in wingtip shoes. I thought it was Robert Redford at first, maybe wanting me to costar with him in a movie, but the shoes were a dead giveaway. He flashed a button at me and said, "FBI. Can I talk to you for a couple of minutes, Lieutenant?"

"Come in," I replied.

"I'm Special Agent John Willick", he said, stepping across the threshold.

"No need to be so formal, I know who you are," I said. "I recognized you immediately, and frankly, I wouldn't let another FBI agent into my house without a warrant. I remember you from your days on the force. In fact, I remember monitoring the radio the night you got shot up on the Westside. I heard sometime later you joined the feebs. Too bad. I heard you were a good copper."

John snickered. "Thank you for the left-handed compliment, Lieutenant. All of the agents aren't bad guys."

"Yeah, I know. It's a shame 99% of them have to give the entire organization a bad name. And call me Devlin."

John didn't like the joke but, being a former copper, understood police humor and police sentiment for the feebs.

"Okay, Devlin, if you have a few minutes, I'd like to talk to you about Charlie Newton and your triple homicide. Maybe we can help each other."

We walked into the living room, and I motioned for John to have a seat in the Queen Anne.

John began, "Have you ever heard of the Golden Triangle?"

"Blond pussy?"

John did laugh at that one. I'd have to remember to restrict my jokes to vaginas instead of FBI agents, though it did sound redundant in the same sentence.

"Not exactly," he was still chuckling, "the Golden Triangle is in Southeast Asia. It consists of four countries: Burma, Vietnam, Laos, and Thailand. Most of the heroin that comes into this country is processed there. However, the opium poppy itself is grown in great abundance in the province of Yunnan, where one of your victims is from. We have evidence the Chinese have set up an intricate drug distribution operation throughout America, and they've been laundering huge sums of cash, hundreds of millions, through bogus accounts set up at the Mercantile Exchange, which brings me to Hiram Goldenstein."

"You think Goldenstein and Chiang Yu were hooked up together smuggling dope from China?" I asked.

"Chiang Yu for sure," Willick said. "We don't think Goldenstein was directly involved in the importation of the drugs, but he was setting up dummy accounts to launder the money for them through the Merc."

"What makes you think that?" I asked.

"Goldenstein used to be a lawyer, did you know that?"

"No, I didn't," I replied.

"He was disbarred from the ABA twenty years ago for unethical conduct when he worked for a law firm concentrated in the insurance industry. He picked names out of the obituaries and established dummy accounts for them, and then he filed claims on their behalf and cashed in. After his law license was taken away, he landed on his feet at the Merc. We have documented evidence he was setting up fictitious accounts there, too. Old habits die hard."

"How about Doherty?"

"We don't have much on Doherty, but we assume he was a courier. Couriers bring in most of the drugs coming into this country from Southeast Asia, and Doherty traveled there more often than he changed his shorts," Willick said. "Any of this sound interesting to you?"

"It doesn't give us our killer, but it ties our three victims together."

"You're right, it doesn't give you your killer. That's why I'd like to talk to you about Charlie Newton."

CHAPTER 18

"Devlin, I've been forewarned you and Charlie Newton are close friends, and you're fiercely loyal to him. I understand that, and I respect that. I've also been told despite the fact you have a few personal quirks of your own, like telling bad jokes, you're a straight shooter and an honest copper, so I'd like to ask you some questions about him."

"Shoot."

"How long and how well do you know him?"

"I've known him over twelve years now, and I know him well," I replied.

"His first book came out in 2008, correct?"

"Yes."

"So, you knew him six or seven years prior to the release of that first book, right?"

"That's about right."

"What did Charlie Newton do for a living those six or seven years you knew him before his book came out?"

"Nothing that I know of."

"How did he support himself?"

"I see where you're going with this," I said. "Charlie had substantial real estate holdings, and he also made a lot of money building resorts and owning restaurants. If you promise not to blab to the IRS, he might have even made a couple of bucks on the ponies."

"Does he still own any, or all, of these things?" Willick asked.

"No, one fine day, Charlie decided to liquidate all of his assets, even his house, and devoted himself, body and soul, to a writing career," I said. "That may seem like an audacious step to take to you and me, but Charlie's a gambler and self-confident, and he's not afraid to roll the dice."

"But you don't know that's where he got his money, correct? Other than the fact that's where he told you it came from?"

"I didn't ask to see his financial portfolio, if that's what you mean."

"Do you know what Charlie Newton was doing last year in Laos and Vietnam, the Golden Triangle?"

"No, but Charlie's a world traveler. I'm sure there were a few unsolved murders in the United Kingdom, Germany, South Africa, and Ireland while he was there but that doesn't mean he did them or that he's an international assassin."

"No, it doesn't. However, we don't have a houseful of dead Irishmen or Germans with Charlie's fingerprints inside the house and his car parked outside, either."

"I know what it looks like, John, but you're shooting low and left of center. If Charlie murdered those three guys, or if he's involved in the importation of heroin, I'll put the handcuffs on him myself. And that's a promise."

"One more thing, Devlin. Did you know Newton was arrested at the airport for Possession of Marijuana in the early '80s?"

"John, c'mon for chrissakes, I pulled his rap sheet. He had about two seeds over the misdemeanor limit. You were a copper; you know that 95% of the American public would be suspect if we took that into consideration."

"That's true, but did you also know that at the exact time Newton was being arrested, about a hundred feet from where he was standing, DEA seized three hundred pounds of heroin off of a C-123K transport plane? Two guys were taken into custody: Adler "Barry" Seal and Wallace "Buzz" Sawyer. Did you ever hear Charlie Newton mention either of their names?" he asked.

"Not that I can recall," I said.

"Did you ever hear Charlie Newton mention Mena, Arkansas?"

"I know he has a few friends in Arkansas, but again, he has friends all over this country, in fact, all over the world."

"Who's in Mena?" I asked.

"Not who, but what. There's a small airport there, nestled amongst the dense pines and hardwood forests of the Ouachita Mountains, which was the hub of gunrunning and dope smuggling activities in the early to mid-eighties."

"I don't understand what you think Newton's arrest for possession of a nickel bag has to do with Seal, Sawyer, or Mena."

"Newton was believed to have been the third guy on the plane with them."

"That's nuts. Don't you think the two mutts would have ratted him out before they got banged with big time in the joint?" I asked.

"Neither one of them was prosecuted. The U.S. Attorney's Office dropped charges against them, and said they lacked probable cause to proceed against Newton. Naturally, when the government declined to prosecute the two primaries, the investigation was terminated altogether and Newton was never charged."

"The U.S. Attorney declined to prosecute? What happened there?"

"I don't know for sure, maybe a faulty warrant, but the case was dropped."

"You know how slick the G is; maybe they're still laying their trap," I said. "Sometimes it takes them twenty or thirty years to put their case together if you're guilty, and two to three weeks if you're innocent, but they always get their man in the end."

"I'm sure the government won't be prosecuting either one of them. Seal was gunned down in front of the Salvation Army in Baton Rouge a few years later by a couple of hit men from the Medellin cartel, and Sawyer was killed when he was copiloting the C-123K and it mysteriously crashed and burned. Columbians don't play nice."

"I hope whoever that U.S. Attorney was who declined to prosecute them runs for Cook County State's Attorney, and soon. They're trying to send me to the joint for calling some guy a douche bag."

John stood to leave and reached for my hand. "Thanks for your time, Devlin. If there's anything I can do for you at the Bureau, give me a jingle."

I walked him to the door, and we shook hands again. His lips pressed into a small, thwarted smile.

"My sources were right, Devlin. You are loyal, and I hope your loyalty is justified at the end. I'd hate to see you get jammed up over this guy. Did you ever hear the saying there is always the threat of tomorrow's treachery? Listen to your eyes and your ears, not your heart."

• • •

The red message light was blinking on my answering machine. I depressed playback.

It was the marijuana totin', international drug smuggling assassin himself. "Devlin lad, I thought perhaps if you haven't already engorged yourself on peanut butter and jelly, you'd like to meet me at Nick and Vito's for a pizza at seven o'clock. I would have called you at work earlier but feared impeding your progress in saving me from the gallows."

If something didn't start to develop soon on the triple, Charlie's last crack may turn out to be visionary.

CHAPTER 19

January 18, 2014
Saturday
1900 hours

Charlie was flirting with the waitress, a raven-haired beauty with big brown eyes, when I arrived at Nick and Vito's. No surprise there.

"Devlin lad, have I been exonerated yet?" Charlie gushed.

"Not yet, funny man, but I'm working on it."

"You seem down," Charlie said. I didn't tell him about my visit from the FBI. I told him instead about Schwartzman.

"While you were on your sabbatical in Mexico, some lump of a reporter wrote a couple of disparaging articles about us. I called him a douche bag, and a couple of days later he showed up with two bullet holes in the back of his head. The deputy superintendent and a few guys showed up at my house at three in the morning and asked me for my 9mm. They think I murdered him. That's why I told you when you called that first night from Juarez my phone maybe tapped. They think you and I are running around playing *Let's See Who Can Kill the Most Guys in the Shortest Amount of Time."*

Charlie was almost gleeful. "So we're both murder suspects?"

"Yes, it seems so," I said and added, "Did anybody ever tell you that you have a strange sense of humor?"

"Are you worried?" Charlie asked.

"Not yet. They don't have any evidence against me, just conjecture, so let's concentrate our efforts on keeping you out of the joint."

The waitress glided across the tiled floor, balancing a pizza overhead with one hand and a tray with a pitcher of Diet Pepsi and a bottle of Miller Lite for Charlie in the other. He slipped her a wink and a conspiratorial smile. She returned the wink and sashayed away.

"I have to pick her up after work," Charlie confided.

We wreaked havoc on the pizza. Charlie dabbed at the corners of his mouth with a white linen napkin, and then holding it high in the air, casually dropped it onto the red gingham tablecloth like a parachute, signaling the end of the meal. "Devlin lad, have you ever considered the possibility that these murders are connected?"

"Connected?" I asked, "No, I don't see any connection between the three homicide victims from Avalon Trails and a newspaper reporter getting whacked downtown a couple of days later. Besides, your killers were in Mexico with you."

"Two of them were, but what about the third guy?"

"Why would he murder the reporter?" I asked.

"I have no idea. Why did they murder the three? But don't you find it strange that you and I are both being looked at as murder suspects?"

It was strange, yes, but I've encountered many bizarre coincidences over the years. "Why would somebody want to set us up as patsies?" I asked.

Charlie waved the waitress over and ordered his second beer for the day. "Devlin lad, you said it the other day yourself; I was targeted, but why? I write fictional books and don't have any known enemies. You, on the other hand, do. Suppose I was set up to discredit you? The murders occur in your area of investigation, and you and I are friends. Even if you hadn't supported me, that alone would have cast you in a bad light. Two days later, a reporter you locked horns with is executed."

"Interesting theory, Charlie; feasible, but unlikely. How many people even know you and I are friends?"

Charlie took a long pull on the Miller.

"My point exactly. Not many people know we are pals, so how did the dead reporter find out so fast?" he asked.

Good question. I recalled having that same thought the morning Schwartzman asked it, but summarily dismissed it because Schwartzman hadn't taken two to the head at that time and it seemed less important. Still, I couldn't see the murders being related, but I did have to admit that Charlie's theory had merit. I wouldn't discard it. How did Schwartzman know that first morning Charlie and I were friends? Who was his source of information? Could his source of information be cunning enough to set all three of us up in some intricate, grand master plan? He'd have to be one hell of a smart dude to make this all come together.

"Not many," I said, after pondering the question for a few seconds. "Two of my sergeants, Bill Peak and Kenny

Abels; Pete and Beth Steffen; and Kerri are all that come to mind. Pete and Beth don't even know me well, so I think we can rule them out. I grew up with Kenny Abels; I've known him my entire life, and I trust Bill Peak completely. And although I'm sure Kerri would have liked to pin me to the mattress with the kitchen butcher knife on a few occasions, she isn't capable of such treachery."

"Only a theory," Charlie said dismissively.

"You write too many mystery novels."

My cell phone rang.

"Hello."

"Devlin? This is the Rat Man. I think I have an ID on one of your guys."

CHAPTER 20

January 18, 2014
Saturday
2015 hours

"Talk to me, Rat Man."

"A friend of mine from Taylor Street told me a couple of your guys were showing the drawings around earlier today. He told them he didn't know them, but he thinks the number-two drawing is of a guy named Johnny Giaccone. He hangs around with a dude named Mario, who has a mole on his face, but he doesn't know Mario's last name or where he lives. Both of them are regulars on Taylor Street. My guy says they're both wannabe wiseguys and are trying to prove themselves. They're both dangerous, so be careful, goomba."

"Thanks, Rat Man. I'd like to kiss you right on your lips."

"Heyyyy, none of that shit, mudderfucker!"

I hung up and called the office. I asked the detective who answered to run John Giaccone's name for me and to call me back as soon as he found anything.

"I think we may have broken the ice, Hemingway. I

believe you're about to be formally introduced to your old friend, Johnny Giaccone, AKA Suspect #2. Finish your beer, and let's start heading toward Taylor Street."

Charlie glanced over at the waitress then back at me with a hangdog expression on his face. "Do you have any idea what you're doing to my social life?"

"Charlie, let's go," I ordered. "You can come back tomorrow and eat pizza again."

Charlie explained to the waitress some urgent business had come up; fifteen minutes later, we were on the Dangerous Dan Ryan Expressway at Pershing Road when my cell phone rang.

"I have the info on Giaccone," the detective said.

"Shoot."

"He has a long sheet for armed robberies and aggravated batteries. He's been in and out of the joint four times. He gave a home address of 815 S. May on his last arrest in November of 2013."

"Do we have any teams available right now?" I asked.

"Everyone is tied up on a job, except Wojcik and Dunnigan. They're up and available."

"Have them meet me ASAP at Taylor and Aberdeen."

Twenty minutes later, Dunnigan and Wojcik arrived for the meet, and I explained the situation to them.

"Let's set up on the house. Charlie and I will take the point. Switch your radio frequency to car to car. If Charlie ID's Giaccone, we'll take him down. His rap sheet says he's a shooter, so be careful."

I parked on the west side of the street about a half block from Giaccone's front entrance so Charlie could get a good eyeball on him. A red Z4 is not the best choice for a surveillance unit, too conspicuous, but Charlie's red Vette wasn't any better. If Giaccone did make us, I hoped he'd make us for coppers and not mistake us for two wiseguys there to whack him.

Hours dragged by. I checked my watch every few minutes. It was 0330 hours, and we'd been sitting there for over seven hours. Charlie was intense, like a kid in line at Six Flags waiting to board the Kingda Ka. He hadn't complained once about his legs cramping or it being past his scheduled bedtime. I was guessing Wojcik and Dunnigan weren't as thrilled.

Taylor Street had shut down for the night; the restaurants and bars were all closed. Residential lights on both sides of the street went dark, and the streets took on an eerie silence.

A black Mustang roared up and parked two car lengths ahead of us. The driver exited.

"That's him", Charlie said.

CHAPTER 21

January 19, 2014
Sunday
0335 hours

I keyed the radio. "Our bad guy pulled up in a black Mustang. He's wearing dark clothing; that's all I can make out from here. Let's take him down."

I turned to Charlie. "Stay in the car."

Exiting the Z4, I called to Giaccone, "Police officer, can I talk to you for a minute?" The police radio was in my left hand, and my snub was pressed tightly up against my right thigh.

Without warning, Giaccone pivoted and fired two shots at me, jumped over the banister, and fled through the gangway before I could get off a shot. The thunderous reports shattered the early morning silence. Everything instantly reduced to slow-mo as I began the foot chase. Sound amplified a hundredfold. Giaccone quietly flipped over the back fence, but it sounded like a train wreck at this hour of the morning. I tried to notify Wojcik and Dunnigan over the radio I had a foot chase and to cover the north end of the alley, but I was breathing hard and over modulating. They couldn't read me. Unable to jump the fence with a radio in one hand and a gun in the other, I had to make the decision to dump one of them. I opted for the radio. I jumped the fence and another shot rang out. I tried to raise my gun to return fire in the direction of the muzzle flash, but I couldn't. My gun was on the ground in the alley, and my right arm was on fire. I'm shot, goddamn it! I tried to reach for my gun but couldn't move my arm. Either Giaccone had great nighttime vision or great predatory instincts, but in either case, he knew I was disabled and came racing back down the alley toward me to finish the job. My mind and my heart were pumping faster than his legs, and my only thought as he came running toward me was that I was going to die in an alley next to a garbage can. The chain link fence behind me rattled. Appearing out of nowhere, Charlie vaulted over the fence like an Olympian, picked up my gun, and took a knee, firing off all of the rounds in rapid succession. Giaccone lay dead in the middle of the alley.

"Are you all right?" Charlie asked.

"No, you asshole, I'm shot! Give me that gun and get your ass out of here, fast," I said.

"Why?"

"Charlie, we don't have time to argue. Go!"

"But why? He shot you!"

"Charlie, please. I'll explain later."

Charlie flipped back over the fence and disappeared as quietly into the darkness as he had come. A moment later, I saw the emergency flashers on Dunnigan and Wojcik's squad car speeding toward me and heard the wail of police and ambulance sirens not far behind. House lights started popping on all over. Within minutes, I was being escorted to an ambulance; twenty minutes later, oscillating red lights bounced off the entrance doors of the emergency room at the Stroger County Hospital. The ER was overrun with people, looking more like a Wal-Mart on Black Friday. It may be considered early Sunday morning for churchgoers, but it was still considered late Saturday night for street people. Two stout EMTs wheeled me through the double sliding doors and through the corridor into the #6 treatment cubicle and, with the assistance of a nurse, hefted me onto a gurney, then dragged the curtain on the U-track around me. Unwashed bodies, feces, and vomit stifled the air. I wished I were back in the alley next to the garbage cans. Italian trash smells like dinner. Unseen faces moaned and groaned and shrieked in pain all around me. I wasn't sure if they sent me here to cure me or kill me.

The nurse slipped a blood pressure cuff around my arm and took my vitals. "How are you feeling?" she asked.

"I need two emergency cans of Febreeze."

She chuckled. "You'll get used to it."

"I hope I'm not here long enough to get used to it."

She removed the cuff from my arm and said, "Your blood pressure is high, but that's expected with a gunshot wound. Can you move your hand?"

I attempted to wiggle my fingers. "Barely."

"The doctor will be in here in a moment to examine you," she said and hurried from the cubicle.

Sirens waned outside the hospital, signaling the arrival of new customers. A harried young intern drew back the curtain and entered the cubicle. I could have mistaken him for Doogie Howser except he was black. I was going to ask him if he wanted to make a career out of medicine when he got out of high school, but it's not wise to get cute with the doctor treating you. He'll anesthetize me, and when I wake up my testicles will be gone. He picked up my chart and walked around the gurney to examine my arm. "There doesn't appear to be any vascular damage or fractures, just soft tissue damage, but I'm going order some x-rays to make sure. If the x-rays look good, I'll give you a prescription for pain management and antibiotics and send you home. You were lucky."

"If I was lucky, he would have missed."

The doctor smiled and said, "I'll be back to see you in a few minutes." He left the room and pulled the curtain closed. A moment later, he returned. "Officer, there's someone from your department here to see you," he said.

Peter Puffer, the IPRA investigator I verbally berated last week, entered. Gosh, my night was going swell. I'm sure the peter puffer wished Giaccone had given me a second asshole and placed it right between my eyes.

I described the events leading up to the shootings, excluding Charlie's presence or participation in the alley.

"Lieutenant, are you right handed or left handed?" he asked.

"Right handed."

"How did you manage to shoot Mr. Giaccone with your right hand after you sustained that gunshot injury to your right arm? Or did you shoot him first? Or did he shoot you after he was dead?"

When I sensed the interview turned adversarial, I called out, "Doctor." The intern reappeared a moment later, and I said, "I'm feeling faint."

"You'll have to leave, sir," the intern ordered the peter puffer.

The IPRA investigator made some disgruntled noises, turned, and stomped out of the room in a huff. I giggled. Sometimes, I amuse myself. The ploy would only postpone the inevitable, though; sooner or later, I'd have to have to answer those questions, but for right now it would give me some time to gather my thoughts.

CHAPTER 22

January 19, 2014
Sunday
0445 hours

The fainting spell ruse almost backfired on me. The ER doctor wanted to admit me overnight for observation because of it, but I convinced him I felt better.

Charlie, Dunnigan, Wojcik, and all on-duty Violent Crimes South personnel were outside in the waiting room when I exited the ER.

Relieved faces and nervous smiles greeted me.

Eddie Wojcik told me they hooked the dead guy's Mustang and were having it towed into the Area to be processed.

"Hey, Lieu, you were lucky. A few inches to the left and he would have shot you in the dick!" Dunnigan quipped.

"How do you figure I was lucky?" I asked, "I still need my right arm."

We were still laughing as we neared the exit. I came to an abrupt halt when I saw Kerri rushing through the lobby toward me, her unbridled weeping drowning out all the extraneous hospital noises. She was wearing pink house slippers and a gray sweat suit. She'd never looked so lovely. Charlie and the coppers vaporized. I stood alone, frozen in space and time.

Kerri threw her delicate arms around my neck, and kissed my cheek hard.

"Are you alright, Devlin?" she asked.

I smiled. "I can't move my fingers on my right hand so I think my sex life is over with for a few months."

Kerri ignored the joke or didn't think it was funny. Tears in multitudes streamed down her face. "Devlin, please, quit this goddamn job! This is the second time in two years you've been shot," she sobbed. "Is it going to take a bullet through your thick Irish skull to convince you?"

"Calm down, it's barely a graze wound," I lied. I brushed the auburn hair out of her eyes with the back of my good hand and dabbed at her tears with my shirtsleeve.

"Kerri, we've been over this a thousand times. What would I do? Be a florist? Do oil changes at a Jiffy Lube?" I asked. "I am what I am. If I quit this job, I wouldn't be me. I can't tell you not to cry or worry because that's who you are, and you can't stop being you any easier than I can stop being me. We're oil and water."

I pulled her tight against me and felt her fragile body melt into mine. She was trembling. "I'll be all right, Kerri. Go home to Emmett the Frog."

She pushed herself away from me, turned and ran from the lobby.

I stood and watched her run away. "Goodbye, Kerri," I whispered as I dabbed at a tear of my own.

CHAPTER 23

January 20, 2014
Monday
0900 hours

The Department put me on the medical and carried me Injured on Duty, but if there was one thing I didn't want to be, it was off of work, not then. I felt like the investigation was gaining momentum. Giaccone, obviously, wouldn't be saying much to assist in the investigation, but the next few days in these investigations could be critical. If the injury was to something other than my right hand, I could lie and say it was better, but under the circumstances, the department would require me to demonstrate I was proficient with a gun before they'd release me from the medical and allow me to return to work. I couldn't fake or lie my way out of that. I could barely pull down my zipper, never mind disassemble a 9mm and put it back together again.

At 0900 hours, Chief Daniels called me at home. "Do you have any coffee on?" he asked.

"I always have coffee on, Chief."

A half hour later, Chief Daniels arrived at my house. I

poured him a cup of coffee with my left hand, and we went into the living room.

He sipped cautiously. "Good coffee."

"Did you come to check on my well-being?" I asked.

The Chief took a second sip and set his cup down on the coffee table.

"Devlin, I want to talk to you off the record. Forget I'm the Chief and think of me as your friend."

"I already do," I replied. "Otherwise I'd be working for Streets and San by now."

"Good. This Schwartzman murder investigation is spiraling out of control. Schwartzman's publisher and chief editor, Aaron Weiss, is putting tremendous pressure on the department to do something about you. IPRA and the BIA want to bring the Schwartzman murder and the triple homicide files to the State's Attorney's Special Prosecution Unit, and they've called in the feds to look at you for violation of civil rights. You calling them names and threatening to beat them up didn't help matters. They are convinced you and Charlie Newton are involved in all four murders."

"How did the geniuses deduce that? Didn't the results come back from the lab yet on my 9mm?" I asked.

"Yes, they did. Unfortunately, the results don't eliminate you as a suspect. One of the bullets Schwartzman took to the head was a through and through, and it was never recovered. The second bullet was a 9mm, but it wasn't suitable for comparison."

"Great! This never happens on CSI," I said. "We need a new lab."

"This is no laughing matter anymore, Devlin. Your *exigent circumstance* and other police rhetoric bullshit isn't going to fly anymore. The federal and state governments are serious about putting you in prison, and the department is going to hang you out to dry. Aaron Weiss and his newspaper will make certain of that; they'll crucify you in the press. Last night, the ADS had to get another complaint register on you for getting involved in the triple after you were taken off of the case. You have one CR# for being a suspect in a homicide, and now this! What the hell were you doing at 8th & May after you were told to stay away from the case?"

"Exigent circumstances," I smiled. "I received information last night from a confidential informant that Giaccone was about to flee our jurisdiction, so I had to move on it fast. The dicks working the case from Area Central were off duty, so I got a team from Area South to assist me. Simple as that."

"Is that the truth?" the Chief asked.

I smiled, "That's my story and I'm stickin' to it."

"How did you ID Giaccone?"

"Charlie Newton was with me. We set up surveillance on Giaccone's house; when he pulled up and exited his car, Charlie ID'd him as the #2 suspect. I got out of the car to question him, and the mutt opened fire on me. Is the department pissed off at me for getting shot, too?"

"Devlin, not one single shred of evidence exists to indicate Giaccone was involved in those murders, nor does anyone believe an abduction of Charlie Newton ever occurred. Charlie Newton is the suspect—not a victim and not a witness. A suspect … and it appears you're covering for him."

I ripped the cellophane off a panetela with my teeth and spit it on the coffee table. "I don't give a shit what it appears like, Boss; Charlie Newton didn't kill those mutts and I'm not covering for him because I don't have to. What am I supposed to do, sit back and watch him get sandbagged? I am not going to let that happen, so they can get CR#s on me, reassign me, suspend me, do whatever they think they have to do, but I am not going to stand idly by and let my friend take the pipe for a triple murder he didn't commit—and, for the record, I didn't smoke the douche bag, either," I said. I lit the panetela. The Chief looked down at his shoes and shook his head.

"I spoke to the IPRA investigator earlier. He told me he asked you how you managed to shoot Giaccone after you sustained the gunshot wound to your arm." It was a question more than a statement.

"I picked up the gun with my left hand and returned fire."

"You're one hell of a marksman with your left hand. Giaccone took five in the 10 ring."

"No shit? I'll bet I couldn't do that again in a hundred years."

The Chief gulped down the rest of his coffee and smiled disingenuously. "I'll bet you couldn't, either."

The Chief stood to leave. "Forewarned is forearmed, Devlin. The stronger you defend this guy, and the more you involve yourself in this investigation, the more complicit it makes you look."

"Thank you, Chief," I said. "I'll tell Charlie to pack his toothbrush because I'm going to leave him out there hanging." Chief Daniels grimaced and shook his head as he walked out the door.

•   •   •

Fuckin' Charlie! Five in the 10 ring?

CHAPTER 24

I called Area Central after the Chief left my house. "Is Barcomb or Donovan around?" I asked.

"Barcomb's here. Hold on."

A moment later, Barcomb picked up.

"Hey, Jack, this is Lt. Cahill. Did anything come back from ballistics yet on Giaccone's gun?"

"Results came in a few minutes ago, Lieu. Not the gun from our triple," he said. "I heard about the fiasco last night. How are you feeling?"

"I'll be able to punch the clown again in a couple of weeks. Bozo will appreciate the rest," I said. "Jack, I hate to impose on you again, but I have to ask you for a large favor. Could you please pull every arrest report, case report, contact analysis report, and any and all court transcripts you can get your hands on for all three of our dead guys from Avalon Trails, as well as on my friend from last night, John Giaccone?"

"Whew, you're burying us here, Lieu."

114

"I know, it's a lot of work. I'm sorry to ask, but I'm getting desperate. I got word a few minutes ago the State's Attorney's Office and the "G" are trying to charge me with the Schwartzman homicide and Charlie Newton with your triple."

"Don't worry, Lieu, we'll get every scrap of paper we can dig up for you, but it's going to take us a couple of days to gather it all up, and that's if we're lucky. I can't even take a stab at how long it will take us to go through all of it—a week, maybe two."

"You don't have to go through it, Jack. Drop it off at my house as soon as you can, and I'll go through it. I'm IOD and have nothing but time. I want to see if Mario's name pops up someplace or try to find some connection between any of them."

"As soon as I have them, you'll have them," Barcomb promised.

I started to hang up the phone and, as an afterthought, I asked, "Jack, do you know who's handling the Schwartzman case on days?"

"Johnson and Lazzaro," he replied.

"Are they around?"

"They're sitting right next to me."

"Tell them to get on the phone."

A moment later, a husky black voice picked up.

"Detective Johnson."

"Hi, Johnson. This is Lt. Cahill. I was expecting you to come talk to me about your case."

Johnson paused. "The two detectives working the case on midnights said they went to your house with the ADS and did talk to you. You told them you were invoking your right to remain silent. No sense me coming to talk to you."

"Good point. I forgot about the Mickey Mouse Club coming to my house. Are you making any progress on the case?" I asked.

"Not much."

"You must have talked to some of Schwartzman's friends, or family, or coworkers?"

"Most of them."

"Any of them have any idea who may have killed him?"

"Yes, sir, his friends and family all think you killed him."

I couldn't help but laugh at his painful honesty.

"How about his coworkers?" I asked, "They think I whacked him, too?"

"Yes, sir, I believe they do, but they haven't been cooperative or forthcoming. Seems they distrust the police for some strange reason."

"Any friends or fellow workers he's especially close with?" I asked.

"There's one guy at work, but we haven't been able to interview him yet."

"Why not?" I asked.

"We can't locate him. One reporter told us the guy was on assignment, one reporter told us he was on vacation, and another reporter told us he quit."

"Did you run him for a driver's license or a voter's registration for a home address?

"No, we were waiting for him to return to work."

"How about if reporter #3 was correct and he quit the job? You'll be waiting a long time."

"Yes, sir," the detective responded meekly.

"What's the guy's name?" I asked

Another long pause. "Lieutenant, this is awkward, but I can't give you the guy's name. We've been ordered not to discuss this investigation with you. I already gave you more than I should have."

"You've been ordered by who not to discuss the investigation with me?" I spat into the phone.

"The Superintendent of Police by way of the Area Commander," Johnson replied.

I knew then Johnson and Lazzaro weren't aggressively searching for Schwartzman's friend because they had already formulated an opinion as to the identity of the offender. Me.

My knuckles went white around the phone. "Johnson, listen to me, those two empty-holstered motherfuckers couldn't put a pimple on a policeman's ass. Neither one of them were ever detectives. They were desk jockeys their entire careers, and the only thing either one of them ever locked up was their desk drawer at night when they were going home."

The phone on the other end was silent, so I continued, "I'm going to help you speed up your investigation, Johnson. Here's something the dicks from midnights and Schwartzman's friends, family and coworkers don't know: I didn't murder the asshole, so don't waste your time focusing your attention on me. Look elsewhere, and maybe you'll clear the case."

I was met with a long silence again, and finally Johnson spoke. "Kiese, Arthur Kiese."

CHAPTER 25

I peered out the window to check the weather conditions. I saw Anthony across the street standing in the window, holding Annie in his arms and watching his wife, Mary, shovel the driveway. The snow was up to her knees.

Good day to take a ride downtown and talk to Aaron Weiss, Schwartzman's editor, if I could get my car out of the garage. I took copies of Schwartzman's articles and stuffed them in the inside pocket of my overcoat. The Department would frown on me talking to Weiss, but I was in shit so deep it didn't make any difference at this point. I was sure I'd be well received.

• • •

Leaving the Z parked illegally in front of the Kinzie Chophouse on Wells Street at noontime didn't seem like a good idea. The Department wouldn't be non-suiting parking tickets for me anytime soon, and getting it towed would cost fifty cents more than paying for parking, so I found a garage on Franklin Street, a few blocks away, and hoofed it. The exercise would do me good anyway.

I trudged through the snow, and fifteen minutes later, I was pussyfooting my way across the slick green and orange terrazzo flooring in the lobby of the Merchandise Mart toward the elevator. Half of the people getting into the elevator with me looked like communists; I was convinced the other half *were* communists. I felt like George Bush at a Democratic convention. I asked one of the pinkos to push 10 for me.

Moments later, I entered the outer office of Aaron Weiss and hurried by his secretary. She shrieked, "Excuse me, is there something I can do you for you?" I told her to tell Mr. Weiss I was there for our appointment as I strode past her desk. She launched out of her seat, biting at my heels as I barged into Aaron Weiss's office.

He sprung from behind his desk, brows knitted, and shouted, "Who the hell are you?"

I introduced myself as he glared at his secretary. "Why didn't you stop him?"

I answered for her. "Mr. Weiss, you should have hired a retired linebacker with nice legs and secretarial skills if you wanted someone who could stop me."

Weiss stared at me for a long moment and dismissed the secretary with the wave of a hand.

I envisioned Aaron Weiss to look like Ed Asner, but he was a svelte, much younger man than I expected. He removed his wire-rimmed glasses and placed them in the inside pocket of his gray windowpane suit jacket.

"So, you are the infamous Lt. Devlin Cahill, just the man I don't want to talk to."

"I don't want to talk to you either. Unfortunately, my current situation mandates I must do so."

"What would you like to talk about?" Weiss asked.

"I want to talk about the rumor your newspaper started about Mrs. O'Leary's cow kicking over the lantern," I said. "What do you think I want to talk about?"

I removed the articles Schwartzman had written from my jacket pocket and tossed them on his desk.

Weiss took a cursory glance down at the newspapers, but made no effort to touch them.

"I'd like you to read those articles, Mr. Weiss."

Weiss remained motionless. "I've read them, thank you."

"Read them again," I said, "Do you remember reading the part where Erik Schwartzman referred to Charlie Newton as a convicted felon and having a history of narcotics violations?" I asked.

Weiss continued to glare at me, and I continued. "What would you infer from reading that article, Mr. Weiss? The truth of the matter is Charlie Newton was arrested one time in his life for possession of a nickel-bag of marijuana, which at that time was a felony. The charge was reduced to a misdemeanor in court, and he received one-year supervision. I don't know if you're aware of it, but when someone meets the requirements of their supervision, it is not considered a conviction," I said and added, "As publisher and chief editor of this newspaper, do you consider that article to be fair and accurate reporting?"

Aaron Weiss casually picked the newspaper up from the desk and held it at arm's length as he skimmed over it with disinterest.

"So, you see I wasn't associating with known felons as Schwartzman alleged. Charlie Newton is a successful, well-respected novelist and a law-abiding citizen."

Weiss still held the article at arm's length, but read it with more interest. His brows relaxed, and his features softened.

"The investigation wasn't taken away from me for any wrongdoing on my part, as one might surmise from reading that article. On the contrary, it was reassigned to *avoid* any allegations of impropriety."

Aaron Weiss laid the paper down on his desk, but remained noncommittal.

Changing the subject, he said, "I don't tolerate anyone being abusive to one of my reporters."

"I'm guessing you didn't appreciate me barging into your office today, anymore than I appreciated Erik Schwartzman barging into mine and thrusting a department directive into my face about two inches from my nose, nor did I appreciate him blocking my path on the way to my office a few weeks ago and insinuating I wouldn't conduct an impartial investigation."

Weiss remained aloof and silent.

"I didn't like Erik Schwartzman, and I may have physically ejected him from my office and called him a couple of names, but I didn't kill him."

Aaron Weiss flumped down into his large, leather swivel chair and asked, "So, you're here why, Lieutenant?"

"I don't think this comes as any surprise to you, but you and your paper swing a big hammer in this city, and right now it's aimed at me. The Chicago Police Department is as tough as they come on the street, but they knuckle under easily to political pressure and adverse publicity. You're using your influence to pressure the Department into initiating action against me, and they will, whether it's warranted or not. They call it damage control. All I did was call Erick Schwartzman a name a couple of weeks ago, and that was the extent of it; for that, you would see me lose my livelihood and go to prison, possibly for the rest of my life."

Aaron Weiss leaned back in his chair, steepled his fingers, and stared at the newspapers on his desk in deep thought. After a moment, he rocked forward and said, "Lieutenant, despite what you may think, I would not like to see you lose your career or go to prison for calling someone a name, *if* that's all you did, but make no mistake about it, I will use whatever influence I may have to bring the man who murdered Erik Schwartzman to justice. Erik may have been over zealous at times, but he didn't deserve to die."

I placed my left hand on the desk and leaned toward him.

"Mr. Weiss, I couldn't agree with you more, but I am not that man. Give me the opportunity to investigate this murder without any interference from you, and I will bring Schwartzman's killer to justice."

Weiss smiled feebly and glanced at the black and blue fingers protruding from the sling.

"I heard about your injury," he said. "Unfortunate."

"Even more unfortunate for the guy who shot me."

The telephone rang, and Weiss told the secretary to hold his calls.

"You haven't convinced me of your innocence, Cahill, but I'll give you the benefit of the doubt. Neither I, nor the newspaper, will comment further on the investigation until there are new developments."

"That's all I ask," I said and turned toward the door. As I was heading for the door, I turned again and asked, "Do you have a reporter here named Art Kiese?"

"We have an employee here by that name, but he isn't a reporter. He's the networking system analyst."

"Could I speak with him please?"

"Erik and Art were good friends, and he was extremely upset after Erik's demise, so I granted him an extended vacation," Weiss said.

"When do you expect him back?" I asked.

"Whenever he feels like coming back."

"Do you have a home address or a phone number for him?"

"Of course we do, but it is our policy not to release that information."

"Not even to the police?" I asked.

"Some police, not you."

"Thanks, I'll find it myself," I said and turned to leave for the last time.

"Lieutenant," Weiss called out. "The next time you pay me a visit, make an appointment first."

"Then I suggest you hire the linebacker and get rid of the tight end."

CHAPTER 26

January 21, 2014
Tuesday
1900 hours

At 1900 hours the following evening, Barcomb and Donovan rang my front doorbell. Donovan was perspiring and gasping for breath as he entered the house carrying a cardboard box big enough to secrete a large midget and more than half-filled with reports and court transcripts.

"This is all we could get our hands on so far, and we had to call in a favor from a stenographer we know to get this, but it's enough to get you started," Donovan said and added, "Have fun," dropping the box to the floor with a thud. "If you find anything of interest, or need us, drop a dime. Have gun—will travel."

Charlie called as I began rifling through the box.

"Any new developments, Lt. Devlin?" he asked.

"No, but we have work to do, Charlie," I said. "Pick up a couple pizzas and two beers and get over to my house ASAP."

"I'm sorry, Devlin lad, but I'm indisposed."

"Tell the young lady to go home, Charlie, and don't forget the pizzas."

"Now I know why everybody hates the police. I'll be there post haste."

Charlie arrived within the hour with two pizzas, a six pack of Miller Lite, and his head shaved bald. A blast of frigid air and flurries rushed in behind him, and I slammed the door.

I nodded toward his baldhead and said, "I see you've opted for the electric chair instead of lethal injection."

"No death penalty in Illinois, remember?" Charlie replied. "How do you like my new 'do?"

I couldn't tell him I liked it because it would make his head swell, and then it wouldn't look good. He'd look like a butternut squash with ears.

"You look like a giant penis," I replied.

"Good. That's the phallic look I was hoping for."

The sweet aroma of savory Italian sausage, red sauce, and oregano wafted through the room, and for the first time in eighteen months, the house smelled like a home.

"Why are you so hell bent on destroying my social life?" Charlie asked.

"The highlight of your social calendar this year is going to be a soirée at Statesville with a guy named Lance if we don't clear these murders."

"Is he cute?"

"He'll look cute after four or five months in the joint."

I ripped the paper off of the pizzas—olives and sardines on both of them.

Charlie went to the kitchen, while I picked off the olives and sardines, and came back with a roll of paper towels, a Miller Lite, and a Diet Pepsi.

We finished most of the pizzas, and then I pulled all of the documents out of the box. I split the workload; I took all the arrest reports and case reports and I handed Charlie all of the court transcripts.

"What are we looking for specifically?" Charlie asked.

"We're looking for the name *Mario*, or anything that connects Mario and Giaccone with the victims from Avalon Trails, or anything that connects me or Schwartzman with any of them. Maybe I locked one of these mutts up years ago and don't remember him."

Charlie pushed back in the recliner, put his cheaters on the tip of nose, and started going through the court transcripts. I began on the arrest reports and worked my way through to the case reports. Giaccone had taken several arrests with codefendants, but nobody named Mario.

I glanced at my watch with bloodshot eyes. It was 0115 hours. The pizzas were gone, and what remained in Charlie's second Miller Lite was piss-warm. Charlie sat so motionless for four hours with his chin tucked into his chest, I checked to see if he was still breathing. I hoped he was engrossed in the material and not dead in my recliner. He peered over his glasses, acknowledged my presence, and went back to reading. Transcripts were piled on the floor halfway up to the armrest of the recliner.

I stood, stretched, lit a cigar, and yawned. "I'm going to put on a pot of coffee," I said as I stumbled toward the kitchen. I threw some cold water from the kitchen sink on my face while I waited for the coffee to finish brewing.

"Devlin," Charlie called, "come in here." Charlie's voice spilled over with excitement.

I rushed back into the great room. "You found Mario?" I asked.

"No. Do you have any cigars?"

"Do I have any cigars?" I asked. "Is that what you so urgently called me in for? Cigars? Do you have a sudden impulse to start smoking after forty years?"

"Do you remember the conversation we had the other day when I suggested we may be getting set up for the murders?"

"Of course I do. Do you think I have Alzheimer's?"

"You said only five people knew we were friends; Sergeants Peak and Abels, Pete and Beth Steffen, and Kerri?"

"I remember, Charlie. Get to the point."

"Well, Devlin lad, I think you overlooked one. There's a sixth. I think I may have cleared the murders, and you owe me a cigar."

CHAPTER 27

January 22, 2014
Wednesday
0130 hours

Charlie handed me a court trial transcript for John Giaccone in which he was tried for an Aggravated Battery with a handgun in 2009. He shuffled through the pile of transcripts on the floor and handed me a second court transcript; this one was for Jerry Doherty, victim #2 from Avalon Trails, in which he was on trial in 2006 for Possession of A Controlled Substance with Intent to Deliver thirty kilos of heroin.

"What am I looking at, Charlie?" I asked.

"Take a look at the defense counsel on both of them."

I transfixed on the page. "Emmett McKittrick! Emmett the Frog?"

"I think he's our common denominator, Devlin lad. He knows both Doherty, the victim, and Giaccone, the shooter; more than likely he knows, through Kerri, that you and I are friends. He may know you carry a 9mm, too, and I'm sure he knows Kerri is still in love with you, as does everyone else. What better way to take you out of the picture?"

I continued to stare at McKittrick's name on the page. "Emmett the fuckin' Frog!"

Without lifting my gaze from the paper, I reached into my shirt pocket and tossed Charlie a cigar. "You earned it, Hemingway."

"What do we do now, arrest him?"

"We?" I asked. "Charlie, you're a novelist, remember? *We* don't do anything. I do."

"I'm getting the hang of this, though, don't you think?"

"Charlie, I've been in on ten thousand busts. You've been in on one and turned the guy into a sieve."

"He shot you!" Charlie exclaimed.

"Point well taken, and in case I failed to mention it, thanks for saving my life the other night. It would make a great action scene in your next book. *The unarmed novelist vaults over the fence directly in the line of fire, drops to one knee, picks up the fallen officer's snub and puts five in the assailant's kill zone.*"

"Ah, you read me like a book, Devlin lad. It's true; my motives were purely heterotelic. Why else would I risk life and limb for an ungrateful Southside asshole other than for a good action scene in my next novel?" Charlie paused. "And you're welcome."

"One other thing, Hemingway—when or where did you learn to shoot a handgun?"

"Norbert, my friend in Germany, is a sniper with the GSG 9 der Bundespolizei, the most elite police unit in the federal police. I often went to the firing range with him during the year I was there. Norbert said it takes forty-three muscles to frown and seventeen to smile, but it only takes three muscles for proper trigger squeeze. Aim at what you want dead, and pull the trigger. I guess he was right."

I relit my cigar and walked into the kitchen to pour a cup of coffee. I called back to Charlie, "Do you want a cup of coffee? I don't have any chocolate milk."

"Please. I'm starting to like it black."

There was hope for Charlie yet. If I could get him to stop using words like heterotelic and profligacy he could walk around the Southside without need of an armed companion.

I brought his coffee and made a second trip to the kitchen to get mine since I lacked the necessary talent to carry two cups with one hand.

"We still have to find Mario. He's the key to this thing, and he has to talk when we snatch him up. We don't have anything on Emmett the Frog. He defends a lot of bad guys. That's his job, and that will be his defense. I don't want to tip him off we're looking at him, but I'm worried about Kerri staying there."

"Can't you tell her the truth?" Charlie asked.

"I'm not sure what the truth is right now. Suppose we're wrong?" I asked. "Emmett *is* a prominent attorney and *does* represent criminals. It could be mere coincidence he's represented two of our five dead guys. If he's innocent, I could ruin whatever chance at happiness Kerri may have … again."

Charlie set his coffee cup on the end table and pushed back in the recliner. "No such thing as coincidence exists in fiction writing."

"This isn't fiction, Hemingway. This is the real deal,"

I said. "I don't believe she's in any danger as long as McKittrick doesn't suspect we're onto him."

Charlie fired up his reward, the panetela. With his shaved head, and a big brown cigar stuck in the center of his mouth, all he needed was a corkscrew tail in the middle of his forehead and he'd look like a pig taking a shit. He drew deep on the cigar and blew it at me, engulfing my head in a nebulous shroud of smoke.

"What's next, Lt. Devlin?" Charlie asked, making a feeble attempt at blowing a smoke ring.

"We find Mario," I said. "And put that cigar out, Charlie. It stinks."

CHAPTER 28

We didn't finish going over the reports until the wee hours of the morning. Charlie fell asleep in the chair. I prayed for sleep, but it wouldn't come. Thoughts of Kerri being in the house with McKittrick tormented me, and I couldn't get the conversation with John Willick off my mind. I also feared Michael Jackson and the dancers would return for an encore if I closed my eyes. That's a benefit of insomnia.

Grunts and groans emanated from the guest bedroom. I didn't know if Charlie was spanking the monkey or doing push-ups, but I knew it was early. Footsteps traipsed into the bathroom, followed by the sound of running water. Charlie was showering, so it was 0800 hours.

I abandoned all hope of sleep and got up to get the coffee started. Ten minutes later, Charlie emerged from the bathroom reeking of Grey Flannel.

"Good morning, Devlin lad. Sleep well?"

Charlie smiled like the Cheshire cat, knowing I hadn't. He was always most amused with himself when he knew he was being most annoying.

"Charlie, I'm beginning to hate you."

We sat down for coffee. Charlie didn't ask for chocolate milk, a small victory for me.

The conversation with John Willick still preyed on my mind. How to ask Charlie about Laos and the marijuana pinch he took thirty years earlier without sounding accusatory? Charlie would see through any attempt I made at subtleness, like trying slight of hand on the magician, so I came right out and asked him.

"An FBI agent was at my house the other day, asking questions about you."

Charlie looked into his coffee cup, grinned uncomfortably, and lifted the cup to his lips. "Such as?"

"What were you doing in Laos?" I asked.

"I was in Vietnam, actually, doing research for a book on Larry Hillblom, the billionaire pedophile who was the co-founder of DHL Worldwide Delivery Service. Have you ever heard of him?"

"No," I admitted.

"Hillblom lived in Saipan and went down in a plane crash; they never recovered his body. While I was in Hue, they predicted a typhoon was about to hit, so I went inland up the Perfume River to the old Ho Chi Minh Trail. The bridge on Highway 9 was open so I entered into Laos."

"What about the three hundred pounds of heroin at the airport in the '70s?"

"What about it?" Charlie answered the question with a question.

"What do you know about it?" I asked.

"Only what I read in the newspaper the next day.

Naturally, I recall the incident because it occurred on the same day, in the same place, and at about the same time I was arrested for the marijuana."

Charlie paused and sipped his coffee cautiously. "Don't you think the feds would have thrown me in jail and deep-sixed the key if I got caught with three hundred pounds of heroin?"

"They didn't bury the two guys they caught with the plane," I said.

"I didn't know that," Charlie replied. "They should have; that's a lot of dope."

"Yeah, that's a lot of dope," I said.

Charlie smiled and asked, "Any more questions?"

"No more questions," I replied.

"Are we straight?" he asked.

"Like Archer Avenue."

"Good. Let's go find Mario," Charlie said.

CHAPTER 29

January 22, 2014
Wednesday
0830 hours

Though identifying and locating Mario ranked #1 on the to-do list, Emmett McKittrick was foremost on my mind that morning. If he were involved in the triple homicide, why would he murder, or have Mario and Giaccone murder, the three victims? Was he the third man in the car? He had represented Giaccone on a shooting case in 2009 and Doherty several years earlier on a drug beef. Was Doherty the target, and the other two victims simply collateral damage? But why would he choose to make the hit at Goldenstein's house? Doherty would have been vulnerable at more opportunistic times and locations. No, there had to be a connection between McKittrick and the other two victims as well, if he was involved at all. That was the only thing that made sense. McKittrick representing both Doherty and Giaccone could have been happenstance, and he could have known, through Kerri, that Charlie and I are friends, but that was conjecture. Maybe Kerri never even mentioned Charlie and me to McKittrick? I could have

135

been assuming facts not in evidence. Was the Schwartzman homicide related to the triple, and if so, why? Was there a connection there, or could Charlie's bizarre hypothesis that Schwartzman was simply a sacrificial lamb to frame me for the murder have been correct? Why would McKittrick want to set me up? I didn't know the man. I hadn't so much as called Kerri on the phone in eighteen months, so he shouldn't have felt threatened. Maybe it was time I did call Kerri, though. Invite her to lunch under the pretext of wanting to apologize to her for being an insufferable asshole and tactfully try to extract information from her about Emmett the Frog.

I put my cup in the sink. "I think I'm going to call Kerri and invite her to lunch," I said.

Charlie swiveled in his seat and said, "That's great news, Devlin lad." Then asserted knowingly, as if he was reading my mind, "Don't let her know the true reason you're asking her to lunch is to interrogate her. She's still in love with you, you know?" Before I could respond, he added, "Why? I have not the faintest, but I do know you'll break her heart if she discovers your real motive for asking her to lunch."

"Thank you, Dr. Ruth. I'll try to be subtle."

I showered, shaved, and picked out Kerri's favorite sports jacket to wear, a brown Donegal tweed with suede-patch elbows. It reminded her of the Irish countryside. I took my Blackberry off the nightstand and stared at it. Kerri's number was still #1 on speed dial. Strange—I've called that number so many times over the years without the least apprehension, and now my stomach was twisted into a knot and my fingers trembled hovering above the #1. At long last, I resolutely stabbed the button.

CHAPTER 30

January 22, 2014
Wednesday
0840 hours

Kerri picked up on the second ring.

"I was wondering … would you be available to meet me for lunch at noon today?" I asked. She likes seafood, so I quickly added, "Red Lobster."

"Why?" she asked.

"Because I get hungry at noon."

"Devlin, you haven't called me in eighteen months, and suddenly you want to take me out for lunch?"

"I want to apologize to you for what I said last week over the phone."

"I've never met anyone who apologizes so often, or anyone who is more insincere."

"I'm sincere this time, Kerri."

"Why can't you apologize over the phone?"

"Because I got shot in the arm and can't crack crab legs with one hand." I heard muffled laughter and her tone softened.

"You are such an asshole, Devlin. I'll see you at noon

...oh, and one other thing: I didn't forget you don't eat crab legs."

• • •

Red Lobster must have been giving fish away. The place was mobbed, and the heat was up too high. It felt like a sauna. The warm, ad nauseam smell of fish stagnated in the air. I told the hostess I'd like a table for two and gave her my name. She told me to wait in the lobby and she'd call my name as soon as a table became available. I hate waiting in lines, and I hate seafood even more. Kerri would know the sacrifice I was making.

Kerri entered while I was still waiting in the foyer and laughed, "Been waiting long?" She reminded me of Charlie sometimes.

"For you or the table?" I asked.

"Why on earth did you pick Red Lobster at noon?" she asked, knowing the answer.

I pursed my lips and frowned.

"Because I love seafood so much."

The hostess called my name and led Kerri and I to a table in the center of the room. I hate that, too. I like a police seat, with my back against the wall facing the door. Now, I'll probably get stabbed in the back with an Alaskan king crab leg.

"How's your *graze* wound healing?" Kerri asked.

I held up my bandaged arm and wiggled my fingers. "It's coming along."

Our waiter, a young blond kid about a sophomore in high school, brought us menus and a basket of rolls and took our drink orders. He appeared nervous, like it was his first day on the job.

"I've been reading about the three murders in Avalon Trails. The newspapers make it sound like they think Charlie killed those men."

"They do think Charlie whacked them, and so do the police."

"You don't think he had anything to do with it, though, do you?" Kerri asked.

"No, of course not, but again, you never know. Sometimes we think we know people well, and it turns out we don't know them at all."

"Was that crack meant for me?" Kerri asked.

"No, don't be so defensive. I'm just saying …"

"Is Charlie worried?"

I snickered. "Charlie is having the time of his life. He thinks this is an adventure, fodder for his next book. He reminds me of Gene Wilder in *Stir Crazy* when he told Richard Pryor the police didn't have anything on them and not to worry because they were innocent. The judge gave them ninety-nine years in prison."

"He couldn't go to prison over this, could he?" Kerri asked.

"Gene Wilder and Richard Pryor did."

The waiter returned with our orders.

"Let's not talk about Charlie. I wanted to take you to lunch today to apologize, *sincerely* apologize, for the mean things I said to you on the phone last week. It was unwarranted. I shouldn't have referred to Emmett as Emmett the Frog, either. We were already separated when you met him; it's not like he was responsible for breaking up our marriage. For all I know, he could be the nicest guy in the world, and I should be happy for you both." I almost gagged as I spat the words out of my mouth.

"Emmett is a nice man, and he treats me well," Kerri said.

"It's odd I don't run into him in court. He is a criminal attorney, right?"

"Yes, but I don't think he handles many murder cases."

"I thought he represented some guy I locked up twenty years ago on a shooting, 'Mario' something or other. I can't remember his last name. Emmett ever mention that to you?"

"No, he said he doesn't know you. Besides, twenty years ago he was doing legal work for some insurance firm."

The waiter brought our meals. A fat ignoramus a few tables over hollered at the already frazzled kid in front of all the other patrons to bring him a goddamn refill. The blood drained from the poor kid's face. He was embarrassed and physically shaken. My right hand may be out of commission for a while, but I have a great left hook.

Kerri anticipated my next move, and her face reddened. "Devlin, please don't say or do anything. Ignore him."

"I wasn't going to say anything," I lied. "I wouldn't want to spoil our beautiful lunch." I popped a scallop in my mouth and chewed the little rubber ball.

I recalled FBI Agent Willick saying Goldenstein was disbarred for insurance fraud many years earlier.

"Do you know what insurance firm Emmett worked for twenty years ago?" I asked.

"Why all the questions about Emmett? Is this an inquisition? What do you care what law firm Emmett worked for twenty years ago?"

"I was trying to make conversation. I thought I should know something about the man cohabitating with my wife."

Kerri slammed her knife and fork on the plate and glared across the table at me. Perhaps it was my phraseology? She stood abruptly with tears welling up in her eyes and stomped away toward the ladies room.

When she left the room, I went over to the table of my fleshy friend.

"Hey, you fatfuck, what did you say to my son?"

He turned the color of the white fish on his plate.

"I asked for a refill, that's all," he whined.

"I hope you leave him a tip that's as big as your fuckin' mouth."

I hurried back to the table before Kerri returned.

"Kerri, I'm sorry; I didn't mean to upset you. You know it's only because I'm concerned about you."

"I know you are, but you have a way of saying things that makes me want to smash this pitcher of Diet Pepsi over that concrete block you call a head."

"I like Diet Pepsi," I smiled.

The anger in her face dissipated and she repressed a smile. She gets mad at me fast, but she forgives me even faster.

"Barton, Karnes, and something."

"Barton, Karnes and something, what?"

"That was the name of the insurance firm Emmett

worked for twenty years ago. He does have a friend named Mario, too, but I've met him and he's only about thirty years old, so he would have had to have been about ten when you arrested him twenty years ago."

"I do vaguely remember the guy showing up for court in a Power Ranger costume. Maybe it is him?"

My fat friend, three tables over, picked up his check and lumbered over to me. "I'm sorry for being rude to your son. I think he'll be pleased with his tip." The cheeks of his ass looked like two watermelons in a condom as he bounced away.

Kerri shook her head. No explanation needed.

I duked our waiter a double sawbuck; between the fat ass and me, the kid should have had a good first day on the job. I paid the bill and escorted Kerri to her car.

I kissed her on the cheek. She picked up my bandaged arm and kissed my black and blue fingers.

"Thanks for taking me to lunch, Devlin. It was nice, despite your big mouth. Please take care of yourself and don't get hurt anymore."

"I'll try my best not to, and you be careful, too. Sometimes lawyers have unsavory characters hanging around them, so keep your wits about you."

Kerri nodded, got into her gray Lexus, and pulled out of the parking lot. Maybe I should have told her the truth after she told me she'd met Mario?

I got in the Z4 and dialed Area Central. The sergeant got Bill Donovan on the line.

"Bill, I think we may have caught a break. Get the home, cell, and work phone MUDDS on Emmett McKittrick. I think we'll find Mario on one or all of them."

I started pulling out when a second thought occurred to me. I stopped and fumbled for the badge case in my back pocket. Special Agent John Willick's business card was in there. I dialed his number.

"John, this is Devlin Cahill. Do you remember the name of the law firm Hiram Goldenstein was working for when he got disbarred twenty years ago?"

"Not off hand, but I can find it and give you a call back."

"Thanks, John. I appreciate it."

CHAPTER 31

January 22, 2014
Wednesday
1500 hours

I was clipping along eastbound on 111th Street when my Blackberry rang. I pulled to the curb across the street from St. Christina's Church to take the call. Dozens of frenzied, apple-cheeked boys on their way home from school, raced around like savages, jackets opened, unfastened boots, with the woolen hats their mothers made them promise to wear in their hands. They screeched and took turns knocking one another into the snow, no doubt for the benefit of the young girls meandering along and pretending they didn't notice them. I thought of getting out and scolding them before somebody got hurt, but I was outnumbered, and they looked dangerous. Besides, I had a phone call to answer.

It was John Willick. "I have the name of that law firm for you; it's Barton, Karnes, & Lambert in Orland Park. I hope that helps."

"That helps tremendously, John, thanks for your help. I'll get back to you when I get more … oh, and John, I asked Charlie Newton about Laos. He was doing research for a book on a guy named Larry Hillblom, some billionaire pedophile who went down in a plane crash."

John Willick thanked me for the information but didn't comment further. I got the distinct impression he wasn't as convinced as I was with Charlie's reason for being in Laos. I wouldn't be either if I were him. Long way to go to research a book. If he knew Charlie, though, I'm sure he'd find his explanation more palatable.

I looked across the street at St. Christina's as I pulled out into traffic and waved thank You to a statue of Jesus. "I owe you one."

• • •

The investigation was coming together but it was still cloaked in fog. Many possible scenarios and a lot of unanswered questions remained.

I entered the onramp of I-57 south at 111th Street. After I merged with traffic, I called the office for an exact address for Barton, Karnes, & Lambert. Twenty-five minutes later, I pulled up to their doors in Orland Square.

I flashed the button on the secretary and told her I'd like to speak with anybody who'd worked there twenty years earlier. She told me to have a seat in the waiting area and someone would be with me shortly. Five minutes later, an elderly, distinguished-looking gentleman with white hair and a ruddy complexion emerged from one of the offices.

"I'm Daniel Barton, Lieutenant, what can I do for you?"

I started explaining the nature of my visit, and he invited me into his office.

"Yes, I read about Hiram in the news," he said. "What a tragedy."

"What can you tell me about him?" I asked.

Mr. Barton shook his head and sighed. "Not much. He was an intelligent man and a gifted attorney, well liked, but greed got the better of him. We were doing a routine audit of our books and found he was involved in some unscrupulous business practices. Naturally, we terminated his employment at Barton, Karnes, & Lambert immediately and turned the information over to the Attorney Registration & Disciplinary Commission. Consequently, he was disbarred."

"How about Emmett McKittrick?" I asked.

"Emmett? Oh, God, don't tell me something has happened to him, too?"

"No, he's fine. Did they work here at the same time?"

"Oh, yes, you might even say Emmett was Hiram's protégé. Emmett was a bright lad, too, industrious and dedicated to the profession. I believe he was greatly disappointed in Hiram when Hiram's skullduggery became common knowledge. Emmett left our firm shortly thereafter on his volition and ventured out on his own."

"Do you know if McKittrick and Goldenstein kept in contact with each other over the years?"

"I'd have no idea. I haven't seen or heard from either one of them in almost twenty years."

"Is there any chance McKittrick could have been implicated in the fraud with Goldenstein, and left the firm before he was discovered?"

"I don't think so. Emmett didn't strike me as that type."

"But Goldenstein didn't strike you as that type either, did he?" I asked.

"Point well taken," Mr. Barton said. "Who knows what evil lurks in the hearts of men?"

I smiled and replied, "The Shadow knows."

Mr. Barton chuckled, rose from behind his desk and said, "Maybe the Shadow knows, but Daniel Barton certainly doesn't. That's obvious."

Mr. Barton escorted me to the door of his office and placed a hand on my shoulder like we were old friends.

"If I can be of any further assistance, please don't hesitate to call or stop by," he said.

"Thank you for your cooperation, Mr. Barton. You've been a great help."

"I'm glad I could be of some assistance," he said.

He shook his head and said sorrowfully, "Despite Hiram's shortcomings, I personally liked the guy. Such a tragic end."

"Dance with the devil and you might get burned," I said as I left his office.

• • •

McKittrick was now tied to Goldenstein and Doherty, two of the three dead guys in Avalon Trails, and Giaccone, one of the two shooters. If the Mario that Kerri met turns out to be our Mario, McKittrick would be associated with all of the players, except the Asian victim. We would still have to prove McKittrick had contact with Goldenstein more recently than twenty years ago, too. I hoped when the phone records came back, they would provide us with some answers.

CHAPTER 32

January 22, 2014
Wednesday
1700 hours

Charlie's rent-a-Vette was parked on the apron of my garage, encased in ice, when I got home. I pressed the garage door opener on the visor and pulled in.

A voice called out from my office, "Devlin lad, I hope that's you and not somebody coming to abduct me again?"

I called back, "I'm sure after a week with you nobody will be coming back any time soon to kidnap you."

"How did your lunch go with Kerri?" Charlie asked.

"Informative. If you can pull yourself away from the computer for a minute, I'll tell you about it."

Charlie came into the living room, sipping a cup of coffee. "Just brewed. Help yourself."

"Thanks. You're a gracious host."

Charlie followed me into the kitchen and I poured a cup of coffee.

"Well?" he asked.

"Well, McKittrick and Goldenstein both worked for the same law firm, Barton, Karnes, & Lambert, about twenty years ago. I took a ride to Orland Park after our lunch and talked to the owner of the law firm, who said they had both worked together. Kerri also told me that McKittrick has a friend named Mario."

"Did you tell Kerri about our suspicions?" Charlie asked.

"No. Maybe I should have. What do you think?"

"Devlin lad, I've been giving this some thought. I don't want to unduly alarm you, but consider this hypothesis, if you will. We've been assuming that as long as McKittrick doesn't know the police are investigating him, Kerri is no danger, and that's probably true, but since Giaccone has been dispatched …"

I interrupted, "You mean since you shot the shit out of him?"

Charlie frowned at the interruption and continued, "Mario may feel the police are drawing near. Giaccone, and everyone from Avalon Trails, are dead. The only person alive, other than myself, that could tie him to the murders is McKittrick. Should he opt to eliminate McKittrick, Kerri could be in danger. So, my answer to your question is I think you should get her out of there now, even if it blows the investigation."

It was a possibility I never considered. Charlie was proving to be as good a homicide dick as he is a writer.

Without responding to his theory, I speed dialed Kerri's cell phone number but she didn't answer. I called several more times in the next few minutes, but there was still no answer.

CHAPTER 33

I glanced at my wristwatch every few minutes. It was 1940 hours, and Kerri hadn't returned any of my calls, which is unlike her. I became increasingly worried.

As a last resort, I called her home number, and McKittrick answered. I had never talked to him before, and I didn't want to talk to him then.

"Is Kerri there?" I asked.

"May I ask who's calling?" McKittrick asked.

"Her ex-husband."

There was a long silence. I should have used some other form of introduction.

"Kerri's not here," he growled. "In the future, Lieutenant, if you want to contact Kerri, call her on her cell phone. Don't call my house."

"I have called her cell phone several times, and she hasn't responded. Do you know where she is?" I asked.

"No, I don't. I assume if she wanted to talk to you she would have called back." The phone went dead in my ear.

Smoke was coming out of my ears. I threw on my jacket as I raced for the garage. Charlie asked, "Where are you going?"

"I'm going to establish a rapport with Mr. McKittrick," I yelled back as I opened the door leading to the garage.

"Do you want me to go with you?" Charlie hollered.

"No."

Charlie called out as I was backing the Beamer out of the garage, "You only have one hand!"

I didn't respond, but I thought one hand is all I'll need. I hoped.

• • •

Ten minutes later, I fishtailed up the long drive to McKittrick's house in Beverly. It's a large estate on top of a hill. I rang the doorbell and heard chimes inside play "Hail to the Chief." Pompous bastard.

McKittrick opened the door; I threw a left hook into his face and knocked him on his ass. Blood gushed from his mouth and his nose.

"Let me introduce myself, asshole. I'm the guy you hung up on."

McKittrick spit blood onto the granite tile and snorted to clear his breathing passages. He started getting up and I gave him the heel of my shoe in the head, knocking him back to the ground. I wasn't physically sound enough to allow him get back to his feet.

"You look shocked, Mr. McKittrick. Perhaps you're under the misconception that I am the TV police? I am not. If you ever hang up on me again, I'll stick your phone so far up your ass they won't find it at your next colonoscopy."

McKittrick glared but made no effort to get back to his feet again. He wiped the blood from his face with the back of his hand and looked at it. "You're in a lot of trouble, Cahill."

"I'm in trouble?" I laughed, "Who's sitting on the floor bleeding from all of his orifices?" I gave him another boot in the head to emphasize my point.

"Now, let me ask you again before I get seriously pissed off, where is Kerri?"

Before he could answer, the door leading to the house from the garage opened, and Kerri rushed in with an armful of groceries. "Devlin, what the hell are you doing?" she shrieked, dropping the bags to the floor.

"I was discussing phone etiquette with the counselor," I replied.

Kerri cried and bent down to help McKittrick to his feet. "Devlin, please leave!" she shouted.

"Kerri, you have to come with me!"

"I'm not going anywhere with you, Devlin. You are truly crazy, do you know that? You need help."

McKittrick rose on unsteady legs and wiped the blood away from his nose with a monogrammed French cuff. His eyes were glazed, lips the size of inner tubes. A black and blue mark the shape of my heel swelled on his forehead.

"Kerri, I think you're in danger. I should have told you today at lunch. You have to get out of here now."

"What do you mean 'I'm in danger'?" she shouted. "I can't leave Emmett in this condition," she said.

"Fuck Emmett. Let him call an ambulance."

"Devlin, please leave this house and don't ever come back. I'm not going anywhere with you," she cried. "Are you going to beat me up, too?"

"Kerri, please …"

She interrupted, "Devlin. Leave."

McKittrick regained his composure, gave me the junkyard dog stare, and said, "This is only round one, asshole."

I threw another left hook into his face and knocked him out. "Round two, motherfucker." Down for the 10 count.

Kerri screamed and was near hysteria. She held her hands over her eyes and ran in place. I tried to capitalize on McKittrick's state of unconsciousness to tell Kerri why it was imperative she leave there immediately. She knew about the Avalon Trails homicides. Time mandated I give her the abridged version of McKittrick's connection to two of the victims and one of the killers, and the Mario she met may be the killer. I gave her Charlie's theory about why she may be in danger, but she was either too upset to understand what I was saying, or she wasn't buying it.

"Devlin, that is preposterous!" she cried. "Emmett is not like that, and Charlie's as fucking nuts as you are." She knelt on the floor next to McKittrick. "I have to call an ambulance for Emmett, so please leave."

"Kerri, I'm begging you. Please come with me."

"I can't, Devlin. I can't. Don't you understand that?"

"Kerri, you're in more danger now than ever. I showed my hand."

"You'd better leave before the police and the ambulance get here. Don't ever call me again."

My mood darkened. "When the frog wakes up, tell him he didn't do too good the first two rounds. Tell him I can't wait for the bell to ring for round three."

I turned and went out into the frigid night air. It was sleeting heavily. My left hand was the size of a catcher's mitt—I thought it was broken—and the frozen rain felt good on it. The driveway was an icy slope, and I'd have to traverse it cautiously or I'd have a catastrophe when I reached the end. There was an analogy there I didn't care to dwell on.

CHAPTER 34

January 22, 201
Wednesday
2145 hours

Charlie was waiting for me when I got home. "How did it go?" he asked.

I held up what used to be my good hand.

"Ah, I see you did manage to establish a rapport," Charlie punned. "Another stunning éclat! Has anyone ever suggested to you that you may have a borderline personality disorder? You are governed by your emotions, think with your fists, and are not often given over to contemplation."

"Charlie, please don't lecture me now," I said as I walked past him into the kitchen. I dumped the ice tray into a dishtowel and put it on my new bad hand.

"Was Kerri there?" he asked.

"No, she walked in while I was thumping the frog. She didn't believe me, and she wouldn't come with me. She's in more danger now than ever. She knows the story, and if she questions McKittrick about what I told her ..."

"Where was McKittrick while you were telling her?"

"Taking a nap."

"Devlin lad, forgive me for being redundant, but you are not goal oriented. There is a distinct hamartia in your character, which I'm certain could be eradicated, or at least alleviated, through extensive psychological counseling."

"Go fuck yourself, Charlie," I said. "I don't even know what you're talking about half the time."

"The object of going over there was to get Kerri out of that house. You bollixed the mission. It seems you've accomplished the opposite of what you went over there to do. Now we may have to go back there and physically remove her from the premises for her own safety."

"Kerri was right—you are nuttier than I am, Charlie. You want to drag Kerri out of the house? She'll never forgive me!"

"Would you rather see her alive and hating you or dead?"

I dwelled on that point but a moment. "I can't drive too well with my hands. You'll have to drive."

• • •

I directed Charlie to McKittrick's block. He turned on their street and pulled up to the curb at the base of the McKittrick estate. The house atop the hill was almost obscure through the driving sleet, and the outline of what appeared to be three police cars parked in front of the doorway was even less perceptible. Charlie backed down the street, parked, and turned his lights off.

"The candy ass called the police on me," I said.

"Wow, what a surprise that is! Just because you punched his face in," Charlie replied.

Ten minutes later, all three squad cars slid down the driveway and turned south on Longwood Drive. Their taillights were still in view when Charlie pulled away from the curb and turned up the drive.

I tapped on the door, hoping McKittrick and Kerri would assume it was the police returning to perhaps ask one more question. McKittrick opened the door. His head was wrapped like a mummy and he was holding a bloody handkerchief to his nose. He turned and ran for the phone. Charlie pushed past me and grabbed him by both wrists as he reached the phone. McKittrick tried in vain to pull away but Charlie held him fast.

"That wouldn't be a wise move, Mr. McKittrick," Charlie warned. Charlie's eyes were cold and his face stern, and for the first time it occurred to me what an imposing, menacing figure he could be if you weren't on his friendly side, like when Fluffy, your cocker spaniel, bares his teeth at you. I'd be wise to remember that face the next time I go overboard busting his balls.

Kerri came running in from another room. "Oh, no!" she screamed. "Devlin, what in God's name are you doing here again?"

I told her again, "Kerri, you can't stay here. You're in danger. I didn't come here earlier to beat McKittrick up, or because I'm jealous, or even because he hung up on me. I came to get you out of here. You have to come with me!"

Kerri was crying and screaming and not emotionally capable of understanding the gravity of the situation. "I told you earlier, Devlin, I am not going anyplace with you. You are fucking insane!"

Charlie released McKittrick's wrists, ripped the phone line out, hurried over to Kerri, and flung her over his shoulder. She was punching and kicking at him as he carried her out the door.

"You ready for round three yet, counselor?"

McKittrick stood motionless and didn't say a word.

• • •

I told Charlie to drop me off a couple of blocks from my house. I was sure the police were already there waiting for me. I told him to take Kerri someplace safe. I tried to kiss Kerri goodbye on her cheek, but she stiff-armed me in the face. Feisty Irish lass. I wasn't sure she was going to forgive me this time.

As I expected, a half-dozen squad cars were parked in front of my house and on my driveway when I strolled up.

Four patrol officers flanked Billy Bartok, the field lieutenant from the 22nd District, whom I have known for years, as he approached me. "Devlin, I'm sorry to have to be the one to do this, but I'm going to have to arrest you for the Aggravated Battery of Emmett McKittrick."

It was embarrassing for me to find myself in this position, but it was harder for Bill Bartok. I felt sorry for him. I've had to arrest a brother-in-blue before, and, regardless of the offense, it leaves you with a sick feeling. I wanted to say something witty to dry out the mood but my upper lip was as stiff as Howdy Doody's from the cold, and my mustache was frozen solid from the two-block walk in the freezing sleet. I couldn't feel my feet, nor could I move my mouth to formulate a word. Otherwise, I'm confident I could have come up with something cute.

Bill Bartok continued, "Devlin, please don't dig a deeper hole for yourself. Tell us where your wife and Charlie Newton are. They put a flash message out on him for forcible abduction, and you know that could put him in a dangerous position."

"I know you're doing your job, Bill," I responded to my peer, "but all I can tell you is that Kerri is someplace safe."

"And Newton?"

"Probably writing a book someplace," I said. "Do you want to remove the snub from my waistband or shall I?" I asked.

Billy Bartok looked down at the snow and shook his head. I handed him my snub. A female patrol officer gently directed my arms behind my back to put on the handcuffs.

She whispered, "I'm sorry, Lieutenant. Procedure."

I smiled at her. "Thank you, officer. I'm familiar with it." She smiled back and led me to the backseat of her squad car. The truth be known, I rode in the backseats of squad cars several times during my troubled youth, and many times as a copper when responding to riots or mass disturbances in four-man cars, but it never felt as ominous as it did that night.

I was transported downtown, instead of Area South Headquarters where persons arrested for felonies in the Mount Greenwood neighborhood are generally taken for processing, for obvious reasons. It would have been embarrassing to be chained up in an interview room right next to my office. It could have been funny, too, though. Bill Peak and the boys would have been laughing and throwing shit at me and threatening to slap me around if I didn't fess up.

When I arrived downtown, there was an entire cavalcade of superstars on hand: ADS Carone, the BIA, IPRA, detectives from Central, and an Assistant State's Attorney from Felony Review. Apparently, given my proclivity for violence, and despite the fact that I didn't have any hands left to fight, they decided handcuffing me to the eyebolt in the wall was the prudent thing to do.

The entire group came into the Interview Room and closed the door. It was like a cattle pen.

The ADS took the lead. "Lieutenant, you know why you're here, and you know the procedures as well as any of us in this room. We are primarily concerned right now about the welfare and whereabouts of your ex-wife, so let's cut through all the bullshit. Tell us where she is."

"Deputy, I can't tell you where she is at this moment because I don't know, but I can assure you she's okay. She was not forcibly abducted, and when you locate her, she'll tell you so herself. As far as McKittrick signing a complaint against me, I am appalled. *I* was the victim of the aggravated battery, not him. He twisted my injured arm without provocation, and a scuffle ensued. He lost the battle, and he's a bad loser."

The ASA jumped to his feet like he'd been goosed. "You're a disgrace to the Chicago Police Department, do you know that?"

I smiled at him. "No, I didn't. Please continue."

"You bet I'll continue!" he shouted. "In the last several weeks, you've been associating with the prime suspect in a triple murder investigation, and you have used your rank and your position to obstruct that investigation. You yourself are a prime suspect in a homicide investigation and now an aggravated battery and an abduction investigation. You have threatened BIA and IPRA investigators with physical violence and called them names, but let me be the first to tell you, I am not amused with your smart mouth, nor am I threatened or intimidated by you. And, when we catch your friend Charlie Newton, I plan on putting both of you in prison for a long, long time."

"Wow, aren't we full of ourselves?" I said. "Since I do not intimidate you, perhaps you'd consider taking this handcuff off of me. As you can see, my arms are injured, and it's hurting my wrist. Besides, there's a half-dozen coppers around to restrain me in case I get an uncontrollable urge to bitch slap you."

I shouldn't have waved the red flag in front of the frothing bull, I knew that, but this guy looked like he could be fun. His upper lip trembled, and I thought he was going to cry.

He screamed, "Take the handcuffs off this mother-fucker!" but nobody moved.

The Deputy said, "That's against Department policy, counselor."

I laughed, which infuriated him more, and I thought with the possible exception of the IPRA investigator, the Deputy and the other policemen thought it was funny, too. They knew I was busting balls.

"Let's see if you're laughing when you're in prison!" the ASA shouted.

"Shhhh, calm down, Junior. Now, let me tell you something. I've been in this business since you were still soiling your diapers; maybe that's a bad analogy because you were probably doing that as recently as last week, maybe even right now. You may see yourself as a big shot, and I can understand why. Here you are, a young punk, barely out of law school, and you can scream at a police lieutenant without getting your ass handed to you on a platter. It's every pussy's dream! It must be empowering. But the truth of the matter is, Junior, you're an inconsequential schmuck and no matter how loud you scream, or how red your face gets, you can't send anybody, let alone me, to prison without evidence. And, you certainly can't kick my ass, whether I have one hand or no hands. When Kerri surfaces, you'll find that there was no abduction, and when the facts come out, you'll find that neither Charlie Newton nor I killed anybody. I don't think any policeman has ever gone to prison for calling an IPRA investigator a peter puffer, otherwise the state would have to build us our own wing. You can charge me with anything you'd like tonight, but you'll never convict me of anything in court, and the State's Attorney's Office will eventually have to chalk up an embarrassing zero in the wins column. So, Micropenis, either lower your voice, or take these handcuffs off of me."

The ASA glared at me and turned to the street deputy. "Charge this fucking asshole with Aggravated Battery. Have somebody run out to Christ Hospital to have McKittrick sign a complaint, and draw up an arrest warrant on Charlie Newton for kidnapping and unlawful restraint."

I called out to the ASA as he stormed out of the room,

"After you arrest Charlie Newton, you're going to have to chalk up two zeroes in the win column, counselor. Now go change your Depends, and I'll be right here when you get back."

When the ASA fled from the room, I caught a glimpse of Chief Daniels standing outside the open doorway. He entered and asked the street deputy if he could have a few words with me alone.

Chief Daniels, like Jim Croce's Leroy Brown, was raised on the south side of Chicago in the baddest part of town and is fluent in both Ebonics and the King's English. He began in his grass-roots language, "Devlin, you about one silly white motherfucker! What the hell did you do to the ASA to make him run out of here like his ass was on fire?" I chuckled, but the chief didn't. "Didn't I ask you a couple of weeks ago not to piss any more people off?" He got up and took the cuff off of my wrist. "You want some coffee?" he asked.

"Yeah, I'd love a cup of coffee—and a cigar."

The Chief smiled and said, "Don't push it."

He strolled to the door and asked one of the detectives to bring two cups of coffee, then he took a seat across the desk from me.

"What the hell happened and where is Kerri?" he asked.

"I can't tell you where Kerri is at this moment because I don't know. I told Charlie to take her someplace safe, but I don't know where he took her." I then told him of my suspicions about McKittrick being involved in the triple homicide from Avalon Trails, and maybe the Schwartman homicide, and my fear that maybe Mario may come to silence McKittrick, putting Kerri in harm's way.

"What about the Aggravated Battery on McKittrick?" he asked.

"I tuned him, but I'm not worried about that. When he's charged with the triple, he won't have much credibility. Besides that, I only had one hand at the time of the incident. How's a one-armed man going to be convicted of beating up a two-armed man?"

Chief Daniels stared at me across the desk. "I'm going to run down the entire story to the Deputy and ask him to overrule Felony Review on this. I'm not sure he's going to be agreeable because it's going to look like we're covering for our own, and I'm sure he doesn't want the heat. Nor do I. They will burn the black off of my ass if you get out of here and screw up again. Do you think, if I can swing this, you can stay out of trouble for awhile?"

"What about Charlie?" I asked.

"There's not much anybody can do about Newton until Kerri materializes in one piece and declines prosecution."

"I could resolve this with one call if Charlie had his cell phone, *and* if Kerri's calmed down, but I don't know where he's at or how to contact him. Kerri's miffed at me right now for redecorating McKittrick's face, but if I can get out of here, I think I can convince her of his involvement in these murders. She's an intelligent woman, and she's not naïve, so I think I can make her listen to reason. If not, she's going to go right back there and put herself back in danger, and I can't let that happen."

Chief Daniels gulped down the last of his coffee and

rose. "Let me go talk to the Deputy and see if we can get you out of here so you can have a cigar." He left the room and returned several minutes later.

"Devlin, the Deputy said he caught your act last week when he came to talk to you at your house about the Schwartzman homicide. He said in his opinion, you are a loose cannon—well, actually he said you're an asshole—and he is not inclined to override the ASA's recommendation."

"I would have described myself as being self-reliant, but asshole and loose canon are good. Semantics."

"You're going to be charged with Aggravated Battery, Devlin." Chief Daniels shook his head, "I'm sorry, there's nothing more I can do."

Moments after Chief Daniels left the room, the ADS re-entered and informed me I was suspended indefinitely pending the outcome of the trial and confiscated my badge and ID card. I felt a rising lump in the back of my throat; my world was crashing down on me. I lost Kerri because of the job, and now I was losing the job because of Kerri. Poetic justice. But perhaps the suspension was for the best. I was going to do whatever I had to do to protect Kerri from harm and prevent Charlie from going to prison. The Department could disavow responsibility for any of my actions from this point forward because, technically, I was no longer a police officer. I was no longer restricted by Department rules and regulations, and, oddly enough, that felt liberating. I wouldn't have to worry about putting the ADS or Chief Daniels, or the Department, in an embarrassing position after I bonded out. Though I believed I stood a good chance of beating the case in court,

I didn't have Charlie's faith in our judicial system. If some political hack, or one of McKittrick's friends in the legal profession, was sitting on the bench, Charlie and I may be spelling justice, *just-us*.

CHAPTER 35

January 23, 2014
Thursday
0930 hours

I spent the night in Central Detention. Aggravated Battery is a felony and there was no preset bond. The bond had to be set by a judge. It was a long night. *Jesus Loves_You* may be comforting words to read on the walls of a church, not so much when it's written on the walls of your jail cell and your roommate is a three-hundred-pound Mexican named Jesus. I was relieved when I found out my cellmate's name was Miguel, not Jesus, and he was locked up for theft and violating an order of protection, not sodomy. He should have also been charged with felony flatulence. He must have OD'd on frijoles. Self-preservation being the first law of nature, my nostrils slammed shut like a clam. I was half asleep with my mouth open when the first bomb shook my cot.

"Dude, are you wearing socks?" I asked him.

He gawked. "Yeah, I'm wearing socks."

"Stick one of them up your ass," I said. "Please. You're fucking killing me."

He rolled over, with his ass still facing me, and went to sleep.

Around 0600 hours, the prisoner van picked us up and transported us to the Criminal Courts Building where I was to be arraigned in Branch 66, Violence Court, before Judge Nielsen. The guards took my sling so I wouldn't hang myself with it, and led us handcuffed together to the bullpen outside the courtroom. I felt like Christ on his way to Calvary, with the good thief hooked up to me on my left and El Farto Miguel on the right. I twisted and turned my wrists to relieve the pressure from the handcuffs. Miguel I designated the impenitent thief for not apologizing after what he put me through all night. Dude was brutal. I considered pleading guilty to Aggravated Battery, preferring to spend six years in Statesville than another night in a cell with Miguel shitting in his pants.

I was the second prisoner called. The bailiff led me before the Honorable Judge Paul Nielsen.

"Mr. Cahill, you're charged with Aggravated Battery. Are you represented by counsel?" the judge asked.

Before I could tell him I was not, Defense Attorney Stephen Kennelly approached the bench and said, "Your Honor, I will be representing Mr. Cahill in this matter."

I knew Stephen Kennelly by reputation, and I also knew that if I liquidated all my assets I couldn't afford his services. He's one of the most prominent, successful, and expensive criminal lawyers in the state.

The judge read the docket file before him. "Mr. Cahill has no prior criminal history."

The ASA interrupted. "Your Honor, if the court

please, Mr. Cahill's ex-wife, Kerri Cahill, was a witness to this crime and has been forcibly abducted from her home, presumably to prevent her from testifying at this hearing. Her whereabouts are still unknown as of this proceeding, so the State asks that a high bond be set in the amount of one million dollars."

Kennelly quickly asserted, "Your Honor, Mr. Cahill is not charged with kidnapping nor unlawful restraint. If the State believes Mr. Cahill is somehow responsible for Ms. Cahill's absence, they should have charged him accordingly. Furthermore, he is a highly decorated police lieutenant with more than twenty years of service with the Chicago Police Department. He was born and raised in Chicago and has both family and community ties to this city. He has no past criminal history and is therefore not a flight risk. We ask that Mr. Cahill be released on his own recognizance."

The judge, never looking up from the docket file in front of him, said, "Mr. Kennelly, I agree Mr. Cahill is an unlikely flight risk and that a one-million-dollar bond seems excessive; however, I am not inclined to issue a personal recognizance bond, either, due to the extenuating circumstances of this case." The judge looked over his glasses at me and asked, "Mr. Cahill, could you make a $400,000 bond, or $40,000 cash?"

I started to ask the judge if he was on a crack pipe, but before the words could leave my lips, Kennelly interjected, "$400,000 would be fine, Your Honor. Thank you."

We stepped away from the bench, and the next case was called. I was allowed to confer with my attorney for a moment before I was taken back to the holding cell to be processed out.

"Mr. Kennelly, I don't know what you're doing here, but I can't afford you, and I certainly don't have $40,000 cash to post bail. You may as well have let the bond stand at a million."

"It's all been taken care of. Charlie Newton asks only that you take notes on your experiences behind bars for his next book, especially your first date with Lance."

• • •

Forty-five minutes later, I was processed out of the Cook County Jail. I walked past the razor wire on 26th Street, sucked in a bucketful of cold, crisp winter air, and savored the sweet taste of freedom on my lips as I trudged through the snow back toward the Criminal Courts Building to see if I could catch a ride home from one of the coppers leaving court. A black Cadillac eased up along the curb and beeped at me. Stephen Kennelly motioned to me to get into the car.

I trotted over to the car and jumped into the passenger seat while the car was still rolling. The car was immaculate and smelled like vanilla, so I didn't bother asking if I could smoke.

"I appreciate the ride, Mr. Kennelly, but I live far south and you're probably not going that far. I can bum a ride off one of the coppers leaving court," I said.

"You're right. In fact, I'm not going south at all. I'm going back downtown to my offices, but you look like you need a cup of coffee. I'll drop you off at Donna's CafeChicago on the way."

I picked up on his suggestion immediately. Charlie knew Donna's CafeChicago is one of my regular haunts, not only because she has the best coffee in town, but because she's a retired copper and a friend of mine. She's a black woman, about one hundred pounds of nitroglycerin, and even the SWAT team couldn't get by her. Police were still looking for Charlie, and it was a safe place for us to meet.

Ten minutes later, Kennelly dropped me off in front of the entrance on State Street south of Roosevelt Road in the south loop. Donna greeted me at the door, rolled her eyes, and kissed me on the cheek. "I heard about your latest escapade on the news last night. You messed up this time, cracker."

"Thank you, Donna," I said. "Sweet as ever." She escorted me to a back room off the kitchen. Charlie sat at a large black lacquered table eating a "Beef Ellington." Charlie, the connoisseur, motioned for me to sit down and swallowed hard. "The sandwich is delicious."

"Bring me two of those and an emergency cup of coffee," I said, and added, "We're not here if anyone should ask."

"Didn't they feed you at the County?" Donna asked, and before I could reply added, "I'll bring you a pot of coffee. You look like you need it."

"So, how did your date go with Lance?" Charlie asked.

"It went well. We're due to be married in early spring."

Donna brought us a pot of hot, steaming coffee and told me my sandwiches would be up in a minute.

"Where's Kerri?" I asked Charlie.

"She's at Pete and Beth's place. She and Beth are getting along famously."

"Is her nose still out of joint?" I asked.

"I think she's perplexed but coming around to our way of thinking. She's still not convinced McKittrick is capable of such duplicity, but she does understand our concern for her welfare."

"That's good. When we leave here, let's take a ride to Pete and Beth's so I can talk to her and see if she's willing to lie to the authorities and say she left McKittrick's house on her own volition," I said.

"She hates you," Charlie said, taking a chunk out of his sandwich, "but she'll probably do it for me."

"I hope we don't get stopped by the police en route and wind up back in the shithouse."

Donna brought my sandwiches, and a bowl of gumbo, which I didn't order.

"Try this," she ordered and walked away.

"I haven't been to the shithouse," Charlie pointed out. "You're the only felon in here." Looking around the room, he added, "You're the only felon at this table, anyway."

"Yeah, but you're a wanted criminal, and with all the bad publicity you've been getting over the last few weeks, the police may shoot you on sight."

"All publicity is good publicity, Devlin lad. It will help increase sales for my next book."

"Speaking of books, I may have to write a book myself, Charlie, to pay you back all this money," I said, slurping up gumbo.

"Great idea, Devlin lad. It should have great mass

appeal among remedial readers across the country, and after it's edited and all the expletives, obscenities, and vulgarities are removed, it should only be about three pages long, mostly definite and indefinite articles of speech. Easy to warehouse and ship."

After we devoured the sandwiches and drained the coffee pot, we got up to leave. Donna returned to our table and kissed me again on the cheek. "If yaw'll not in jail Saturday night, we're going to have a great jazz band here."

Charlie's eyes sparkled. "I love jazz," he said.

"If neither one of you silly sons-of-bitches are incarcerated, stop by."

"You're hot for my body, aren't you?" I asked.

Donna rolled her big brown eyes again, like only Donna can do, and replied with an insincere, "Hmmm, hmmm."

CHAPTER 36

Pete and Beth Steffens' residence surpassed even those of Goldenstein or McKittrick. Everybody must make more money than coppers. Charlie pulled his rent-a-Vette into the drive of the faux chateau. My eyes scanned the broken roofline and the intricate cupola as we approached the front entrance. I whistled in awe. "Pete's not the capo di capo, is he?" I asked.

"No," Charlie replied, "Beth is."

Before Charlie could ring the bell, the front door opened wide, and Beth invited us in. She kissed us both on the cheek when we entered the foyer and led us into the living room.

"Make yourselves comfortable. I'll get Kerri."

I minced across an azure and yellow wool area rug, larger in square footage than most people's homes, to a built-in French provincial display cabinet, which graced the entire length of the wall, fraught with baroque antiques. I traipsed to the white French doors and peered out at a garden pathway, lined with sculpted topiary art, terminating at an enormous water fountain in the center of the grounds.

"Do all Northsiders live like this?" I asked Charlie.

He tiptoed around one of six Parisian odd tables scattered about the room and pointed smugly to a rustic pair of fluer—de—lis bookends, which contained only two books: *Calumet City* and *Start Shooting*.

I nodded toward the books. "If you knew your books were going to be displayed in a place like this, you should have at least had them bound in goat leather."

"I tried, but the publisher wouldn't go along with it," Charlie responded.

Beth and Kerri entered the room. Kerri gazed at the floor and avoided eye contact with me.

"Would anybody like something to drink?" Beth asked.

"Not for me, thank you," I said, never taking my eyes off of Kerri.

Beth turned to Charlie and said, "Why don't we leave them alone to talk for a few minutes." She and Charlie left the room.

"I'm getting bad vibes, Kerri," I said. "You're still mad at me?"

"Yes, I'm mad at you, you friggin' idiot. If you thought I was in danger, why didn't you tell me at lunch? You could have avoided beating up Emmett and this whole fiasco."

"Would you have listened to me?" I asked.

"No."

"I thought as long as Emmett didn't know the police were looking at him, you were safe," I replied contritely.

Kerri frowned. "And what changed your mind an hour later?"

"Charlie suggested you could be in more danger from this other guy, Mario, and we had to do whatever was necessary to get you out of there. You wouldn't come voluntarily."

"So, you beat Emmett half to death and kidnapped me?"

"I beat Emmett half to death, but *Charlie* kidnapped you."

"You are not funny, Devlin!"

"I know. This is no time to be humorous, I'm trying to make you smile." I walked across the room and stood in front of her. "Kerri, I would rather have you never speak to me again than to see anything happen to you." I put my fingers under her chin and lifted her face to look me in the eyes. "Until we catch Mario, you have to remain out of sight. These are dangerous people, Kerri. They've killed three people for sure, and maybe four, and tried to kill me. One more won't make any difference to them."

"You truly believe that Emmett is one of those dangerous people?" she asked.

"I think so, and so does Charlie. If I'm wrong, I'll apologize to Emmett the Frog and let him beat *me* half to death."

"If you're wrong, can I beat you half to death?" Kerri asked.

"Certainly," I smiled, "I may even enjoy that."

Kerri smiled, or at least her eyes did. "Not half as much as I would."

The tension dissipated.

"There's a warrant out for Charlie's arrest for kidnapping you, and as long as he's wanted, he's in danger, too."

"What do you want me to do?" Kerri asked.

Charlie peeked around the corner. "Quiet in here; safe to come in?" he asked.

"Yeah, come in. Let's sit down and map out a strategy."

Beth offered us refreshments again, and when we declined, she excused herself from the room.

"There's nothing the police can do about an arrest warrant after it's been issued," I said. "Charlie, you'll have to appear in court for the judge to vacate the warrant. We'll give Kennelly a call in the morning and see if we can meet him in his office or at 26th & Cal for you to turn yourself in."

"Kerri, you'll have to tell the judge you weren't taken against your will," I said.

"How the hell am I going to say that, Devlin, when nitwit #2—nodding at Charlie—carried me out of there over his shoulder? I don't want to lie to a judge," she protested. "Can't I tell him I don't want to prosecute?"

"You can say anything you want to say, but unless you want to see me and Charlie go to prison, I'm asking you to heed Kennelly's counsel. Remember, Kerri, if the judge looks like he's pissed off, Charlie kidnapped you, not me."

Charlie shook his head. "I don't know why I have anything to do with you."

CHAPTER 37

January 24, 2014
Friday
0900 hours

Southbound traffic on the Ryan flowed well until we hit downtown. Black clouds swallowed up the top floors of the skyscrapers to the east and hovered over the city like a pall. With Kerri seated on my lap, I didn't mind the congestion or the delays, and I enjoyed every pothole we hit. I relished the warmth of her body against mine and the smell of her hair. A profound yearning oozed from every fiber of my body, and I fought the temptation not to grab her by the hair, spin her head around, and kiss her with the passion we once knew, but why start a fire I couldn't put out.

I glanced at my Seiko as we entered the parking garage across the street from the Criminal Courts Building at 26th & California. It was 0910 hours. Donovan and Barcomb would be starting their tour of duty. I wanted to talk to them about the status of McKittrick's phone records and ask them to run Art Kiese.

We plodded down the concrete ramps and exited the parking garage on California Avenue. I clenched Kerri's arm as we jogged across the northbound traffic onto the parkway, and again across the southbound traffic. Dozens of people with upturned collars and pulled down hats scurried past us and up the salted concrete staircase of the Criminal Courts Building. Stephen Kennelly stood outside the entrance, securing his trademark tweed Irish walking hat on his head against bone-chilling winds and constantly stomping his feet to keep the circulation going. Looked to me like he had to make pee-pee. He tugged at the tartan scarf under the upturned collar of his black cashmere overcoat and, pulling it higher around his neck, nestled his chin into the coat. His gloved hand held a leather attaché case, which cost as much as my Beamer. His nose and ears glowed.

Kennelly removed the glove from his right hand and extended his hand to Charlie but looked at me. "My two favorite criminals. And this lovely lass must be the enviable Mrs. Cahill, the victim du jour."

At $500 per hour, he could afford to be funny.

"Don't shake his hand too long, Charlie," I said, "this is costing us money."

Within a half hour, Charlie and Kerri were standing before the Honorable Judge Nielsen. I sat in the back of the courtroom and listened. Kerri nervously shifted her weight from one foot to the other, constantly running her sweaty palms alongside her slacks.

"Has anyone threatened or intimidated you into dropping these charges, Ms. Cahill?" Judge Nielsen asked. I couldn't hear her tiny voice and I was afraid for a minute she would respond, "Yeah, that asshole back there" and point to me, but she didn't. The judge discharged the case for want of prosecution, and we all walked out of there one big, happy family. Kennelly was happier than the rest of us, of course; he just made another grand or two.

We rode the elevator down to the ground floor and whispered about the status of the other pending investigations as we strolled through the marble corridors. We stopped behind the metal detectors at the front entrance.

Kennelly said, "Let's see, Lt. Cahill is still the defendant in the Aggravated Battery Case and a suspect in the newspaper reporter's murder, and Mr. Newton is still the prime suspect in a triple homicide."

"You don't have to sound so glib about it," I said.

Kennelly giggled. "At the rate you two guys are going, I can give up my practice and represent you exclusively."

"If we go to prison, your annual income will be severely reduced," I said.

Kerri started crying. "I don't see the humor in any of this."

Kennelly put a reassuring arm around her shoulders and said, "Don't worry, Ms. Cahill, I'm not going to let that happen."

We stepped outside the Criminal Courts Building. Kerri's tears were flash-frozen on her cheek.

"Why don't you give Kerri a ride back to Beth's house?" I asked Charlie. "I'll try to catch a ride to Area Central. I want to see if Donovan and Barcomb are making any progress."

CHAPTER 38

I caught a Second District uniformed officer coming out of Narcotics court and bummed a ride off of him to Area Central Headquarters.

Donovan and Barcomb were the first detectives I saw as I entered through the back door of the second floor. They were seated at a long laminate table perusing a huge stack of MUDD records when I came in, and they looked to have been at it for a while.

Barcomb stood and shook my hand. "Can I get you a cup of coffee, Lieu?"

"You don't have to call me 'Lieu'; I'm a civilian now," I responded.

Barcomb chuckled and reassured me, "Only temporarily, Lieu."

"But I'd still love some coffee," I added.

While Detective Barcomb was getting my coffee, I asked Donovan about their progress.

"Nothing yet. No Marios, no Fontanettas, but we do

have a few people that use only the first initial 'M,'" he replied.

"I'm guessing 'Mario' is his real first name," I said.

"That's our guess, too. We're looking for anything Italian with an M initial for a first name," Donovan said.

Barcomb came back with the coffee. "How's the arm healing, Lieu?"

"I should be able to sign a confession soon," I joked.

Barcomb chuckled. "When you're able to sign, turn yourself into us. We need the clear-up."

"While I'm here, could you do me one more favor?" I asked. "Run a guy named Art Kiese for me. I need a home address on him."

Barcomb went over to the computer and ran the name. A few moments later he returned and said he pulled up two Art Kieses: one was a seventy-year old man and the other one was thirty-seven.

"The thirty-seven year old should be my guy," I said.

"He lives downtown in Presidential Towers according to his driver's license," Barcomb replied.

"You'll let me know if you come up with something on Mario?"

"Sure thing," Barcomb said.

"Is anyone available to give me a ride home?" I asked.

Before Donovan or Barcomb could reply, I saw the young State's Attorney from Felony Review strutting about, the one that wanted to beat me up.

"Oh, wait a minute," I said, "I see a friend of mine. I'll ask him."

I yelled across the room, "Yoo-Hoo, Micropenis, would you be going south?"

He yelled back, "Go fuck yourself, asshole."

I turned to Donovan and Barcomb and smiled. "He said no."

CHAPTER 39

January 24, 2014
Friday
1700 hours

Kennelly should have at least offered to buy us breakfast this morning, or a new car or something considering the prices he charged, but he didn't. I'd have to settle for peanut butter and jelly again. I slathered peanut butter on six slices of bread and had to rest before I started smearing jelly on the next six slices. My arm was a nuisance. I went to the fridge and pulled out a half-gallon of milk. As I was pouring it into the glass, lumps the size of snowballs fell out and splashed sour milk all over. I poured the milk down the drain, threw the sandwiches in the garbage, and headed for the Mexican restaurant on 111th Street, which is what I should have done in the first place.

I was pulling into the parking lot when my Blackberry rang. It was Detective Donovan.

"Lieu, we might have something. We found a listing on the MUDDS for McKittrick's home phone for an M. Pellegrino in Melrose Park. We checked with the phone company, and the guy's first name is Mario. We ran him and he fits our physical, so we pulled up his mugshot on the computer—dead ringer for the composite. Can you reach Charlie Newton to have him come in and view a photo lineup?"

"I'll get a-hold of Charlie right now," I said, "and we'll be in as soon as we can."

I ended the call and dialed Pete and Beth Steffens' house. Beth answered, and I asked her if Charlie was still there. A moment later, Charlie picked up the line with his usual aplomb. "Devlin lad, more mischief, pray tell?"

I told him Donovan and Barcomb may have ID'd Mario and to start heading south and meet me at Area Central.

"It's Friday, Devlin lad. Date night."

"Prioritize," I said.

"I did. See you in a couple of days."

"I'll see you in a half hour."

I pulled out of the parking lot of the Mexican Restaurant. Mario was more important than a burrito ... and Charlie's date.

CHAPTER 40

January 24, 2014
Friday
1730 hours

Reclining the seat in the Beamer, I kicked back in the parking lot of Area Central, smoking a cigar and listening to porno music, watching the world go by as I waited for Charlie to arrive. No relief from Mother Nature. Wet, heavy snow began falling; within minutes, a blanket of white covered the hood of my car. A steady stream of blue and whites and unmarked squad cars silently pulled into, and out of, the lot. All I could hear was Dave Brubeck playing *Take Five*. Some incoming had prisoners with hands cuffed behind their backs and an officer on each arm to make sure they didn't slip on the sleet and fall face first on the pavement, a certain complaint of police brutality. Mouths moved but words were muted, like mimes, outside the confines of my car. I didn't have to hear their words, though, to know what they were saying. I've heard them all thousands and thousands of times, and I was sick to death of listening to their dribble. Most of the coppers were young, uniformed officers, brimming with enthusiasm and just beginning their careers; I was like that once, naively believing I could somehow make a difference. After getting punched in the face a few hundred times, suspended and sued every time they stepped out the squad car, their enthusiasm will wane.

Sade began singing *Nothing Can Come Between Us*. Her voice was cool and relaxing. I closed my eyes and leaned back on the headrest. My thoughts drifted back to the day I met Kerri in 2007, the happiest day of my life, and my lips pressed into a thin, mirthless smile. I went to Carson Pirie Scott to buy a La-Z-Boy recliner for my La-Z-Ass, something big and leather and overstuffed. The night before, I caught an elbow in the face making an arrest, and I had a two-steak shiner. After assisting me for about twenty-five minutes, the salesman got annoyed with me and said he'd send the interior designer over to help me. I began to tell him I didn't need a goddamn interior designer to help me pick out a recliner, but he stomped off in a huff. As Kerri neared a couple of minutes later, though, I changed my mind and decided an interior designer was exactly what I needed. I forgot why I was there. I think I told her I was shopping for drapes, something in black and blue to match my eye. Her smile lit up the showroom. She laughed and told me she didn't think I'd be happy with black and blue drapes once my eye healed. A year later, I had a La-Z-Boy recliner, a wife, and salmon-colored carpeting.

A few years after we were married, I convinced her to leave her job and go back to school full-time at Columbia College to get her Master of Fine Arts degree in interior design. She was reluctant to quit her job, but after much cajoling, she acquiesced. Our marriage was idyllic for the next several years, until I got shot. Kerri's mood and demeanor blackened overnight. She obsessed about me quitting the job or becoming a pencil pusher in some geek job. I couldn't, or wouldn't, do either. Finally, she gave me the ultimatum: the job or her. I don't do ultimatums well, so my stubbornness led her to the door. I thought she would only be gone a day or two, realize this incident wasn't worth ruining our marriage, and then she'd return, but I was wrong. The 158-grain bullet, which passed through my chest, hurt me in more ways than I ever could have imagined. I underestimated Kerri's obstinacy … and mine. I was wrong about a lot of things. I was wrong about everything. She took a furnished room at a motel and subsisted on whatever little money she had saved up, quit school because she couldn't afford it, and refused any financial support from me. No school. No job. No money. No family in America. I drove her right into McKittrick's arms. God am I a fool.

• • •

Charlie pulled into the police parking lot in his rent-a-Vette like he was driving at the Indy 500. He whipped into an available parking space about three rows behind me, and I braced for the sound of metal grating on metal. I got out of my car and held up my bullet-ridden arm to get his attention. He sidled through the parked vehicles toward me, careful not to brush against the salted cars in his date-night clothes.

"What's the hurry, Hemingway"? I asked.

"No hurry, Devlin lad. If I wanted to drive slowly I would've rented a Yugo."

The wet end of the panetela unraveled in my mouth, and I spit out a chunk of tobacco. Disgusting habit. "Let's go upstairs and I'll introduce you to some of my friends."

"That shouldn't take long," Charlie quipped.

• • •

When we got to the second-floor offices, Donovan and Barcomb introduced us to a third detective, Art Breckenfield, who would be conducting the computer-generated photo lineup. Breckenfield didn't know squat about the investigation, and could therefore be considered impartial to avoid later defense claims that the investigating detectives influenced Charlie's ID of Pellegrino. Breckenfield asked Charlie if he would consent to the viewing being videotaped, and I nodded to Charlie. With the camera rolling, Breckenfield pulled up five random photos of subjects fitting the general description of Pellegrino; before he could ask Charlie if anyone of them looked familiar, Charlie jabbed his finger into the face of Mario Pellegrino.

Charlie came out of the interview room and said, "That, gentlemen, is the ubiquitous Mr. Fontanetta."

Barcomb and Donovan looked at each other and then at me.

I told them, "He always talks like that."

"We'll grab a couple of guys and go set up on Pellegrino's house. We won't go to the door until we're sure he's in there so we don't spook him."

"Can we ride with you?" I asked.

Donovan's cheek ticked and Barcomb grimaced. "Lieu,

I think it would be better if you sat this one out. You're on suspension already, and if anything goes wrong, it will be our asses along with yours," Barcomb said.

I was disappointed, but I knew he was right. Giaccone was dead, Charlie saw to that, but if there were any hope of getting to McKittrick, we'd need Pellegrino alive and talking.

"You're right, Jack. Charlie and I will go back to my house. Be careful and give me a call when you take him into custody."

"Will do, Lieu."

As Charlie and I headed back toward the parking lot, he wistfully echoed my disappointment. "I wanted to go on that surveillance, Devlin lad."

"Why, so you could turn another asshole into a watering can?"

• • •

We picked up a few gyros sandwiches at the Greek joint in Oak Lawn and took them back to my house. Charlie drank his customary two Miller Lites, and we both zonked out watching a rerun of one of the most sensational bouts in boxing history, the first fight of the Mickey Ward/Arturo Gatti trilogy. I thought I heard the bell ring for the next round, but it was my telephone. I glanced at my watch as I reached for the cell phone on the coffee table. It was 0100 hours.

"We got him," Barcomb said.

CHAPTER 41

I was beginning to get that unwelcome feeling whenever I entered Area Central. As Charlie and I strode through the second floor, a few of the dicks waved halfheartedly to me, sans the friendly banter, lowered their heads, and went back to whatever they were doing. I know how policemen think. I'm out on bond for tuning up McKittrick, on indefinite suspension, and I'm a suspect in a murder. My friend, Charlie Newton, is a suspect in three. The coppers didn't want to appear too unfriendly in case I beat the beefs, but they did want to keep a comfortable distance between us in case I didn't. If I do get fired or wind up wearing an orange jumpsuit, they won't have any sympathy for me. Sympathy is a word in the dictionary between shit and syphilis. I waved back at them.

I didn't get any negative vibes from Donovan and Barcomb, though, and as far as I was concerned, they were the only two that mattered right now.

Donovan was seated outside the interview room,

leaning back in the chair with his feet up on the desk, sipping coffee and reading a report.

"What's our guy have to say, Bill?" I asked.

"Nothing so far. Arrogant son of a bitch. Jack's in there with him now trying to soften him up." Donovan let his chair fall forward and dropped the report on the desk. "Do you guys want some coffee?" he asked. "We might be here awhile."

Bill was right. About three hours and six cups of coffee later, Barcomb came out of the interview room. Lips pressed tightly and a slight shake of his head told me he wasn't having much luck.

"Anything, Jack?" I asked.

He shook his head and threw his notebook on the desk in frustration. "No, this guy thinks he's cute. The last words out of his mouth as I was leaving were to go fuck myself."

"Good, is it on video?" I asked.

"Yeah, the camera's rolling."

"Tell your sergeant you're through interviewing this mutt and to turn off the camera in there," I said.

Donovan and Barcomb understood what I was suggesting, and from the twisted expressions on their faces, it didn't set well with them, but they had the midnight-watch sergeant log them out of the interrogation room and shut off the camera. I had a narrow opportunity to establish a rapport with Mr. Pellegrino.

Pellegrino bore a remarkable resemblance to the composite sketch. Kudos to Charlie and Officer Melton, the sketch artist. Body thicker and heavier muscled than what I imagined, but there was no mistaking him. His left arm was chained to the O-ring in the wall, the same one I had been chained to a few days earlier, and his feet were up on the desk.

"Get your feet off of the desk, Topolino," I said.

"You must have the wrong guy, dude, my name is Pellegrino."

I slapped his feet off of the desk. With both feet now firmly planted on the floor, he scooted to the edge of his chair, leered at me, and poised for combat.

"Did you know that Native Americans change their names two or three times during their lifetimes?" I asked.

His brows knotted and his lips puckered. "What?"

"It's true," I continued. "Native Americans are given descriptive names later in life according to their deeds or achievements, like Running Bear, Crazy Horse ..."

"Thanks for the history lesson, asshole" he interrupted, "What does that have to do with me?"

"Topolino. It means Mickey Mouse in Italian. I'm going to name you because your mama didn't."

"I get it. Now we're going to play good cop–bad cop, and you're the bad cop," he said.

I bitch-slapped him with my bad hand, and the pain shot up to my eyeballs. "Right again, Topolino."

Red welts rose on his face, outlining my imprint.

His face twisted into a scowl, and he sneered, "You hit like a bitch."

The lab could have lifted my prints off of his face after I delivered the second blow.

"Any better?" I asked, but he wasn't so verbal now. I detected a glimmer of fear in his eyes, a look I've seen many times before.

The desk made a loud screeching noise on the floor, like fingernails on a blackboard, when I threw it across the room and raced to unshackle him from the detention ring. I roughly removed the bracelet from his wrist and flung my chair within inches of his, violating his personal space. He lowered his head, and his shoulders slumped. Tough guys are like dogs; they exhibit aggression only when they're on a leash. It's called barrier frustration. Unleash the dog, or remove the handcuffs, and they become pussycats when they realize their false bravado is of no avail. He began tapping his foot in the direction of the door.

"Now that we've established a rapport, Topolino, let's start over. Unlike the good cop, I don't plan on spending three hours in here with your monkey-ass playing patty-cake. If you'd like to call me an asshole again, or tell me to go fuck myself, like you did the other detective," I said through clenched teeth, "now's your chance, tough guy. You're unhandcuffed, so there's nothing to stop you but cold, hard, motherfucking fear." I gave Pellegrino a few seconds to respond, but he didn't. My tough-guy/dog simile is usually right, but I have to admit, I have been bitten in the ass by unleashed dogs before, so I was delighted when Pellegrino didn't jump up and start mopping the floors with me.

"Let's begin by telling me what you know about Charlie Newton," I said.

He leaned back in his chair and hesitated a moment, like he was thinking of something clever to say, but rubbed the welts on his face and thought better of it. "I never heard of Charlie Newton," he replied in a more courteous, subdued tone. Good start; he was lying, of course, but at least he was responding to questions and didn't call me asshole.

"What were you doing in the bookstore the day of his book signing?" I asked.

"What would I be doing in a bookstore?"

"Buying a book on basic phonics, I'd imagine," I answered, "or setting up Charlie Newton to take the fall on a triple homicide."

Pellegrino folded his arms across his chest and lowered his head. "I'll tell you the same thing I told your friend, the good cop; I don't know Charlie Newton, I haven't been to a bookstore since I was ten, and I didn't kill anybody."

"What do you know about John Giaccone?" I asked.

"Giaccone was a friend of mine, until one of you fu-" he caught himself before he finished the sentence. "You killed him, didn't you?"

I held up my bad arm. "Yeah, you shoot me, I shoot you. That's how the game's played."

"I want to talk to my lawyer," he said.

"If all goes well, you'll be sharing a cell together and you can talk to him as often and as long as you'd like for the next twenty years to life."

Pellegrino looked puzzled. "What does my lawyer have to do with this?" he asked.

"You tell me. What do you know about Emmett McKittrick?"

"I don't know shit about Emmett McKittrick. He's a lawyer. He represented me on a couple of beefs, and I couldn't pay him, so I do odd jobs for him once in awhile."

"Like murders?" I asked. "Those are odd jobs."

He proffered a tight-lipped smile and said, "No, like building a deck behind his house."

"Why did Giaccone shoot me?"

"You'll have to ask him," Pellegrino replied.

I moved my chair closer to him until our knees touched. "Let's not start getting cute again, Topolino, or we may have to reestablish a rapport."

He made a long, soft sigh of exasperation and responded, "I don't know why, for chrissakes. Maybe he had a few parking tickets and he thought you there to arrest him."

"Or maybe he committed a few murders and thought I was there to arrest him for those?"

"If he did, I wasn't aware of them."

"Let me run a few other names past you: Hiram Goldenstein."

"Never heard of him."

"Jerry Doherty."

"Never heard of him."

"How about an Oriental guy named Chiang Yu?"

"Unless he's the guy who owns the Lao Sze Chuan in Chinatown, I don't know him either."

"How about McKittrick's girlfriend?" I asked.

"No."

"You've never met McKittrick's girlfriend?"

"No, I met his wife a few times. Or maybe she's just some broad he's shacking up with, I don't know."

I felt the urge to light him up again for referring to Kerri as some broad, and I didn't like the sound of shacking up either, but I didn't.

"Have you ever heard of Eric Schwartzman?" I asked.

"Yeah, I've heard of him. He's the reporter that got tapped, right?"

"Right. What do you know about him?"

"I don't know anything about him other than what I read in the paper." Pellegrino shifted in his chair, leaned forward, and reestablished eye contact. "Jesus Christ, do you think I killed every motherfucker in Chicago?"

"Not all, Topolino," I replied. "Just four."

Pellegrino fixed his eyes on his lap again and shook his head, then began tapping both feet.

"We're going to go pick up your attorney now, Topolino, bring him in here and ask him the same questions we're asking you. He's smarter than you, though, and knows how to play this game. It's what he does for a living, and he knows that he who talks first gets the best deal. You'd better pray he doesn't say you did anything more than build a deck for him. Let's see if he's willing to risk his career and his freedom to cover for you, or if he trick-bags your stupid ass. I'm guessing the latter."

Pellegrino called out to me as I was exiting the interview room, "He can't trick-bag me because I didn't do anything."

I left the door open and called Charlie to the doorway. "Have you ever seen this guy before, Topolino?" I asked.

Charlie glared at him and addressed him by his alias, "Hello, Mr. Fontanetta."

Pellegrino stared hard at Charlie for several seconds, looked at me bewildered, and said, "I've never this guy before in my life."

• • •

Outside earshot of the interview room, I conferred with Donovan and Barcomb again. I suggested we pick up McKittrick and let both McKittrick and Pellegrino know the other was in custody; maybe one of them would break. I preempted Donovan or Barcomb's suggestion that I make myself scarce by offering to take a hike. I saw the relief in their faces. Interrogating Pellegrino was one thing, but since I was already charged with tuning up McKittrick, that was something else again. Even if McKittrick did cop out, he'd claim duress, and his confession would go out the window.

Charlie and I left the building for the second time that day. I was tired of driving back and forth from my house, so we drove to an all-night truck diner on Pershing Road in the Irish Riviera, not far from Area Central Headquarters. The restaurant didn't meet with Charlie's standards but we had few options at that time of the morning.

"I'm not eating here," Charlie said when he saw the ashes from a cigarette, dangling from the corner of the short-order cook's mouth, fall onto the griddle. The cook flipped an egg over on them and they magically disappeared.

We sloshed across the wet tile floor to an orange plastic booth in the back of the diner and sat down. I ordered the truckers' special, the largest breakfast on the menu, and Charlie ordered coffee. The cook returned a moment later and dropped two cups of coffee in front of us, mine spilling out onto the table. Charlie refused to drink it. It would be a long night without coffee.

A few minutes later, the cook reappeared and plunked the plate of pancakes, eggs, ham, and hash browns in front of me with the same decorum, then turned without a word and went back to his griddle.

"Friendly chap, isn't he?" Charlie asked.

"Parolee—not fond of coppers."

"How do you know he didn't spit in your food?"

I broke a yolk, swabbed the ham around in it, and took a big bite. "I don't."

Charlie looked at my plate and said, "Please let me know in advance when the bowel evacuation is beginning."

"I'm potty trained, Charlie, but if I have an accident in my pants, you'll be the first to know."

A smile crossed my face at the thought of Charlie having to use the bathroom. The Board of Health won't go in there to inspect it without a HAZMAT suit. I put my Blackberry on the table and waited for Donovan or Barcomb to call. This may be the last opportunity Charlie and I would have to extricate ourselves from this mess.

I was relying heavily on Donovan and Barcomb's investigative skills. If they couldn't pull the proverbial rabbit out of the hat, it wouldn't be Pellegrino and McKittrick going to prison, it would be Newton and Cahill, and I am sure prison standards aren't up to Charlie's.

As if reading my mind, Charlie asked, " Do you think Donovan and Barcomb are as good as you purport them to be?"

I shrugged and raised my brows. "I'm told they once cleared a murder in Canaryville."

Charlie's face, a blank sheet, waited for further

explanation. When none was forthcoming, he asked, "Why is that so astounding?"

"No dental records in Canaryville, and everybody's DNA matches."

We both laughed, it eased the tension, and then Charlie added, always having to get in the last word, "You're from Canaryville, aren't you?"

CHAPTER 42

January 26, 2014
Sunday
0600 hours

At dawn, the over-the-road truck drivers emerged from their sleepers and filtered into the restaurant for Sunday breakfast. The griddle hissed, and the aroma of frying bacon hung in the air. Condensation on the windows made it impossible to see out, but I was confident the weather hadn't changed much. A trucker dumped a pocketful of change into the jukebox, and some hillbilly started moaning a song about his broke-down pickup truck and his po' ass mama. Still no word from Donovan or Barcomb.

Charlie suggested I call them. It couldn't hurt, so I called Central and asked to speak to either Donovan or Barcomb. A moment later, Donovan picked up the phone.

"What's going on, Bill?" I asked.

"Nothing at the moment. We have McKittrick in here, but neither one of them are talking. Jack's arguing with the ASA from Felony Review about probable cause to get a search warrant for both of their houses."

Donovan and Barcomb had been working around the

201

clock and I could hear the exhaustion in Donovan's voice.

"I hope Jack's not arguing with that young ASA I asked for the ride home yesterday?" I asked.

"No, it's a different ASA who probably doesn't hate you as much."

Donovan changed the subject and asked what I was doing awake so early. I told him Charlie and I spent the night in the truck diner hoping something would break. He suggested we go home and get some sleep. It didn't look like there was going to be a break in the case anytime soon, and if they were successful in obtaining the search warrant, it promised to be an even longer day than the day before.

I felt guilty going home and resting while Donovan and Barcomb were dragging their tired asses around town, but I was as useless as a jockstrap on ASA Micropenis. Charlie asked me if I could arrange for him to participate in the execution of the search warrant.

CHAPTER 43

I was in total darkness when I awoke. I wasn't sure where I was at first, but the lack of flatulence in the air told me I was no longer in a *cell with Miguel*. Nice—it rhymes. I propped myself up on one elbow, flicked on the lamp next to my bed, and checked my Blackberry to ensure I hadn't missed Donovan or Barcomb's call. No messages. I glanced at the LCD display on the clock radio and it read 4:25 PM. What the hell were Donovan and Barcomb doing all of these hours? Did they get the warrant? Did they execute it? Or had they collapsed from exhaustion? Why hadn't they called?

I crept to the bedroom door and quietly opened it so as to not disturb Charlie in the other room. The house was dark except for a sliver of light emanating from under the door of my office. As I neared the room, I heard the rat-a-tat-tat of fingers on a keyboard.

Charlie was showered and shaved and busy at work. His exuberance was making me ill.

"Don't you sleep?" I asked.

"Indeed I do, Devlin lad, but this constant running back and forth to Area Central and staying up all night in filthy diners has necessitated me to adjust my commitment from writing so many words a day to writing so many words a week. I have to capitalize on every spare minute. So, I've been slaving away at my craft while you slept."

"You have baby shit for brains," I said.

Charlie ignored the remark as usual. He was becoming desensitized to my barbs. "There's fresh coffee and a half of a grapefruit in the kitchen if you're interested," he said.

"A half of a grapefruit? I may be suspended, but I'm still a copper. We eat doughnuts. Besides, it's four-thirty in the afternoon. Peanut butter and jelly time."

I poured a cup of coffee and lit a cigar, with full intention of waiting until I heard from Donovan or Barcomb, but I couldn't stand the suspense. I had to know what was going on.

The sergeant who answered the phone in Area Central sounded cool toward me after I identified myself. He told me Donovan and Barcomb were still in the office and put me on hold. A couple of minutes later, Barcomb came to the phone.

"I'm sorry to keep bothering you, I know you're busy, but I'm dying here," I said.

"No problem, Lieu. I have good news and bad news. The ASA approved the warrant for McKittrick's house. We had a hard time finding a judge to sign it on a Sunday morning, but we got Judge Nielsen out of bed, and he signed it for us. We executed the warrant hours ago and didn't come up with anything of evidentiary value, but we did recover a double-door, six-foot-high safe. McKittrick's lawyer is in here now and contends documents in the safe are protected under lawyer/client privilege, and he intends on filing a motion to stop us from opening it."

"Why don't we have our guys rip it open before he can file his motion?" I asked.

"Two reasons. First, our guys say the safe's locking mechanism has an upgraded security feature called glass relockers; if you break them trying to defeat the locking mechanism, it would take days, or weeks, to get it open. The second reason is the ASA already knows about the safe and told us we're to let a judge make the decision."

I shook my head in utter disgust and spit a piece of tobacco onto the back of my hand. "What about McKittrick and Pellegrino?" I asked.

"The ASA says there's insufficient evidence to charge either one of them. They're going to be released without charging."

Engorged veins in my head pulsated, and I felt tremendous pressure behind my eyes, like a tornado whipping its way around in my head that couldn't find a way out.

"I can understand Felony Review releasing McKittrick without charging. Without any admissions, we don't have anything against him, but what about Pellegrino for chissakes? Charlie witnessed the murders and ID'd him."

"You're not going to want to hear this, Lieu, but the ASA says Charlie Newton still looks like a better suspect than Pellegrino. Newton's prints were in the house, his car was left on the scene, and then he disappeared for a week. We have no physical evidence to link Pellegrino to the scene or the murders other than Newton's word. The ASA says he wouldn't consider charging Pellegrino with three murders without some independent corroborative evidence."

I thanked Barcomb for his and Donovan's tireless efforts and told him to go home and get some well-deserved sleep. I hung up the phone, ripped it out of the wall, and smashed it against the wall.

Charlie came out of the office and strolled by me toward the kitchen, glancing at the hole in the drywall and the phone fragments on the floor.

"Not good news I gather," he said as he continued on his way to the kitchen.

CHAPTER 44

I made breakfast. Our bacon was cooked, figuratively and literally, and well done I might add. We identified the murderers, found them, and arrested them, and still we were the ones under the cloud of suspicion. Maybe the plan to abduct Charlie, hold him for a week, and release him wasn't as ludicrous as it first seemed.

I lowered the heat and cracked a half-dozen eggs onto the electric griddle. "Do you want bacon and eggs?" I asked.

"No, thank you," Charlie replied, "bad for the cholesterol and the waistline. I'd like two poached eggs, dry toast, and I'll have that other half of grapefruit."

"I wouldn't worry about your cholesterol or your waistline. You're going to die by lethal injection soon anyway. You may as well enjoy yourself."

"Such an optimist," Charlie said, sipping his coffee while reviewing his notes for his next novel. "I talked to my agent yesterday, and he said he likes the premise of my manuscript so far."

"Did you tell him he may have to find a ghost writer to finish it for you posthumously?" I asked.

"No death penalty in Illinois, remember?"

We finished breakfast, and I lit a cigar. Charlie volunteered to do the dishes, which was out of character for him, and his motives worried me.

"I'll do my own dishes," I said.

Gladly refusing to argue the point, Charlie said, "In that case, if you don't mind my using your office, I'd like to write for awhile."

"Be my guest, Hemingway."

I believed Charlie's nonchalance toward the investigation, and the world in general, was genuine. Mine, on the other hand, was a sham. My confidence was dwindling. If McKittrick doesn't get charged with these murders, or—worse yet—he isn't involved in these murders, the best-case scenario for me is that I've lost my job and my pension. Worst-case scenario, I go to the joint, which wouldn't matter much if I lost my job. What difference would it make?

My fingers began trembling as I was drying the dishes and I had a strange metallic taste in my mouth, like I was sucking on a washer. A moment later, my left hand and the left side of my face went numb. Within seconds, it passed.

The telephone rang, and I hurried into the front room to answer it; realizing I no longer had a phone in the front room, I rushed to the bedroom and picked up my Blackberry from the nightstand.

It was Bill Donovan. "I have some breaking news. Judge Nielsen authorized opening the safe. He ordered

McKittrick to give us the combination and advised him the safe would be forcibly opened if he refused. The judge said he would first review the files in the safe to determine what, if any, files were protected under lawyer/client privilege before releasing the contents to the police."

I began pacing. "Did McKittrick give him the combination?" I asked.

"He did."

"When is the judge going to open it?"

"He did."

"Bill, don't make me pull this out of you," I said. "Was there anything in there?"

"No papers or files pertaining to our dead guys, or Giaccone or Pellegrino, but we did recover $1.2 million ..."

I interrupted. "That's great, maybe he'll go to prison for income tax evasion, but that doesn't do squat for me or Charlie."

"You didn't let me finish, Lieu," he said, "and a 9mm like the one used in our triple. We didn't get any prints off of it, but it's on the way to the lab for test firing. If it's our murder weapon, we're going back to arrest McKittrick, and I don't think he'll be going home this time."

I was glad the numbness in my face was gone because I had to pucker and kiss the phone. "Charlie," I hollered from the bedroom, "we may have gotten a game changer!"

Charlie appeared unconcerned when I gave him the news, and responded with a dispassionate, "Great," turned around, and returned to the computer and his manuscript. I don't know what it takes to get a rise out of this guy.

I paced the floor for the next half hour, from window

to window, not knowing what I expected to see. I fired up a panetela and checked the Blackberry in my shirt pocket to ensure it was charged. When I got tired of wandering around the living room like a caged animal, I grabbed the feather duster and gave the rooms a once over, praying Charlie wouldn't emerge from the office and catch me. It was emasculating, and Charlie isn't the type of guy who would ever let me live it down. In Charlie-world, such menial duties are relegated to maids and houseboys. I successfully avoided detection, and started cleaning the bathroom when I was done.

I was on my knees scouring the toilet when the long shadow of a figure loomed behind me. Latrine duty was almost as denigrating as feather dusting—almost. At least it required elbow grease and the ability to get down on one's knees.

"What are you doing?" Charlie asked.

"This is what they call scouring the toilet, Charlie," I responded. "This is what your maids do when you're not around and the reason your toilets are always sparkling."

"How novel," he replied.

My Blackberry rang. I scooted away from the toilet so I wouldn't drop it in the drink as I was pulling it out of my shirt pocket.

"Lieutenant, the lab called," Jack Barcomb said. "We got our murder weapon."

For one of the few times in my life, I was at a loss for words. I lowered my head and exhaled.

"We're going back to pick up McKittrick and Pellegrino. The ASA from Felony Review has already contacted his supervisor, and charges on each of them for three counts of murder have been approved."

When I found my voice, I asked, "Did the gun come back registered to McKittrick?"

"The serial number has been obliterated," Barcomb informed me, "but the lab tech thinks he can raise it."

"Thanks, Jack." I returned the Blackberry to my pocket, let out a sigh of relief, and rested back on my haunches to savor the moment. A minute earlier, I was in the toilet with a can of Comet between my knees, and now I was on top of the world, still on my knees but thanking God. In all probability, the criminal charges against me would be dropped, and IPRA would have to exonerate, or unfound, the complaint register investigation against me. I'll soon be a lieutenant of police again, and Charlie is no longer the prime suspect in a triple homicide.

"You can grow your hair back now, Charlie," I said. "It doesn't look like you'll be getting the electric chair after all."

Sunlight spirited through the blind slats and cascaded down the wall like a sign from God, promising brighter days ahead. *Thank you, Jesus. I owe you two now.*

CHAPTER 45

January 28, 2014
Tuesday
0930 hours

The next morning, Charlie and I drove separately to the Criminal Courts Building and appeared at McKittrick and Pellegrino's arraignments in Violence Court. A big money lawyer named Jacob Belkind, reputed to be on a par with Stephen Kennelly, represented McKittrick. Pellegrino's attorney, Aaron Cox, a familiar face at homicide trials, was also a formidable adversary. Two high-priced mouthpieces, and my guess was McKittrick was footing the bill for both of them. He must have a couple million more stashed away someplace.

Both defendants were dressed in jeans and sweatshirts, in sharp contrast to their lawyers' bespoke three-piece suits. McKittrick probably had a closet full of them at home.

McKittrick and Pellegrino both pled not guilty, which came as no surprise, waived their rights to a preliminary hearing, and requested a jury trial. They were both held without bond, and their respective attorneys indicated they planned on filing a stack of pretrial motions, including motions to quash the search warrants and suppress the evidence, and motions for severance. If the court ruled in favor of the defense on either one of those motions, the case was in jeopardy. If the court granted the motion for severance, Pellegrino would be subpoenaed as a witness at McKittrick's trial. McKittrick's attorney would put him on the stand and ask him if he put the gun in McKittrick's safe without McKittrick's knowledge. Pellegrino would take the fifth, and McKittricks's jury would infer his refusal to answer the question meant he was guilty and come back with an NG on McKittrick. It's an old ploy. Pellegrino's case, if tried separately, would be even more difficult to convict. The only evidence against Pellegrino was Charlie's identification, and Charlie's story still sounded hokey, even to me. Eyewitness identifications are deemed to be unreliable in many cases. The murder weapon was found in McKittrick's safe, not Pelligrino's. A talented defense attorney, such as Aaron Cox, could blow a hole right through the prosecution's case.

The motion to quash the search warrant and suppress the evidence in McKittrick's case was even more critical to the prosecution. If the court threw out the warrant, the gun would go out under the exclusionary rule; without the murder weapon, there was no case against McKittrick. The prosecuting attorney had his work cut out for him. If Marcia Clark lost the OJ trial, anything was possible.

The arraignments lasted a few minutes. McKittrick and Pellegrino were led away by the bailiff back to lock-up.

McKittrick turned and leered at me when he got to the

door leading back to lock-up. I held up three fingers and mouthed the words, "Round three."

He held up three fingers back to me, then dropped two of them. The finger left standing indicated he didn't think I was funny.

CHAPTER 46

January 28, 2014
Tuesday
1000 hours

I pulled out of the parking garage across the street from 26th Street directly behind Charlie, but as soon as his tires hit California Avenue, he started banging gears. Within four blocks, he left me in the dust, and I couldn't see him anymore.

With the arrests of McKittrick and Pelligrino, and the recovery of the murder weapon used in the triple, there wasn't any heat on Charlie anymore, so it was time I started devoting more time to the Schwartzman murder and trying to pull my own ass out of hot water.

A few minutes later, I jumped on I-290 East and headed toward the West Loop. Even before exiting at Canal, I could see the four staggered, forty-nine-story brownstone skyscrapers called The Presidential Towers Complex casting their shadows over the West Loop.

For a meager fifteen bucks, I parked across the street and entered the building at Madison & Clinton. I nodded at the doorman as I passed toward the concierge desk. A well-preserved middle-aged woman stood behind the high concierge desk. An enormous oval wooden fixture, with recessed lighting, was suspended from the ceiling overhead by thin decorative chains. It looked like a leftover prop from *Close Encounters of the Third Kind*. I'd be pissed off if they beamed her up before I got to ask her in which tower Art Kiese lived.

The woman directed me to the security desk in Tower #2. The security officer asked my name and rang Kiese's apartment.

"I'm sorry, sir, there's no answer."

I handed him my business card and asked him to tell Kiese to call me at his earliest convenience, which better be in the next few hours.

I doubted Kiese would call me, but it was worth a shot.

CHAPTER 47

Three loud, officious raps at my front door jolted me out of bed. Staggering toward the door, I ran my fingers through my hair and tried to press down the bed head to make myself more presentable in case it was somebody I gave a shit about, which was unlikely.

Bad news on the doorstep. Two suits with G.I. Joe haircuts and wingtip shoes were standing at my threshold when the door swung open.

"I didn't know Jehovah's Witnesses came out in this weather," I said.

Both men flashed FBI badges.

"Mr. Cahill?" the shorter of the two asked.

"Lieutenant Cahill," I quickly corrected him, not to be a pompous ass, but not addressing a police officer by his rank is an old trick used by the feebs and lawyers to demean or lower one in stature.

"Sorry we woke you, Lieutenant. We'd like to discuss an incident you had with Emmett McKittrick. May we come in?" the taller one asked.

"I'm sorry you woke me, too. I would not like to discuss Emmett McKittrick with you, now or ever—and, no, you may not come into my house, not without a warrant."

"We can do this here, Lt. Cahill, or we can subpoena you and do this in our office."

"Get the subpoena."

The two looked at each other, and then back at me.

"Thank you, Lieutenant. You've been most cooperative."

"Thanks for stopping by—I closed the door—dickwads."

PART II

CHAPTER 48

June 21, 2014
Saturday
0730 hours

Sparrows chirped merrily outside my bedroom window, and a wisp of warm, sweet summer air slipped in under the sash, billowing the curtains. The first official day of summer. I stumbled from the bed and went room to room, opening all the windows. The morning dew was still on the ground, and there wasn't a cloud in the sky. A glorious morning.

Winter of '13-'14 would go down in the history books as one of Chicago's worst with a snowfall accumulation of eighty inches. Though the weather had gotten better, not much else had. The last five months hadn't turned out like I expected, or hoped. I anticipated a notification from the State's Attorney's Office informing me of their intent to decline prosecution against me on the Aggravated Battery charge against McKittrick, since they were trying him for three murders, but it didn't come. I was still on indefinite suspension, and the likelihood of me saving the job was growing dimmer each day. I hadn't heard back from the

FBI either, but that didn't mean they weren't still building a case against me for violating McKittrick's civil rights. Every copper with more than two days on the job knows the G can indict a peanut butter and jelly sandwich, so I'd be lying if I said I wasn't worried. IPRA's investigation was still ongoing, too, but that didn't surprise me. As a rule, they wouldn't render their findings until the criminal and civil charges against me were adjudicated. In most cases, their findings concurred with those of the federal and state authorities, but the possibility of being fired for violations of Department rules and regulations, still loomed overhead. I had made some powerful enemies on the job.

To celebrate the first official day of summer, I drank my coffee and smoked a cigar on the patio. Kerri always enjoyed dining al fresco, and we ate out there every opportunity we could, weather permitting, behind the privacy of a six-foot redwood fence. Many a warm, summer evening we sat out there, chatting under the stars and the moon until they disappeared.

I finished the pot of coffee and another cigar before slipping on a pair of jeans and a sweatshirt and packing my duffel bag. My hiatus from the gym was over. Ennui has its advantages. Working out kept my stress level down and helped me to forget about the world for a few hours, and it helped me sleep at night. I was running three miles a day, every other day, and pushing the iron around on the alternate days. On Friday and Saturday afternoons I went to Scottsdale Park and sparred a few rounds. I also honed my housekeeping skills to stay busy. Dusting was still gay, but vacuuming was a physical, manly chore, like scouring toilets, at least that's what I kept telling myself, but today the maid was taking off. I glanced out the window and saw the mail carrier coming up my walkway.

"Good morning, Willa, how are you doing today?" I asked.

Willa lumbered up the walkway and smiled as she handed me the mail.

"Mornin' Mr. Cahill, how y'all doin'?

"I never had a bad day," I lied.

Two envelopes on top of the stack of bills were both from the Cook County State's Attorney's Office. I waited until I got inside the house to open them.

The first envelope contained a subpoena for Devlin Cahill, which read "The State of Illinois vs. Emmett McKittrick and Mario Pellegrino." The second envelope contained a subpoena for Charlie Newton, who had given my address as his temporary residence in the states. The date and time on the subpoenas was for Monday, July 7, 2014, at 0900 hours. The trial wouldn't commence on that date; it was only for the purposes of a pretrial briefing. The ASA's name on the subpoena was Dina Bernichio. I didn't know her, but I knew of her. A few of the detectives who worked for me had cases with her in the past and said she was an outstanding prosecutor. Her claim to fame was she had never lost a jury trial. I prayed ours wouldn't be her first. My career, if not my life, depended on it.

The buzzer on the clothes dryer sounded. I tossed the mail on the sofa table, and as I was stuffing a towel into my duffel bag, my cell phone rang. I didn't recognize the number on the caller ID.

"Hello."

"Lt. Cahill, this is Lt. Gracyk from Bomb and Arson. I'm calling to notify you that a bomb went off in Charlie Newton's car when he attempted to enter."

CHAPTER 49

June 21, 2014
Saturday
0830 hours

"Is Charlie all right?" I asked.

"Yeah, he's fine, but his car wasn't so lucky."

"Where is he?"

"Standing about twenty feet away from me. We're still on the fourth level of the parking garage behind the Congress Hotel on Wabash Avenue."

"Will you still be there in about a half hour?" I asked.

"Yeah, we'll be here for a while yet processing the scene."

"I'm on my way. Thanks for the phone call."

• • •

Twenty-five minutes later, I pulled up to the entrance of the Park One Garage on Wabash. Without a badge or gun, and driving a Beamer, the Mexican attendant refused to let me enter. I tried to explain to him that I was a policeman but he spoke less English than I did Spanish. I don't know if he didn't understand me or if he wasn't buying it. I grew impatient. "Yo soy la policia, motherfucker," I kept repeating. He continued smiling at me and shaking his head. I got Lt. Gracyk's number off of my caller ID and called him back. I asked him if he could send a uniformed officer to the entrance so I could get in.

Two minutes later, a uniformed patrol officer from the First District came down and escorted me up to the fourth level.

A couple of blue and whites were parked by Charlie's car, and I saw Charlie talking to two plainclothes guys. I recognized one of them, Curt Scheer, a Bomb and Arson investigator. I worked with Curt, better known as Cur-teese the po-leese, years earlier in Narcotics. Crime scene tape was wrapped around several concrete pillars and cordoned off the area around Charlie's car. The windows were blown out of the car, and glass fragments were spread out over a ten-foot area.

"Well, Hemingway, you did it again. More of your literary fans?" I asked.

"More likely mutual friends of both of ours, I would suspect," Charlie answered.

"I think this is one of those rare occasions where I have to agree with you. I received two subpoenas in the mail for you and me about ten minutes before they bombed your car. It seems news travels at warp speed and someone doesn't want you to testify."

I introduced myself to Lt. Gracyk, thanked him again for the notification, and turned my attention to Curt.

"Cur-teese the po-leese, what do we have?"

"Obviously, a VBIED," Curt responded.

"No, not so obvious. Let's pretend I don't know anything about bombs," I said.

"Vehicle Borne Improvised Explosive Device, commonly known as a car bomb."

"Have you been talking to Charlie? Couldn't you say car bomb?"

"It makes me sound like I know my shit if I say VBIED. I won't be able to tell you any more about it until we examine it in the lab."

"Do they have security cameras in here?" I asked.

"Yeah, my partner's reviewing them now. I'll let you know if we get anything."

Charlie strolled over by the vehicle and inspected the interior damage from a few feet away outside the yellow tape.

I joined him. "I'm sure Hertz will be pleased when you return the vehicle."

"I don't think Hertz will mind at all," Charlie said. "I rented it from Avis."

I told Charlie, under the circumstances, I thought it was better if he returned to my house and stayed there until the trial. There is safety in numbers. Charlie said staying with me for a few days would be bearable, but being without a car wouldn't be. He asked if I could give him a ride to Hertz, since Avis probably no longer sought his patronage, to lease another car.

We left the garage on Wabash and drove to the car rental agency, where Charlie leased another Corvette, same make, model, and color, right down to the interior. It's like the bombing never happened.

Charlie followed me for a couple of miles in his new Vette, abruptly changed lanes, and launched past me like a scud missile. Apparently, I was driving too slowly for a civilian.

A question gnawed at me on the ride home: If Giaccone was dead and McKittrick and Pelligrino were in jail, who planted the bomb? Perhaps the security cameras would give us the answer.

CHAPTER 50

July 7, 2014
Monday
0850 hours

Monday morning, Charlie and I bumped into Donovan and Barcomb in the congested commissary on the first floor of the Criminal Courts Building. We each got a cup of coffee and a doughnut, except Charlie who got a carton of orange juice, and waited in the queue to pay at the register amongst the criminals and defense attorneys, which, like FBI and vaginas in the same sentence, is redundant. Two future inmates behind us, with baseball caps turned sideways and dusty narrow asses hanging out of their dirty drawers, shouted above the din, no doubt intended for our ears. Heads on rubber necks flopped side to side in sync with every word uttered, accompanied by wild, jerky hand gestures. Joe Cocker on acid. I couldn't catch every word they were saying, but it was something about suing the police after they beat their case, and I learned that both of their names were Dog, which they used to address each other at the beginning and end of every sentence.

As a courtesy, I made a suggestion, "Dog, you better

pull up them drawers and cover that narrow ass before you get to Statesville, or they'll be calling you Bitch when you get out, Dog."

Both Dogs began flailing their arms, like they were trying to take flight, and doing the Curly shuffle. One more stooge and the trio was complete. They both kept repeating, "Oh, hell no!" as they scuffed their Michael Jordans around the floor. I don't know what they were trying to communicate, but I got the distinct impression my guidance wasn't well received. Some people can't accept constructive criticism.

Charlie grabbed Donovan by the arm, preventing him from reaching into his pocket to pick up the tab, and handed the cashier a $100 bill. The old black man at the register frowned as he counted out Charlie's ninety-dollars change in ones and fives. No seats in the commissary, counters for standing only, so, rather than stand and eat, we brought our continental breakfasts with us to eat in the witness room.

Court was not yet in session when we entered through the heavy, wooden double doors. With the exception of the court clerk who was arranging docket files next to the judge's bench, the room was empty and quiet as death. Our footsteps sounded like stampeding horses as we clopped across the tiled floor to the witness room, which is annexed to the courtroom. Prosecuting attorneys use the room to brief witnesses before a trial, and sequester them during a trial. Shaughnessy and Zemaitis were already seated in the witness room when we arrived.

It had been a long time since I was required to testify

in a murder trial, not since I became a lieutenant, a benefit of rank, but the hours and days I sat sitting in this room when I was a detective came rushing back to me when I took the first sip of commissary coffee. It was every bit as bad as I remembered. It made the midnight watch's coffee taste like Starbucks. The sweet rolls were worse yet. Cook County Jail inmates call the stale rolls <u>duffies</u>. One bite and I knew what the jail did with the duffies the inmates refused to eat.

I was hiding a large chunk of the duffy in my mouth, hoping my saliva would moisten it sufficiently to choke it down. I was about to spit it out on the conference table, when a statuesque brunette with a layered pixie hairdo barged into the room. Spitting was no longer an option. Etiquette demanded I swallow it.

"Good morning everyone," Ms. Bernichio chirped and flashed a Julia Roberts's smile at everyone.

"I'm sorry I'm late," she said and introduced herself as she dropped a stack of files onto the conference table. She plopped into the chair at the head of table, inhaled deeply, and let the air escape through puckered lips like she was blowing us a kiss. She nodded at the files in front of her. "These suckers are heavy," she said, her voice just above a whisper, and smiled wider. I knew at once why jurors loved her.

"Now you know who I am; let's see who you are," she said, and added, "I already know detectives Donovan and Barcomb, and Shaughnessy and Zemaitis."

"I'm Lt. Cahill, and this is Charlie Newton," I said, nodding toward Charlie.

"I've read your books, Mr. Newton, and they were fabulous; I thoroughly enjoyed them," she said.

Charlie's passion for writing is only exceeded by his passion for women, and Ms. Bernichio said the exact words to set him on fire. Charlie's patented gaga look washed over him. I've seen it hundreds of times.

"Thank you, Dina," Charlie said. "My third book, *Canaryville,* is soon to be released. Perhaps I can personally deliver an autographed copy to you when it comes out?"

Charlie and Dina smiled at one another and held eye contact for a prolonged length of time, making the rest of us uncomfortable, like we were intruding. We hadn't started the pretrial briefing yet, and Charlie was already making goo-goo eyes at the ASA. She knew it, we knew it, and he knew that we knew it, but he didn't care. There's no shame in Charlie's game.

During the awkward hiatus in conversation, Barcomb and Donovan gawked across the table at me with raised brows. I pursed my lips, rolled my eyes toward Charlie, and shook my head.

Ms. Bernichio broke the silence at long last. "Gentlemen, as I am sure you are aware, we have several problems with this prosecution."

"Aren't there always?" I asked rhetorically.

Ms. Bernichio continued to smile but didn't respond. She stood, thrusting her chest forward as she removed her ecru suit jacket, and removed a fresh legal pad from her attaché case.

Charlie ogled her as she wriggled out of her jacket. We all did, to be honest, but not with Charlie's unabashed lust.

Ms. Bernichio was endowed with two undeniable assets, besides her dimples, which I don't believe were purchased at Busts R' Us.

"The defense strategy is going to be that the defendants were framed by the police, in particular by Lieutenant Cahill, who has a vendetta against Mr. McKittrick due to Mr. McKittrick's intimate relationship with his ex-wife. They will attack the veracity of Mr. Newton's claim he was abducted and contend Lt. Cahill and Mr. Newton conspired to frame Mr. McKittrick after Mr. Newton murdered the three victims in Avalon Trails. That contention will be bolstered by the facts that Lt. Cahill fatally wounded one of the two alleged offenders, after having been removed from the investigation by the Chicago Police Department, and the subsequent physical altercation between Lt. Cahill and Mr. McKittrick. They will assert the investigating detectives were manipulated and misdirected by Lt. Cahill due to his position of authority."

"Why don't we release them now and go home?" I asked.

Ms. Bernichio, still smiling, shot back, "That may be a bit premature." She added, "We could have had a *real* problem with this prosecution had the murder weapon been found in a location other than the locked, virtually impregnable safe, in Mr. McKittrick's home. A judge opening the locked safe, outside the presence of the police, makes it difficult for the defense to allege the police planted it there, and that's our case in chief. They will have to come up with a plausible explanation as to how it got there, and I don't think they can."

"Is the gun in the safe all we have going for us?" Barcomb asked.

"No," Ms. Bernichio replied, "the <u>voir dire</u> went well. I think we have a good jury." Turning her attention toward me, she said, "The State can counter that Emmett McKittrick, like Lt. Cahill, also had a personal relationship with Kerri Cahill and had personal relationships with everyone involved in this case—Hiram Goldenstein, Jerry Doherty, John Giaccone, and Mario Pellegrino—which we can establish through prima facie evidence, such as phone records, court transcripts, and employment records. Chiang Yu was the only one with whom we have been unable to tie him. If the jurors consider the unlikelihood of Lt. Cahill being personally involved with Kerri Cahill, Emmett McKittrick, and Charlie Newton, they must also consider the unlikelihood of Mr. McKittrick being involved with Kerri Cahill, two of the three victims, and two of the alleged offenders. Tit for tat."

Charlie's ears perked up before she could say tat.

Ms. Bernichio scooted her chair closer to the conference table, picked her pen up off of the legal pad, and squirmed around in her seat until she was in a comfortable writing position.

"I'm going to put you on the stand in chronological order, with the exception of Mr. Newton. I think his eyewitness identification of Mr. Pellegrino will be the most damning testimony, and I want it to be the last thing the jury hears before retiring for deliberation." She turned to Shaughnessy and Zemaitis and said, "You had the scene, so we'll start with you."

The witness-room door opened. and Bill Sheridan, the firearms expert from the state crime lab, entered.

"I'm sorry I'm late," he said.

"No problem, we're just getting started," Ms. Bernichio said. "And you are?"

Bill introduced himself and pulled up a chair next to Barcomb.

Ms. Bernichio began her questioning of John Shaughnessy.

Charlie balanced his glasses on the tip of his nose and leaned back in his chair. With legs crossed into a figure four and writing pad on his knee, he began taking copious notes at the other end of the table, either fodder for his next book or love notes to Dina Bernichio. I didn't know which.

Sunbeams lasered through the south windows with such intensity I expected the wooden conference table to begin smoldering. Dust particles flitted in the light beams. Four stories below me, razor wire glistened in the sunlight, and the gravel on the rooftops of the Cook County Jail complex across the way sparkled like chopped glass.

I became aware of a tiny voice floating on the airwaves. "Lt. Cahill? Are you still with us?" Ms. Bernichio asked.

"I'm sorry," I said.

Ms. Bernichio turned to a fresh page on her legal pad and scrawled my name on the top line. "Lieutenant, your testimony is going to be the State's greatest liability."

"Thank you for your candor," I said.

"I believe I can successfully explain away your interpersonal relationships with Mr. Newton and Mr. McKittrick, but I cannot explain away the decision of the Cook County State's Attorney's Office to charge you with assaulting Mr. McKittrick or the Chicago Police Department's decision to place you on indefinite suspension as a result of the encounter. This will hurt us in front of a jury."

There wasn't a question pending, and I didn't know how to respond, so I didn't. I maintained eye contact with Ms. Bernichio and waited for her to continue.

"Furthermore, your attorney, Stephen Kennelly, called me this morning and told me that he has advised you to exercise your Fifth Amendment right to remain silent when asked anything relative to the altercation with Mr. McKittrick," Ms. Bernichio said. "You know how juries view witnesses who invoke the right to remain silent."

"Ms. Bernichio, the successful prosecution of this case is of prime importance to me, both professionally and personally," I responded. "I couldn't tell you why the ASA from Felony Review chose to believe McKittrick's version of what transpired between us instead of mine and subsequently charged me with Aggravated Battery. My guess is because I'm a copper and McKittrick and the ASA are both members of the American Bar Association." I smiled at her and added, "No offense."

Without looking up from her legal pad, she replied flatly, "None taken."

I felt a chill in the air, but continued. "I would have thought by now, under the current circumstances, someone in your office would have had the common sense to drop the charges against me instead of risking the outcome of a triple homicide prosecution. The feds, and the police department, will be relying heavily on the outcome of this trial, and it will have great impact on their findings," I said. "If you think waiving my right to remain silent will bolster our case, I will."

Ms. Bernichio smiled. "I cannot, and would not, advise you not to heed your attorney's counsel. That is strictly your decision to make." She ran her long fingers through her hair and returned to her notes. "Let's get down to specifics."

• • •

Four hours later, after having gone over all of our testimonies, Ms. Bernichio concluded the pre-trial briefing. "We're set for trial on Wednesday, the 16th. Your subpoenas are still in effect. Any questions or concerns?" Ms. Bernichio asked.

"I'm concerned about your marital status," Charlie said.

Ms. Bernichio smiled and pivoted toward the door. Without turning around as she was exiting the room, she called back, "Unattached."

Court was in session when we left the witness room. Our footsteps no longer reverberated in the emptiness of the courtroom. Judge Franjo Karlovich, a behemoth of a man, was seated on the bench. He would be our trial judge. He must weigh himself at a dairy farm, I thought.

"How would you like to be his colon?" I asked nobody in particular.

The bailiff admonished me for talking in the courtroom, and I shut up. I hoped the Croatian sumo wrestler didn't hear what I said. He'd eat me for lunch on Wednesday.

As we were riding down in the cramped elevator, Ms. Bernichio asked me, as if an afterthought, "Lieutenant, have you spoken to your ex-wife recently?"

Strange question to ask, I thought. "Not in the last several months," I replied. "Why?"

"She didn't tell you she's been subpoenaed as a defense witness?"

CHAPTER 51

July 7, 2014
Monday
1430 hours

Kerri had moved back into the McKittrick house in Beverly, which didn't set well with me, but since Pellegrino was being held without bond, she didn't feel she was in danger any longer. She was never in fear for her physical safety from McKittrick, and now that he's also being held without bond, neither am I. I thought her decision to move back into McKittrick's house was a mistake. It could send the wrong message to a jury.

I punched the #1 key on my cell phone as soon as I got home from the pretrial briefing. Kerri answered.

"How are you holding up?" I asked.

"Okay, I guess."

"I had a pretrial briefing today with the ASA. She told me you've been subpoenaed as a defense witness?"

"Yes, I have, and I'm scared. I don't know what to say, Devlin. Emmett's attorney asked me if I witnessed you beat Emmett up. Of course, I had to say yes. I was there, but I don't want to get you in any more trouble. What should I do?" She was sobbing.

"Don't cry, Kerri," I said. "You tell them the truth and don't worry about it. I got myself into this, I'll get myself out."

She wept openly. "I don't want to be responsible for you going to prison or losing that stupid, stinking goddamn job."

I changed the subject. "I wish you weren't staying in that house."

"Where else am I going to go, Devlin? I couldn't impose on Pete and Beth Steffens anymore," she said, "and I don't have the money to go anywhere else."

"How about back here?" I asked.

There was a long silence. "Thank you, but no. Coming back, under these circumstances, would not be for the right reasons. Our situation hasn't changed. In a week, or a month, I'd be packing again, and I can't go through that pain a second time."

"How about if I get fired and I'm no longer a policeman?" I asked.

"So, if you're forced off the job, we get back together, but if you have the option of quitting, you'd choose the job over me. Is that what you're saying?"

"It was not my intention to upset you more. I'm sorry. I'll call you later," I said, circumventing her last question. If I did lose the job, maybe Kerri and I could get back together and live happily ever after? As I was putting the cell phone back in my pocket, I remembered Napoleon Hill's saying: In every adversity lies the seed of an equal or greater opportunity. The job without Kerri, or Kerri without the job? The ambivalence of pain and joy.

CHAPTER 52

July 16, 2014
Wednesday
0825 hours

We stood in the marble corridor outside of Judge Franjo Karlovich's courtroom, dressed in our Sunday best, chatting in hushed tones about anything other than the case in which we were about to testify. Several other people, unrelated to our case, lingered about the hallway, too, occasionally meandering over to the court calendar sheet posted on the wall to ensure the case they were there for was scheduled to be heard.

At 0830 hours, the bailiff opened the courtroom doors from the inside, and we all entered. Four shackled men in orange DOC jumpsuits were seated in the jury box with a deputy sheriff beside them. The gold-frocked court clerk stood next to the judge's bench arranging docket files for the morning call, and an attractive court reporter with legs up to her neck sat in front of the judge's bench loading paper into her steno machine. Charlie gave me a sideways glance, raised his eyebrows, and made the goo-goo face. We continued toward the witness room while the others scattered themselves about the first few rows of benches.

• • •

I stuck a finger in the throatlatch of my heavily starched white collar and stretched it away from my neck. Either the dry cleaners shrunk my shirt or I was two tacos away from outgrowing it.

An array of aftershaves and colognes coalesced in the air and filled the witness room. Charlie removed an engraved Mont Blanc pen and a pair of Ben Franklins from the chest pocket of a silk Hawaiian shirt, placed a notebook on the knee of his cream linen slacks, and began scribbling in his notepad. Far be it from me to play the fashion critic, but I couldn't help but notice Charlie wasn't wearing any socks with his Michael Toschi chocolate suede slip-ons. Miami Vice retro.

"Didn't you have any money left over for socks?" I asked.

Charlie continued writing, never lifting his gaze from his notebook. I didn't know if he hadn't heard me or if he was ignoring me, but after several moments of dead air, he countered, "I gave all my money to Stephen Kennelly to defend you." He heard me.

I responded, "Those shoes wouldn't look good with socks, anyway," and I shut up.

As near as I could tell, everyone was seated in the same seats they were seated in the other day for the briefing. Though coppers are trained to be systematically unsystematic, they're creatures of habit like everybody else. The two Johns, Shaughnessy and Zemaitis, both bespectacled and both wearing gray pinstripe suits—Men's Warehouse must have had a twofer sale—sat on the far end of the table, perusing their copies of the case report. Zemaitis clamped an unlit Lucky Strike in the corner of his mouth, head cocked oddly, as if to avoid the imaginary smoke getting his eyes, and turned the pages of the report.

Jack Barcomb and Bill Donovan were seated in the center of the long conference table, cramming for their upcoming testimony. They were actively involved in every facet of the investigation other than the scene: the interrogations and arrests of McKittrick and Pellegrino, as well as the procurement and execution of the search warrants. It was going to be a long day for them.

Bill Sherwood, the lab tech, relaxed, leaning against the window reading the morning newspaper. His testimony would be straightforward. He'd testify to the methods of firearms identification, as he had in a thousand other cases, and state with scientific certainty that the firearm recovered from McKittick's safe was the weapon that murdered Moe, Larry, and Curly.

I did not foresee a pleasant day ahead for Charlie and me. If Charlie had any apprehension about testifying for the first time in criminal court, he didn't show it. He continued jotting down notes, his face devoid of emotion. He bobbed the naked ankle supported on his knee up and down, to some tune playing in his head. His calm was unsettling.

The door to the witness room burst open, and Dina Bernichio entered smiling. "Good morning, everyone."

Charlie stopped taking notes, and at long last, an expression appeared on his face.

"The judge has four cases on the calendar he has to

dispose of this morning, which should only take a few minutes, and then we'll bring our jury out. Are there any questions before the trial starts?" Ms. Bernichio asked.

Charlie said, "I have a question," and gave her the goo-goo grin.

Dina Bernichio laughed. "I already told you my marital status, Mr. Newton. Talk to me after the trial."

She stared at the unlit cigarette flopping from Zemaitis's mouth as she bustled toward me.

"It's not lit," he protested before she could say anything.

"Good, let it remain so," she said.

Standing before me, she yanked the silk pocket square from my breast pocket.

"Too ostentatious," she said, handing it to me.

"Too ostentatious?" I pointed to Charlie and his Hawaiian shirt. "How about Don Ho?"

"Mr. Newton's not a police officer and expected to dress in conservative business attire."

I frowned and said, "You and Charlie should get along fine."

"I think the judge has taken the bench; I have to get out there," she said as she hurried toward the door.

"Did you say the judge has taken the bench or eaten the bench?" I asked.

Ms. Bernichio stopped at the door before exiting and addressed us. "Review your reports and the testimony we went over the other day. The trial will begin in the next few minutes. Wish us all luck."

CHAPTER 53

July 16, 2014
Wednesday
0915 hours

Subdued voices and indistinguishable words filtered through the closed door. I turned my wrist to check my watch. It was 0915 hours.

The silence in the room was disquieting. All the detectives were engrossed in their reports and took advantage of every moment to prepare. Bill Sherwood read the newspaper from front to back, including the obituaries and comics. Charlie continued to write in his notebook, his tranquil demeanor and bouncing ankle irritating me to the point of self-destruction. At the other end of the table, Shaughnessy turned a page of a report. I welcomed the disruption. I glanced at my Seiko again. It was 0925 hours.

The bailiff stuck his head in the room and said, "Detective Shaughnessy."

Shaughnessy rose and followed the bailiff into the courtroom. The atmosphere in the room changed. Tension became palpable.

The trial was underway.

• • •

I glanced at my watch. It was 1010 hours, and Shaughnessy was still on the stand, much longer than I expected given his limited participation in the investigation. What the hell could they be grilling him on?

At 1020 hours, Shaughnessy returned to the witness room, face flushed, accompanied by the bailiff. The bailiff said, "Detective Zemaitis." Zemaitis stuffed the Lucky back into the pack and followed the bailiff from the room.

Shaughnessy picked up his file from the conference table and said wryly, "You're going to love these guys," and slipped out the door. During the few seconds the door was open, I heard Zemaitis testifying about prints being recovered in the house and car.

Zemaitis was still in the hot seat at 1115 hours, Donovan and Barcomb continued to peruse their files, and Charlie wrote in his notebook.

"What the hell could you be writing about all morning?" I asked.

"My manuscript ... and you're disturbing me," he said.

"Excuse the fuck out of me," I said. "You're disturbing me, too, Don Ho, with your foot bouncing for three hours. I'm about ready to put a bullet in your ankle."

Charlie remained withdrawn, continued to write, and replied dispassionately, "You don't have a gun."

More annoyed, I asked, "Are you prepared to testify?"

After a long, exasperated intake of breath, Charlie returned his glasses and his pen to his shirt pocket, and faced me.

"Devlin lad, I've been prepared to testify in this matter since the day I was abducted, so relax."

"I am relaxed, but you're too relaxed," I said.

"You've checked your wristwatch twenty times in the last half hour," Charlie pointed out.

"How would you know?" I asked. "You haven't had your head out of that notebook since 8:30 this morning."

Charlie grinned, that irritating, pretentious smirk he gives when he knows he's irked me to the point of discombobulation, and said, "Such a hothead, Lieutenant."

Zemaitis returned to the witness room to pick up his files. I was too self-conscious to check the time, thanks to Charlie. The bailiff next called Detective Donovan. Donovan rose and faced us with the grin of a constipated man, held up his hand and wiggled his fingers bye-bye, like he was going to the gallows, and followed the bailiff into the courtroom. Zemaitis slid out the door with them.

I kept my wrist under the table and peeked at my watch. It was after noon. Experience told me the court would break for lunch after Donovan's testimony. More than likely, Jack Barcomb and Bill Sherwood's testimony would be heard after lunch, and Charlie and I may not testify at all today.

At 1245 hours, a browbeaten Bill Donovan slinked back to the witness room, sopping sweat from his forehead with a handkerchief.

"The judge recessed for lunch," Donovan said.

Barcomb glanced up from the file, smiled, and spoke for the first time in hours. "You look like you got your ass whooped and your pocketbook took."

"Belkind and Cox are a trip," Donovan said, tossing the damp hankie to Barcomb. "It should be dry by the time you're called to testify. You can give it back to me at work."

Ms. Bernichio pranced into the room, not showing any strain from the morning's jousting tournament, and formally notified us the court had recessed for lunch.

"Be back here by 1:30," she advised.

"It'll take us fifteen minutes to get out of the building and walk to a restaurant and fifteen minutes to get back, leaving us fifteen minutes to eat, ten of which will be waiting for our food to arrive," I said.

"Eat little and eat fast, Lieutenant," Ms. Bernichio replied.

"I hope I don't pass out from hunger on the stand," I said. "The defense team may get the wrong impression."

Charlie asked, "Will you be joining us, Dina?"

"No, I'll have to pass on lunch to prepare for this afternoon's witnesses," she said. "I'll see you all back here at 1:30 sharp."

• • •

Dozens of Mexican restaurants are within walking distance of the Criminal Courts Building, and I had a taste for Mexican, but Jean's Restaurant was closer, and time was of the essence. Charlie, Jack, and I nipped our way northbound on California Avenue. People with time to spare ate leisurely lunches on the grassy parkway, which lay in between the north and southbound traffic on California Avenue; others basked in the warmth of the sun and read newspapers.

The food at Jean's was good, cheap, and fast but not Mexican. Lunch was over before it began. My stomach thought I had been garroted.

We were back in the witness room at 1330 hours. I heard the clerk announce in a loud voice that court was back in session. Several minutes later, the bailiff opened the witness-room door and called Detective Barcomb. I expected Barcomb's cross-examination to be the most grueling of all the detectives. In addition to being the arresting officer for both defendants, he also conducted both interrogations and was the affiant on the search warrants.

Muted voices and vague words rose and fell outside the witness-room door.

"How was your lunch?" Charlie asked.

I didn't have to look at his face to see the smirk.

"Will you shut the fuck up?" I said. "Go back to scribbling in your notebook."

The door swung open at 1600 hours and Jack Barcomb returned after two-and-a-half hours on the stand. Bill Sherwood, the firearms expert, laid his newspaper and the latest edition of Evidence Technology Magazine on the table and followed the bailiff into the courtroom.

Barcomb glanced sideways toward the door and said, "I don't think you'll be getting on today, Lieutenant. Bill was right about Cox and Belkind. Bring a lubricant with you tomorrow."

Just like the Ten Little Indians, then there were two, Crazy Horse Charlie and Cochise Cahill.

Dina Bernichio and Bill Sherwood returned to the witness room together at 1615 hours.

"Court has been adjourned until 9:00 AM tomorrow," she informed us. "Go home and get plenty of rest. You'll both need it for tomorrow."

CHAPTER 54

July 16, 2014
Wednesday
1730 hours

Charlie and I went to the Chi Tung Restaurant on Kedzie Avenue in Evergreen Park for dinner. I ordered Kung Pao Chicken, and Charlie ordered Thai food. I ate with a fork and, of course, Charlie asked for chopsticks, which he used with the precision and dexterity of a native.

"Are you worried about testifying tomorrow?" Charlie asked.

"I should be asking you that," I said.

Charlie nimbly scooped a portion of food onto his sticks. "You didn't answer my question."

"No, no, no, I'm not worried at all. I haven't been sleeping or eating because I'm stressed out over not worrying," I said. "Yes, I'm worried, and if you were normal, you would be, too."

Charlie swallowed his food. "I would think you'd be used to testifying at murder trials by now."

"This is not a typical murder trial," I said. "I'm usually not out on bond for a felony and on indefinite suspension from the police department when I testify. The defense attorneys are not going to attack the legality of the arrests or Chicago Police Department policies and procedures; they are going to attack me, personally, and you, too."

"I'm not worried about it," Charlie said.

"Would you be worried about it if your writing career was dependent upon the outcome of the trial?" I asked.

"Point well taken," Charlie said. He laid the chopsticks on the plate and gazed seriously across the table. "Devlin lad, this is going to turn out all right. The bottom line is McKittrick and Pellegrino will be convicted. The murder weapon in McKittrick's safe is irrefutable evidence."

"Kerri looked like she was going to faint when she went to court to drop the kidnapping charges against you," I said. "Wait until she has to testify at a trial."

"She's a defense witness. The defense team isn't going to grill her, and what could Ms. Bernichio ask her on cross?" Charlie asked.

"Amongst your many talents, are you now studying law?" I asked.

"In fact, I have been doing legal research, primarily for my book."

"Please don't tell the judge he erred when he sustains an objection, or we'll both wind up in the shithouse," I said.

"Nothing new for you."

Charlie grabbed the check, and I dropped a sawbuck on the table for a tip. He moseyed to the cash register, winked twice at the Asian cashier, and paid the bill.

When we got back to my house, Charlie had his

mandatory two beers, and we retired for the night. Tomorrow would be a long day.

I wasn't able to follow Dina Bernichio's advice to get plenty of rest. I sat on the edge of my bed and smoked cigars until the wee hours of the morning. Despite all the time I had to consider my testimony, I still didn't know what I was going to say on the stand. The defense was going to destroy me. The last time I was this nervous was at my first murder trial. It was several months after I graduated from the police academy. I don't think I had even testified at a traffic court hearing up until that time. I feared something I might say would lose the case and I'd feel like a fool. An old, seasoned copper I worked with the day before the trial began said, "Listen, kid, when you testify in court tomorrow, the judge knows the defendant is lying, and he knows the defense attorney is lying. He also knows the prosecutor is lying, and he knows you are lying. His job is to determine who lies best." A lesson to remember.

I laid out a conservative gray pin-stripe suit for the morning, a drab gray tie, and omitted the pretentious pocket square to make Ms. Bernichio smile. It was a short, restless night's sleep.

CHAPTER 55

July 17, 2014
Thursday
0700 hours

The alarm clock went off at 0700 hours. The last time I looked at it, it read 0430. "You've got to be shittin' me," I mumbled as I strained to lift myself out of bed.

Charlie was showered, dressed, and had the coffee made when I entered the kitchen.

"Good morning, Devlin lad. D-Day."

I frowned, poured a cup of coffee, and lit up a cigar.

"I didn't wake you doing my exercises this morning, did I?" Charlie asked.

"No, would you care if you did?"

"No," Charlie replied. "I was curious, not apologetic."

"That's what I thought."

"Speaking of exercising, I meant to ask you, how are those twenty cigars you smoke a day working out for your health regimen?"

"Fine, I had to increase them, though. I was getting too much oxygen in my lungs."

"I'm glad it's working out for you," he said.

"I'm glad you're not wearing your Hawaiian shirt with the parrots on it," I said. "I felt like I was at a luau."

"My wardrobe, I admit, is limited, albeit well tailored and tasteful," Charlie said, rolling up the sleeves on his yellow tattersall shirt. "I can't accommodate business suits, or clothes I don't wear, in my suitcase," he said. "You, on the other hand, were a vision of sartorial splendor yesterday with your silk pocket square, until you were denuded by Ms. Bernichio."

I gulped down the coffee and said, "I'm going to get ready."

• • •

Charlie dropped the convertible top of the red rent-a-Vette as he backed out of my drive onto Central Park Avenue. He put it in first, popped the clutch, and banged second before we reached the end of the block.

"Don't hit the brakes," I said as I bent under the dashboard to light a cigar.

"Do you know what I was thinking?" Charlie asked.

"How many awards you're going to receive for your next book?"

"If you convict McKittrick of these murders, and he convicts you of the beating him up, you two could be cellmates. Wouldn't that be an irony?"

"You insufferable prick, Charlie. Would you please refrain from speaking until we get to court." Had I known twelve years ago, when I called him an anal retentive asshole from the Northside, that I was talking to the Boris Spaasky of ball busting, I would have kept my mouth shut.

Charlie downshifted at 31ˢᵗ & Kedzie, and punched it again. The light was stone-cold red when we went through it.

"Made it," he smiled.

Ten minutes later, we were sitting in the witness room. Ms. Bernichio entered moments later, happier than usual.

"Good news, gentlemen," she said. "The lab raised the serial number on the gun and ran a registration on it. The gun is registered to Paul Pellegrino, Mario's brother."

I smiled, "That is good news, but I'm sure the defense is going to contend Paul's our shooter, not Mario."

"They'll have a hard time doing that. Paul was killed in a motorcycle accident last year. I don't think it will be a far stretch for the jury to assume his brother was heir to his gun."

"Is that why you look particularly lovely this morning, Ms. Bernichio?" Charlie asked.

She smiled, "I'm sure it is." She scampered toward the door and said, "I have to get back out there; they're about to bring the jury out. Lieutenant Cahill, you're up next."

My stomach knotted. I heard the jurors shuffle into the jury box, and I heard the court clerk say, "All rise. Court is now in session. The Honorable Franjo Karlovich presiding."

A moment later, the bailiff stuck his head in the door. "Lieutenant Cahill."

CHAPTER 56

July 17, 2014
Thursday
0932 hours

Butterflies fluttered in my stomach as I entered the courtroom, the kind you get before a fight, but experience has taught me they leave after the first blow is struck. The courtroom was eerily quiet. Twelve pairs of eyes, with twelve different mindsets, studied me like a lab rat as I self-consciously made my way toward the witness stand. McKittrick and Pellegrino sat at their respective tables, their attorneys seated next to them, leering at me. With each step, the witness chair moved further and further away.

I stole a cursory glance at the jury as I moved toward the clerk to be sworn and tried to size them up: seven men—three white, three black, and one Hispanic—and five women—four white, all young, and one elderly black woman. Contrary to what Ms. Bernichio said, it didn't look like a great jury to me. Minorities are, in general, anti police, and there were a total of five of them on this jury. Young, white women educated in our liberal colleges live in a make-believe utopian world, and they weren't any better. White men suck, too. The candy-asses have a glove compartment full of parking tickets and hate the police. The whole jury sucks. The whole world sucks.

I put my hand on the Bible, praying it wouldn't burst into flames.

"Do you solemnly swear to tell the truth, the whole truth, and nothing but the truth, so help you God?" the clerk asked.

"Some of it" would have been the honest reply, but I said, "I do."

"Please be seated," the clerk said.

Dina Bernichio approached the stand. "Sir, would you please state your full name and your occupation, and spell your last name for the court reporter?"

"Devlin Cahill. C-A-H-I-L-L. I'm a lieutenant with the Chicago Police Department."

"How long have you been a sworn member of the Chicago Police Department?"

"Twenty-four years."

"What is your current assignment, Lieutenant?"

"I'm the commanding officer of Area South Violent Crimes Unit."

"How long have you been assigned as the commanding officer of the Area South Violent Crimes Unit, sir?"

"Seven years."

"Were you working on January 6, 2014, at 3:30 AM?"

"No, ma'am."

"Did you have occasion to be notified of a triple homicide investigation that occurred at 12859 S. Carondolet in the Avalon Trails community on that date?"

"Yes, ma'am, I was."

"When, where, and how did you receive that notification?"

"I was notified by phone at home by Sgt. William Peak."

"Is that standard procedure for you to be notified at home?"

"Yes, ma'am. I'm notified of all potentially high-profile incidents."

"What, if anything, did you learn that was out of the ordinary relative to this investigation?"

"I learned that a car had been recovered from the scene that had been rented by Charlie Newton. His fingerprints were found both inside the vehicle and inside the house."

"Did you know, or had you ever heard of, Charlie Newton?"

"Charlie Newton is a friend of mine."

"What, if anything, did you do next?"

"I proceeded into Area South Headquarters to ascertain if any progress was being made in the investigation."

"Progress such as what?"

"Such as had Charlie Newton been located or anything of an evidentiary nature been discovered."

"What did you learn?"

"Charlie was missing, and two spent bullets were recovered from the floor of the residence."

"Did you know where Charlie Newton was?"

"No, ma'am."

"Did you eliminate Charlie Newton as a suspect at that time?"

"No, ma'am."

"Now, Lieutenant, calling your attention to January 7, 2014, the following day, was the investigation reassigned?"

"Yes, ma'am, it was reassigned to Area Central."

"Do you know why the investigation was reassigned?"

"The Chief of Detectives called me into his office and told me that the investigation was being reassigned because of my personal relationship with Charlie Newton. He didn't want the perception of impropriety."

"So, it had nothing to do with you personally, or the manner in which the case was being investigated?"

"No, ma'am."

"Calling your attention to January 18, 2014, were you actively involved in this investigation?"

"No, ma'am."

"What, if anything, occurred on that date that was out of the ordinary?"

"I received a phone call from a confidential informant who told me that the offender we were looking for may be named John Giaccone and that Giaccone was about to flee this jurisdiction."

"What did you do next?"

"I attempted to contact Area Central with the information but was unable to reach them. I called Area South and ran a name check on Giaccone, and I was provided with a home address. I requested a back-up unit to meet me in the vicinity of Giaccone's residence and initiated a surveillance of the location."

"Who, if anybody, were you with at that time?"

"Charlie Newton."

"What, if anything, occurred next?"

"At or about 3:30 AM, a black Mustang parked in front of the residence. When the driver exited the vehicle, Mr. Newton positively identified him as one of the two men that had abducted him and murdered the three victims in Avalon Trails. I got out of my personal vehicle, announced my office, and attempted to arrest John Giaccone."

"Did you have your weapon drawn?"

"Yes, ma'am. He was a suspect in three murders and his criminal history record indicated he was involved in several previous shooting incidents and had a propensity for violence."

Belkind rose. "Objection, your Honor. Speculation. There's no evidence before this court Mr. Giaccone murdered anyone."

"Objection overruled, counselor. Lt Cahill didn't say Mr. Giaccone murdered anyone. He said he was a suspect in three murders," Judge Karlovich ruled.

"Lieutenant, did you believe John Giaccone was a murderer at the time you confronted him?"

"Yes, ma'am, I did."

"Did you believe he could be armed and dangerous?"

"Yes, ma'am, I did."

"What happened after you announced you were a police officer?"

"He opened fire on me, jumped over a banister and fled through a gangway."

"What did you do next?"

"I pursued him on foot into an alley."

"Did you call for assistance?"

"I attempted to call for assistance, but I was over modulating and the back-up unit couldn't hear my transmission."

"What, if anything, occurred after that?"

"I chased Giaccone into the alley, he turned and fired on me, and there was an exchange of gunfire."

"Did you sustain any injuries in that exchange of gunfire?"

"I was shot in the arm."

"Did John Giaccone sustain any injuries in the exchange of gunfire?"

"He was mortally wounded."

"Lieutenant, other than the first day when the murders occurred in Avalon Trails and were under your area of responsibility, until the day you felt exigent circumstances existed necessitating direct police action be taken before John Giaccone fled this jurisdiction, were you actively involved in any part of this investigation?"

"No, ma'am."

"Did you coerce or influence Charlie Newton at any time, in any manner, to identify John Giaccone as one of the offenders in these murders?"

"No, ma'am."

"Did you at any time, or in any manner, coerce or influence the direction of this investigation by Area Central Violent Crimes detectives?"

"No, ma'am."

"That's all for direct, Your Honor."

• • •

The easy part was over. Cross-examination, I suspected, wouldn't go so smooth. Cox and Belkind licked their lips like wolves over a carcass. McKittrick and Pellegrino continued to drill holes through me. I'd like to step down off of the stand for a minute and give each of them another slap upside the head, but it wouldn't look good in front of the jury. The elderly black woman gave me a faint smile. I didn't know if that meant she liked me or if it meant she knew I was full of shit.

Cox stood and strolled over to the jury box to begin the cross. Here we go.

CHAPTER 57

July 17, 2014
Thursday
1000 hours

"Mr. Cahill, you said you're a Chicago Police lieutenant, is that correct?"

Cox wasn't going to address me by rank. I knew where he's going with his line of questioning.

"Yes, sir."

"What is your current duty status?"

"I'm on suspension."

"Suspension? Whatever for?" he asked theatrically.

"Conduct unbecoming."

"What conduct did you engage in that warranted a suspension?"

"I didn't engage in any conduct that *warranted* a suspension," I replied.

"What circumstances caused the Chicago Police Department to place you on suspension?"

"I was suspended for having a physical altercation with the defendant, Emmett McKittrick."

"Isn't it true, Mr. Cahill, the Chicago Police

Department not only saw fit to suspend you, but the Cook County State's Attorney's Office saw fit to charge you with a felony count of Aggravated Battery?"

"True."

"You do know Aggravated Battery is a felony, don't you?"

Dina remained seated and said, "Objection, Your Honor, asked and answered."

"Objection sustained."

"Why aren't you in jail, Mr. Cahill?"

"I'm out on bond."

"When you're suspended, Mr. Cahill, does the Chicago Police Department take away your badge and identification and your police authority?"

"They do."

"Let's see if I got this right. As you sit here on the stand today, you are technically not a police officer. In fact, you are a felon out on bail. Is that correct?"

"I am a Chicago Police Officer until such time I am discharged from the department, Mr. Cock."

"Which should be in the near future, I'd guess."

Dina Bernichio jumped to her feet. "Objection, Your Honor."

"Objection sustained."

"Have you ever been the subject of other disciplinary investigations?"

"Yes."

"How many?"

"I don't know."

"Would it be fair to say that you have been the subject of disciplinary investigations on at least five other occasions?"

"Yes, that would be fair, Mr. Cock."

Cox slapped his yellow legal pad against his thigh and rushed the bench. He shouted, "Your Honor, would you please order the witness to stop calling me Mr. Cock?"

I looked up at the judge contritely and said, "I'm sorry, Your Honor, I thought that was the counselor's name."

Judge Karlovich leaned over the bench, repressed a smile, and said, "The counselor's name is Cox, Lieutenant."

"Oh, plural," I said.

Cox continued with his cross. "How about twenty times?"

"Yes, that would be fair."

"Fifty?"

"I don't know."

"Would it surprise you to learn you have been the subject of forty-seven excessive force complaints and twenty-one verbal abuse complaints?"

"No."

"Mr. Cahill, did you know a newspaper reporter named Eric Schwartzman?"

"Yes."

"Isn't it true you called him a douche bag when he was attempting to interview you relative to the Avalon Trails homicides?'

"No, sir."

"That's not true?"

"No, sir."

"Why did he write an article saying you did?"

"Apparently, he misunderstood me. I thought his nickname was *Deutsche*, which means German in German. I may have mispronounced it."

"Do you know what, if anything, happened to Eric Schwartzman the day after he wrote the disparaging article about you?"

"He was murdered."

Judge Karlovich said, "Court is going to recess for twenty minutes. Lieutenant, you may step down."

"He was murdered" were not the last words I wanted the jury to hear before recessing. They'd be chewing on that for the next twenty minutes.

The clerk said, "All rise."

The bailiff led the jury out of the room in double file. Judge Karlovich lumbered in the other direction toward chambers. A twenty-minute recess should give him enough time to devour a small calf or a large pig before we broke again for lunch. Court spectators slipped out the back doors into the hallway. Cox and Belkind remained seated with their clients, conversing in whispered tones. I wouldn't have time to go outside and grab a cigar, so I returned to the witness room. Charlie was doing dips between two chairs when I entered.

"Are they beating you up, Devlin lad?"

"I would say yes."

Charlie finished his last rep and stood, then tucked his shirt into his slacks.

"I thought being a homicide detective would be more exciting than this, but this is boring, isn't it?" Charlie asked.

"Let me ratchet up the excitement for you. I'm going to grab a few drags off of a cigar and blow the smoke out the window. You watch the door and let me know if anybody's coming," I said.

A minute later, Dina Bernichio was standing next to him.

"Lieutenant Cahill is smoking," he snitched.

"Put that out," Ms. Bernichio ordered.

I tossed the cigar out the window. "Remind me not to rob a bank with you," I said to Charlie. He smiled.

"The lieutenant says you're letting the defense attorneys beat him up," Charlie said.

Dina said, "I'm not *letting* them, but there is no defense for the indefensible." She and Charlie chortled— and Cox told *me* I wasn't auditioning for *Saturday Night Live*. He should catch Sonny and Cher's act.

"You're doing fine, Lieutenant. We'll clean some of this up on redirect," Ms. Bernichio said. "Don't get combative and no more comic relief."

"10-4," I replied.

"Please tell me I'm going to testify today?" Charlie asked. "I'm going stir crazy in this room."

"Why don't you do some butt crunches?" I suggested.

"I'm sure you'll get on today, sometime after lunch," Dina said. "I better get out there."

The clerk said, "All rise," and I heard the jurors scuff back into the jury box. After the jury was seated, the clerk boomed, "Court is back in session."

The defense team was certain to turn up the heat on the second half of my testimony. They would drag Kerri into this mess. I shouldn't have promised Ms. Bernichio I wouldn't be combative.

The bailiff came to the door and said, "Lieutenant, please return to the stand."

CHAPTER 58

July 17, 2014
Thursday
1040 hours

The clerk asked, "Lieutenant Cahill, you are aware you are still under oath?"

"Yes, sir."

Cox removed his silver wire-rimmed glasses, returned them to his shirt pocket, and strolled back over by the jury box.

"Ms. Court Reporter, could you please read my last question and Mr. Cahill's response back?"

The court reporter unraveled a roll of steno paper and said, "Do you know what, if anything, happened to Eric Schwartzman the day after he wrote the disparaging article about you?" Answer: "He was murdered."

Cox knew what the question was, and he knew what my answer was; he wanted to inculcate the point in the jury's mind.

"Wow, that was some coincidence, don't you agree Mr. Cahill? The day after Eric Schwartzman wrote a scathing article about you and your friend, Charlie Newton, he was found dead with two bullet wounds in the back of his head?"

"I don't know."

"You don't know what, Mr. Cahill? That Eric Schwartzman sustained two gunshot wounds to the back of his head or that it was a coincidence?"

"I don't know if it was a coincidence."

"Are you saying you shot Eric Schwartzman in the head?"

"No, I'm saying one of your clients did."

Ms Bernichio bolted from her chair. "Objection, Your Honor. Lieutenant Cahill is not on trial here."

"Perhaps he should be," Cox said, "Your Honor, the defense intends to prove that Mr. Cahill has an interpersonal relationship with my client, who cohabitates with Mr. Cahill's ex-wife, a classic love triangle if you will, and that he, with the assistance of Charlie Newton, had the means, manner, and motive to frame my client for this triple slaying."

"Objection overruled. The court will allow you to continue this line of questioning, Mr. Cox, but let's dispense with the Perry Mason drama."

"Isn't it true, Mr. Cahill, that police officials seized your weapon after Eric Schwartzman was murdered and that you were subsequently presented with a criminal rights form informing you that you were under investigation for Eric Schwartzman's murder, which you signed, but you refused to give a statement?"

"Which question would you like me to answer?"

Judge Karlovich told Cox to rephrase his question.

"Okay, isn't it true, Mr. Cahill, police officials seized your weapon after Eric Schwartzman's murder?"

"No, that is not true. I voluntarily surrendered my weapon, it was not seized, to eliminate my weapon as the possible murder weapon in an effort to expedite the investigation."

"Were you later presented with a criminal rights form by the Independent Police Review Authority, which you refused to sign?"

"Yes, I refused to sign on advice of my attorney and exercised my constitutional right against self-incrimination."

"Why did the police department consider you a suspect in that murder investigation?"

"I assume because he alleged I called him a douche bag a day or two earlier."

"Isn't it true you were also the subject of a complaint investigation for throwing Eric Schwartzman down a flight of stairs a year earlier?"

"True."

"And did you do that?"

"No, sir."

"So, you were wrongly accused then, too?"

"Yes, sir."

Cox returned to the defense table, briefly conferred with Belkind, and picked up his legal pad. Then he turned his attention toward me again.

"How long have you known Charlie Newton?" Cox asked.

"Twelve years."

"Would you consider Charlie Newton to be a close friend?"

"Yes."

"When you first received notification of the triple homicide in Avalon Park by Sgt. Peak, and you were informed Charlie Newton's fingerprints were found both inside the house and outside in the vehicle parked in the drive, did you consider your friend, Charlie Newton, a suspect?"

"I considered him a person of interest," I replied.

"Isn't it true if the fingerprints inside the house and inside the car belonged to anyone other than your friend, Charlie Newton, he or she would have immediately been regarded as a suspect?"

"No, he or she would have also been regarded as a person of interest."

Cox paced before the jury box with his hands clenched behind his back at parade rest and gazed at the floor.

"Certainly, as a trained homicide detective and a close personal friend of Charlie Newton's for twelve years, you must have formed some opinion as to his involvement in these murders?"

"I didn't form any opinions based upon the evidence available."

"If you did believe Charlie Newton, your close personal friend for twelve years, was responsible for these homicides, you would have rushed right out and arrested him for murder and saw to it that he spent the rest of his natural life in prison, correct?"

"Correct."

Cox jeered at my response for the jury's benefit.

"When was the next time you saw or heard from Charlie Newton?"

"Seven days after his abduction."

"Were there any witnesses to this alleged abduction?"

"Not that I'm aware of," I said.

"So you have only Charlie Newton's word an abduction ever occurred?"

"Yes."

"You believe him because he's your friend, right?"

"I believe him because there's no evidence to the contrary."

"Where did Charlie Newton tell you he was for his mysterious seven days of absence?"

"He said he had been held against his will somewhere in Mexico."

"Somewhere in Mexico? Hmmm. But nobody has ever found that location in Mexico?"

"Mexico's a few miles out of my jurisdiction," I said.

"Isn't it true that on January 22, 2014, you went over to Mr. McKittrick's home in a rage looking for your ex-wife and when Mr. McKittrick opened the door, you punched him in the face, knocking him to the ground and breaking his nose?"

"Objection, Your Honor," Ms. Bernichio shouted. "The incident in question is pending in criminal court and Lieutenant Cahill has been advised by his attorney, Stephen Kennelly, to invoke his constitutional right to remain silent."

"Ms Bernichio, Attorney Kennelly is not in court, and

Lt. Cahill can speak for himself. I'm sure he's familiar with his Fifth Amendment rights. Objection overruled."

Dina Bernichio knew the objection would be overruled, but she wanted the jury to know I wasn't clamming up on my own volition.

"You may answer," Judge Karlovich informed me.

"I'm familiar with my Fifth Amendment rights, and I voluntarily waive my right to remain silent," I said.

Ms. Bernichio shook her head faintly.

I continued. "I did go over to McKittrick's house to check on my ex-wife's well-being, but I wasn't in a rage. I did strike him in the face, and I did knock him to the ground—I don't know if his nose was broken—but I only struck him after he grabbed me by my right arm, which had recently sustained a gunshot wound, and began pushing me toward the door. When I tried to pull away, he gripped my arm tighter and I was in extreme pain, so I instinctively swung at him."

"How many times did you strike Mr. McKittrick, *instinctively*?"

"Once that I recall."

"Did you *instinctively* kick Mr. McKittrick in the head while he was laying helplessly on the floor?"

"No, sir." I'll discuss my testimony with Father Nangle in the confessional box later. A few Hail Marys and a few Our Fathers should get me off the hook.

Cox picked up a file on his desk and strode over to show Ms. Bernichio. "Your Honor, we ask that the emergency room records from the Little Company of Mary Hospital, and a photograph of the injuries sustained by

Mr. McKittrick that night be submitted into evidence as Defense Exhibit A."

Cox hustled to the witness stand and handed me the report and the photograph. "Does this photo accurately depict what Mr. McKittrick looked like when you left his house?"

"I don't know what he looked like when I left. I didn't pay any attention to him. My arm was bleeding, and I had to go home to rebandage it."

"Would you read the injuries section of the report to the ladies and the gentlemen of the jury?"

"The patient suffered a broken nose and a large contusion on the forehead."

"Do you see that large contusion in the photo?"

"Yes, sir, I do."

"Looks like a heel print, doesn't it?"

"Yes, sir, it does."

"How do you suspect a heel print got on Mr. McKittrick's forehead?"

"I didn't say it was a heel print, I said it looks like one. I think he must have hit his head on the floor when he fell. Maybe he landed on a shoe."

"You mean when he fell to the floor because you knocked him down?"

"Yes, when I knocked him down."

"Was anyone else present when you struck Mr. McKittrick?"

"No, sir."

"Was anyone else present when you kicked Mr. McKittrick?"

"I didn't kick him."

"So, if anyone says they were present when you punched or kicked Mr. McKittrick, they would be lying. Is that your testimony?"

"Yes."

"Now, Mr. Cahill, you stated Mr. McKittrick grabbed you by the arm in which you had recently been shot and you were in tremendous, unbearable pain, is that correct?"

"Correct."

"How long were you in the hospital as a result of that gunshot wound?"

"I was treated and released."

"No broken bones? No arterial damage?"

"No, sir."

"But you were in all this pain?"

"I once smashed my finger with a hammer. No broken bones or arterial damage, but it hurt nonetheless and I wouldn't have liked anyone grabbing me by it."

"If they would have grabbed you by that finger, you would have *instinctively* smashed their face in again, correct?"

"Yes, sir."

Cox paused for several seconds to let my answer sink in with the jury. How would they view my candid response that I would *smash someone's face in?* Two points for honesty? Two points for appropriate reaction? Or minus ten points for unwarranted excessive force?

Cox flipped the page on his legal pad and glared at me.

"Let's talk about the shooting itself, Mr. Cahill, shall we?"

CHAPTER 59

July 17, 2014
Thursday
1055 hours

Cox glared at me, and an extended silence filled the courtroom. The jurors stared at me as if waiting for a response.

"Is there a question pending, counselor, or are you asking my permission to continue cross-examining me?"

"How were you shot?" Cox asked, annoyed.

"I'm not sure I understand your question, sir."

"What's not to understand? It's a simple question; how—were—you—shot?"

"I—was—shot when a projectile, commonly referred to as a bullet, traveling approximately 2,500 feet per second, came out of the barrel of a gun, which John Giaccone was firing at me, and passed through my arm."

Cox bounced from the jury box to the bench.

"Your Honor, I ask the court once again to please admonish the witness from trying to be a comic and to answer the question."

"Counselor, Lt. Cahill told you he didn't understand

your question, and you had the opportunity to rephrase it. If that is not the answer you were looking for, perhaps you may want to ask him under what circumstances he was shot."

I was beginning to like Judge Frankovich and regretted making fat jokes about him. I still wouldn't want to pick up the tab for his lunch, though. Cox ambled back near the jury box.

"Under what circumstances were you shot?" he asked exhaustively.

"I was attempting to arrest John Giaccone for investigation of a triple homicide when he turned and opened fire on me."

"Is that when you were shot?"

"No, sir."

"What happened next?"

"He jumped off a porch and fled through a gangway into the alley, and I pursued him on foot."

"Was it then you were shot?"

"Yes, sir, I was shot in an exchange of gunfire."

"When you say an exchange of gunfire, did he shoot you first?"

"I'm not sure when I was shot."

"If he shot you first, you wouldn't have been able to return fire, would you have?"

"Apparently, I could, because I did."

"*Apparently*? You don't know if you shot John Giaccone five times in the chest after you sustained a gunshot wound to your right arm?"

"It was a life-and-death situation, Mr. Cox, one of

which I'm certain you've never experienced in a courtroom. My adrenalin was pumping. The entire incident occurred in less than thirty seconds, and I'm not sure at which point I was shot. I didn't realize I was shot until he fell down."

"Why did you shoot Mr. Giaccone five times?"

"That's all the bullets I had."

A few of the male jurors smiled; Cox didn't.

"So, what you are saying is that if you had more bullets, you would have shot him even more times?" Cox asked.

"I would have continued firing until I was absolutely certain he was physically incapable of returning fire, that's what I'm saying. You would too, Mr. Cox, if your life depended on it."

Cox turned to the next page on his yellow note-pad.

"Let's move on to Mr. Pellegrino," Cox said. "When was the first time you saw him?"

"At his arraignment."

"Isn't it true, that you were at Area Central the night he was taken into custody?" Cox asked.

"Yes, sir, but I didn't see him. He was in an interrogation room with the door closed."

"Is it your testimony, you did not see Mr. Pellegrino at all that evening?"

Ms. Bernichio objected, "Asked and answered."

"Who is Topolino?"

"I have no idea."

"Do you know what Topolino means in Italian?"

"I don't speak Italian."

"I didn't ask if you were fluent in Italian, but you do know some words in Italian, correct?"

"Cannoli."

A few of the jurors laughed. The defense team didn't.

"Your Honor, would the court admonish the witness? This is a murder trial, and two men's lives are at stake here. This is not an audition for *Saturday Night Live*."

Judge Karlovich said, "Mr. Cox, you asked him what words he knew in Italian. He told you."

Cox shook his head in frustration and strolled back over by the jury box.

"Would you explain to the ladies and gentlemen of the jury what a Chicago Police Department ERI report is?" Cox asked.

"It's an initialism for Electronic Recording of an Interrogation," I replied.

"Meaning the interrogation of a suspect is being videotaped, correct?" Cox asked.

"Yes."

"And when is this report prepared?"

"In all instances relating to homicide investigations and sometimes in other cases of a serious nature."

"The detectives log in at the beginning of the interrogation and log out when the interrogation in terminated. Is that true?"

"Yes, sir."

"Could you explain why the videotaping was shut off hours before Mario Pellegrino was released from police custody?"

"I assume because Mario Pellegrino's interrogation was going to be interrupted for hours, maybe days, while the detectives went out to arrest Emmett McKittrick. We don't leave the camera run constantly."

"Isn't it true, the camera was shut off because you went into the interview room and physically abused Mr. Pellegrino, or Topolino as you called him?"

"No, sir. I didn't see him that night."

"So, Eric Schwartzman lied when he said you threw him down the stairs; Eric Schwartzman lied when he said you called him a douche bag; Emmett McKittrick lied when he said you came over to his house and physically assaulted him; and, Mario Pellegrino lied when he said you called him Topolino and slapped him around the interrogation room?"

"Yes, sir."

"Mr. Cahill, in your twenty-four year professional experience as a police officer, would you say a police officer with an extensive disciplinary history for brutality and verbal abuse, such as yours; a police officer recently involved in a fatal shooting incident; a police officer suspected of a homicide; and a police officer charged criminally with a vicious attack on a citizen, has a ... what were your words? ... propensity for violence?"

"Objection, Your Honor," Ms. Bernichio shouted.

"Objection sustained."

"The defense rests," Cox said over his shoulder as he returned to the defense table.

"Any redirect?" the judge asked Ms. Bernichio.

"Yes, Your Honor." Dina strolled over to the jury box and assumed Cox's position.

"Lt. Cahill, how many years again do you have on the Chicago Police Force?"

"Twenty-four."

"Your personnel jacket indicates you've been the subject of sixty-seven disciplinary investigations. If my math is correct, that means you receive one complaint register approximately every four-and-a-half months, or less than three a year. How many people do you arrest in a one-year period?"

"Two hundred, or thereabouts."

"That would mean less than one percent of all people you arrest file a complaint against you, is that correct?"

"I've never done the math, but it sounds right."

"Have you ever received any awards?"

"Yes, ma'am. I've received 22 Department commendations, 417 Honorable Mentions, 17 letters of commendation, one Blue Star Award, and a second Blue Star Award is pending."

"Would you tell the ladies and the gentlemen of the jury what a Blue Star Award is?"

"The Blue Star Award is granted when you have been seriously injured in the performance of your duty. I've been shot twice."

"Would it be fair to say you are one of the most decorated officers in the Chicago Police Department?"

"Yes, ma'am."

"One last question. When the Cook County State's Attorney's Office charged you with Aggravated Battery, were they aware you only had use of one arm and that the complainant was a suspect in a triple slaying?"

"They were aware I only had use of one arm, but they weren't aware we were looking at McKittrick as the offender in a triple homicide."

"Did the police department?"

"The police department knew I had been recently shot, but they didn't officially know we were looking at McKittrick in the triple homicide investigation. Once the State's Attorney's Office decided to charge me criminally, the Department had no option but to suspend me. That's standard procedure."

"Thank you, Lieutenant."

"Recross?" the judge asked.

Cox stood. "One last question, Your Honor," he said and faced me. "You said you were shot on two occasions, Mr. Cahill; what happened to the man in the first shooting incident?"

"He was mortally wounded."

"Shot to death?" Cox asked.

Dina hollered objection. "Your Honor, Mr. Cox said he had one more question. He's up to two now."

"Objection overruled. Mr. Cox has a right to recross. The witness may answer."

"Yes, mortally wounded means shot to death, counselor."

"How many times was he shot?"

"I don't recall," I answered.

"Isn't it true he was shot nine times?"

"Could be."

"Mr. Cahill, did you think the victim was still capable of returning fire after the fifth or sixth bullet passed through his body?"

"Could be; I'll never know."

Cox turned and hurried back to the defense table. "That's all for recross, Your Honor."

Judge Karlovich said, "The witness may step down. Court will recess for lunch. Be back at 1:00 PM."

I wanted to kiss Dina Bernichio as I passed her table for turning a zero into a hero.

CHAPTER 60

July 17, 2014
Thursday
1145 hours

It was a hot, sweltering Chicago afternoon, and the concrete underfoot was burning the soles off of my shoes. Still, I would have preferred to walk the half-mile to Mi Tierra restaurant in Little Village than risk my life riding with Speed Racer in his rent-a-Vette. But these short recesses and lunch breaks didn't leave us an option, so I strapped myself into Charlie's car, said a prayer, and we blasted off.

The aromas of cayenne pepper, chili powder, and grilled carne asada stagnated in the hot, humid, and windless air over Little Village.

Mi Tierra was crowded, but the service was fast and the food was better. Charlie and I both ordered the sampler.

Charlie prescribed to European fork etiquette, cutting enchiladas into bite size pieces and conducting them into his mouth with tines turned downward. It was like eating lunch with Prince Charles.

"Don't eat frijoles with sour cream before you take the stand," I said, "You may be up there for a while, and I don't want to see you shit in your pants. The defense team might get the wrong idea."

"I hadn't planned on it," Charlie said.

He wolfed his food down like he was playing *Beat the Clock* and was unusually quiet. His stoic composure was sometimes hard to read. Was it a case of nerves? Or merely time constraints? Or was he simply hungry?

As he crammed the last morsel of food into his mouth, I asked, "Are you worried?"

He looked at me quizzically and asked, "About what?"

That eliminated *a case of nerves* as one of the answers.

After I testified, the motion to exclude witnesses was no longer in effect for me, so I took a seat in the back of the courtroom to listen to Charlie's testimony.

Charlie was confident enough while he was in the witness room, and at Mi Tierra, but I've seen lawyers fall apart on the witness stand when they're sitting in the hot seat.

When the bailiff called "Charles Newton," Charlie swaggered into the courtroom with his usual air of self-confidence, and I knew at once I didn't have anything to worry about. Pellegrino and McKittrick sneered as he passed their tables. Charlie smirked at them briefly and quickly turned his attention to the jury and cheesed. The clerk swore him in, and Charlie took the stand.

Ms. Bernichio asked, "Would you please state your name and spell your last name for the court reporter?"

Charlie adjusted the microphone. "Charles Newton." He leaned over the witness stand and ogled the court reporter with the long legs, probably blowing any chance he had at wooing Ms. Bernichio, and said, "N-E-W-T-O-N."

"What do you do for a living, Mr. Newton?"

"I'm a novelist."

"Calling your attention to January 4, 2014, what, if anything, of an unusual occasion occurred?"

"Nothing."

Ms. Bernichio raised her brows in surprise to his response, as did I. She waited for a moment or two for him to expound on his answer, but he didn't. Maybe Charlie was not as cool as he appeared.

Unflustered, as if that was the response she expected, Ms. Bernichio continued, "Did you have occasion to meet anyone you see in this courtroom today?"

Charlie pointed toward Pellegrino. "The man in the gray tie."

"Indicating for the record Mr. Newton has pointed out Mario Pellegrino."

"Under what circumstances did you meet Mr. Pellegrino?"

"He attended one of my book signings, introduced himself as Mario Fontanetta, and struck up a conversation, which, by the way, is not *unusual* at a book signing."

"Do you recall the nature of that conversation?"

"Yes, we discussed a manuscript I was writing about a Mercantile Exchange broker. He told me he had a friend who was a broker at the Merc and that he would introduce me to him to assist in my research."

"What happened next?"

"I called him on my cell phone the following afternoon

and made arrangements to pick him up at the train station in Beverly that evening so he could introduce me to his friend."

"Did you, in fact, pick him up at that location?"

"Yes, ma'am, I did. We drove to a neighborhood I now know as Avalon Trails, and he rang the doorbell. A man opened the door and let us in. Two other men were in the house. As soon as we entered, Pellegrino produced a semi-automatic pistol and opened fire, killing all three occupants."

"What did you do when the shooting started?"

"I fell to the floor and rolled behind a sofa for protection. A second man entered the house, secured my wrists with flexi ties, and duct-taped my eyes. I was led out of the house and put into the trunk of a car."

"So, there were two offenders?"

"Three. Another man waited in the car. I didn't see him but I heard three distinct voices while I was being put in the trunk of the car."

"Where were you taken?"

"Mexico, where I was held prisoner for seven days and released."

"Did you have occasion to see your abductors while you were being held captive or were you kept blindfolded?"

"I saw two of them all day, every day."

"So you had a good opportunity to see them?"

"I'll never forget them," Charlie answered.

"When did you next see any of your abductors?"

"On January 18, 2014, Lt. Cahill told me there was a man he wanted me to see in the neighborhood of Taylor

Street. We drove there in his personal vehicle and initiated a surveillance. Several hours later, a man pulled up in a black Mustang and exited. I immediately recognized him as one of my two abductors and I identified him. Lt. Cahill got out of the car and told the man he was a police officer and wanted to talk to him. The man pulled out a gun and started shooting at Lt. Cahill."

"What did you do when the shooting started?"

"I stayed in the car as Lt. Cahill instructed me to do."

"What happened next?"

"The man jumped over the porch railing and ran through a gangway with Lt. Cahill in pursuit. I heard several more shots, and then I heard police and ambulance sirens wailing."

"Did you subsequently learn the identity of the man?"

"John Giaccone."

"As you sit here today, Mr. Newton, is there any doubt in your mind whatsoever that John Giaccone was one of your abductors?"

"None whatsoever."

Dina strolled over by the defense table. "When did you next see the defendant in this matter, Mario Pellegrino?"

"On January 24, 2014, Detective Barcomb contacted me and told me he'd like me to look at some photos. I went into Area Central Detective Headquarters and picked out the photo of Mario Pellegrino."

"Are you sure the man who attended your book signing; the man you witnessed murder Hiram Goldenstein, Jerry Doherty, and Chiang Yu; and the man you spent seven days with in Mexico is the defendant, Mario Pellegrino?"

"Positive."

"Now, Mr. Newton, two days prior to your testimony here today, what, if anything, of an unusual nature occurred to you?"

"Someone …" Cox shouted an objection, but Charlie blurted out, "planted a bomb in my car."

"Objection, Your Honor. These two defendants have been in custody, and there is no evidence indicating Mr. Newton's unfortunate circumstance is related to this case.

The judge sustained the objection, and instructed the jury to disregard Charlie's response and that it be stricken from the record, but it was too late. Once the jury heard it, they couldn't it erase it from their minds.

"The State rests, Your Honor."

Judge Karlovich turned to the defense. "Cross."

CHAPTER 61

July 17, 2014
Thursday
1310 hours

Jacob Belkind studied his legal pad for several moments before rising and approaching the witness stand.

"Mr. Newton, indulge me here, if you will. So I'm certain I understand your story, is it your testimony that a perfect stranger approached you at a booksigning, invited you to his friend's house, executed everybody on the premises, except you of course, the only witness to a triple homicide and then held you hostage for a week in Mexico? No ransom demands? Nothing?"

"Credo quia assurdum," Charlie responded.

Belkind stared at Charlie and blinked. Judge Karlovich turned toward the witness stand. "Mr. Newton, you will answer in English."

"Believe it because it is absurd," Charlie translated.

Several of the jurors laughed, and I did, too. Wait until Charlie starts throwing some profligacy and heterotelic at his ass. Belkind will think he's still speaking Latin.

"You are a writer of fiction, are you not?" Belkind asked.

"Yes."

"Would it be fair to say that writers of fiction have to be creative to make up things, which are not true yet sound convincing?"

"It worked for Shakespeare."

"Answer yes or no."

"Yes."

"Would it be fair to say that you are a successful and talented writer, hence, gifted at spinning yarns?"

"I'm also gifted at separating truth from fiction," Charlie responded.

Belkind approached the bench. "Your Honor, would you please admonish the witness and instruct him to answer yes or no?"

"Mr. Newton, please restrict your answers to yes or no," Judge Karlovich said.

Belkind continued, "Isn't it true your fingerprints were found inside the house where the murders occurred, as well as outside in the car you had rented?"

"Yes."

"And then you were whisked away in the trunk of a car all the way to Mexico. How long of a drive was that?"

"A long time. I couldn't see my wristwatch with my eyes taped and my arms bound behind my back."

"Have you ever heard of a medical condition called hypoxia?"

"Yes, oxygen deprivation."

"Very good, Mr. Newton. Are you familiar with the effects of hypoxia?"

"Double vision, dizziness, disorientation."

"Would it be reasonable to believe a person purportedly locked in the trunk of car for twenty-four hours could suffer from one or all of these symptoms?"

"Reasonable, yes."

"Are you also aware of the fact people suffering from hypoxia oftentimes are unaware they are even afflicted with the disorder?" Belkind asked.

"I am."

"So, wouldn't it be possible for someone in a disoriented state to misidentify someone? Answer yes or no."

"Yes."

"Now, calling your attention to your direct testimony, you stated that you and Lt. Cahill 'initiated a surveillance,' is that correct?"

"Yes."

"Interesting choice of words; the exact words Lt. Cahill used when he was on the stand. It sounds like cop-speak, like Lt. Cahill put those words in your mouth."

"I am not a parrot, counselor. No one puts words in my mouth. I've been writing police novels for twelve years now, and I'm familiar with police jargon."

"What is a 10-1 call, Mr. Newton?"

"Officer needs assistance."

"A 19-Paul?"

"Miscellaneous incident, miscellaneous action."

Belkind abruptly dropped that line of questioning.

"Isn't it true Lt. Cahill escorted you to Area Central Headquarters and told you the police had identified Mario Pellegrino?"

"No, that's not true. He told me the police wanted me

to view photos and went with me, but he didn't tell me that police, or anyone else, had identified Mario Pellegrino."

"From a group of photos, correct?"

"A group of computer photos; correct."

"How many photos were you shown in addition to Mr. Pellegrino's?"

"Four, in addition to his."

Belkind casually drifted over to the jury box again and asked, "Mr. Newton, would you please tell the jury what the other four men looked like? Were they blond? Auburn?"

"I don't recall what they all looked like," Charlie answered.

"Could they have been four black men?" Belkind asked.

"Abolutely not."

"Hispanic?" Belkind asked.

Charlie pondered the question and replied, "They could have been."

The response set Belkind back on his heels. He rushed the witness chair and boomed, "So the other four men in the photos could have been brown-skinned men?"

"I didn't say that, Mr. Belkind. Now who's trying to put words in my mouth?" Charlie asked. "I said they could have been Hispanic. Nine percent of this country's population is classified as white-Hispanic, such as actors Martin Sheen, Emilio Estevez, and Cameron Diaz. Race and ethnicity are two separate and distinct categories. I was shown five photos of white men. I don't know if they were German, Irish, Italian, or White-Hispanic, and I don't recall the color of their hair, but Mario Pellegrino was the

.

only man in the group of photos who abducted me, and I would have picked his picture out if the police had shown me a thousand photos."

Belkind's window of opportunity slammed shut in his face; the wind gone from his sails, he sneered, "Isn't it true, Mr. Newton, you were never abducted at all and that you, in fact, murdered the three men in Avalon Trails and your close, personal friend, Devlin Cahill covered for you?"

Dina Bernichio shot to her feet; her voice filled the room. "Objection, Your Honor."

"Objection sustained."

"No more cross," Belkind said, turning abruptly and returning to his seat.

"Redirect?" Judge Karlovich asked.

"Yes, Your Honor," Dina responded.

"Mr. Newton, prior to January 6, 2014, had you ever met or heard of Hiram Goldenstein, Jerry Doherty, Chiang Yu, or John Giaconne?"

"No, ma'am."

"Prior to the day Mario Pellegrino attended your book signing on January 4, 2014, had you ever seen or heard of him before?"

"No, ma'am."

"That's all. Thank you."

"Recross?" the judge asked.

"No, Your Honor."

Judge Karlovich turned toward the witness stand. "You may step down, Mr. Newton."

CHAPTER 62

July 17, 2014
Thursday
1440 hours

Charlie swaggered back to the witness room in a businesslike manner, stealing a glance at Dina Bernichio for praise or approval. She told him with her eyes he got an A on his report card. Judge Karlovich recessed the case until 9:30 the following morning. Everyone stood as the jurors were led from the courtroom.

When Dina and I re-entered the witness room, Charlie beamed, "How did I do?"

"Outstanding, Mr. Newton," Dina replied, "It couldn't have gone better."

"19-Paul?" I asked.

"You shouldn't be surprised, Devlin lad. You're the one that gave me the police codes," Charlie said.

"Yeah, but that was twelve years ago!"

Ms. Bernichio stuffed her files into a large brown accordion-type envelope on her pushcart. "The defense will start to put on their case in the morning." She glanced toward me. "They're going to put on your ex-wife as their first defense witness to impeach your testimony relative to your version of the altercation between you and McKittrick, which could hurt us; that's why you should have taken the fifth on the stand like you were instructed."

"I wasn't thinking of it from that angle," I said.

"I'm sure you weren't, Lieutenant, that's why you should have listened to the advice of your counsel."

"Reprimand accepted."

"If your ex-wife's testimony contradicts your testimony, you realize I will have to go on the attack?"

"No, if you and I are to remain friends, Ms. Bernichio, don't do that. Kerri didn't ask to be involved in this mess, and I don't want to see her hurt or humiliated on the stand."

"Lieutenant, so you and I understand one another, we are not friends. We are thrown together in a common cause, to put two men in prison for the murders of three human beings, and I intend to do that. If I have to ruffle some feathers, so be it, but they are not walking out of this courtroom because I don't want to hurt someone's feelings." Dina spun her pushcart around and sped from the room.

Charlie smiled, "I guess she told you. Her pushcart left tire tracks on the floor when she peeled out of here."

I shook my head. "Women."

"Look at the bright side, Devlin lad, at least she still likes me."

CHAPTER 63

July 18, 2014
Friday
0930 hours

Kerri was ashen as she approached the stand, clutching a handkerchief in her sweaty palm. Beads of perspiration formed above her lip, and my heart ached for her.

"Swear in the witness," Judge Karlovich ordered from the bench. Kerri was sworn in and took her seat in the witness chair.

Cox began, "State your name and occupation for the record and please spell your last name."

"Kerri Cahill, C-A-H-I-L-L. I'm unemployed."

"Ms Cahill, what is your relationship with Devlin Cahill?"

"Devlin is my ex-husband. We've been divorced for two years."

"And what, if any, relationship do you have with Emmett McKittrick?"

"Emmett and I have lived together for the last eighteen months," Kerri responded awkwardly.

"So, would it be accurate to say you have had an intimate relationship with both men?"

Biting her bottom lip, she replied, "Yes."

"Calling your attention to January 22, 2014, did you have occasion to witness an attack on Emmett McKittrick by Devlin Cahill?"

"I didn't witness an attack. I witnessed Emmett on the floor bleeding and Devlin standing over him," and then quickly added, "and Devlin's arm was bleeding."

"So, you didn't witness the initial attack, but you were present when Devlin Cahill kicked Emmett in the head while he was on the ground, correct?"

Dina was back on her feet. "Objection, Your Honor. Leading."

"Objection sustained. Rephrase the question, counselor."

"Ms Cahill, did you see any strikes or kicks thrown by either party in your presence?"

Kerri's eyelids flitted nervously, and her complexion turned the color of milk. I wanted to run up there and scream, "Yes, I knocked him on his ass and booted the living dogshit out of him," to avoid her having to answer any more questions. I could feel her heart fluttering like a wounded sparrow inside my chest. She looked down into her lap, her upper lip trembling and her eyes brimming over with tears, and responded with a sigh, "No, sir."

Cox eyebrows furrowed, and he stared at her menacingly. Kerri wilted like a beautiful flower in her seat.

The tone and volume of Cox's voice changed. "Ms. Cahill, do you remember having a conversation with me relative to this incident in which you stated, 'Devlin kicked Emmett in the head'?"

"I'm sorry, Mr. Cox, I must have misunderstood your question at that time, or you misunderstood my answer."

Cox was outraged. "Your Honor, may I approach the bench?"

Cox, Belkind, and Dina Bernichio stood before Judge Karlovich and spoke in muted tones.

"Your Honor, I request to treat Ms. Cahill as a hostile witness," Cox said.

"Granted."

Cox hustled over near the jury box. His voice blared, "Ms. Cahill, please remember you're under oath. I will ask you again, didn't you tell me that you were present when Devlin Cahill kicked Emmett McKittrick in his head?"

Dina sprang to her feet again, "Objection, Your Honor. Asked and answered."

"Objection sustained," the judge ruled.

"What if anything do you recall about our conversation, Ms. Cahill?"

"I recall you asking me if Devlin kicked Emmett in the head, and I responded, 'Devlin kicked Emmett in the head?' It was an interrogative, not a declarative, statement."

Emmett glared at her from the defense table. Cox was flustered and paced before the jurors, collecting his thoughts for his next line of attack.

"Ms. Cahill, you previously testified that you have cohabitated with Emmett McKittrick for eighteen months, is that correct?"

"Yes, sir."

"Emmett McKittrick provided you with food and shelter and financial support all during that time, is that correct?"

"Yes, sir."

"Would it be fair to say Emmett McKittrick treated you well during your eighteen-month relationship?"

Kerri began crying. "Yes, sir, he did."

"And you show your gratitude by lying against him here today on the stand, isn't that true?"

Cox stood two feet directly in front of the witness chair and leered at her. Swollen purple tributaries filled his forehead.

"Objection, Your Honor," Dina sighed wearily from her seat.

"Sustained."

Judge Karlovich asked, "Are you through with the witness, counselor?"

"One last question, your Honor. Are you still in love with Devlin Cahill?"

Kerri lowered her head, paused before answering, and then whispered, "Yes."

Cox sped to the far end of the jury box and said, "Would you repeat your answer loud enough for the jurors to hear?"

Kerri's eyes swept the jurors, then looked at Cox defiantly. "Yes."

"That's all for this witness, Your Honor," Cox said and strode off to the defense table in a huff.

Judge Karlovich looked over his glasses at Dina Bernichio and asked, "Cross?"

Dina stood, smiled at the defense table, then smiled at the jurors and shrugged her shoulders. "No cross, Your Honor."

Kerri stepped down from the stand and rushed from the courtroom, head bowed low and handkerchief pressed tight to her eyes. I ran out after her, but an elevator must have been waiting. She was gone.

I re-entered the courtroom as Dina approached the jurors to begin her closing arguments. She smiled warmly, making eye contact with each of them. I studied their faces, and it was my guess she was being well received.

"Ladies and gentlemen of the jury. The State of Illinois and the Cook County State's Attorney's Office thanks you for your time, patience, and attention in this matter. You've heard the testimony of the witnesses, and you've heard and seen the physical evidence in this case. The defense had the audacity to try to shift the blame for these heinous crimes from their clients,"—Dina strolled over to the defense table and pointed her finger inches from McKittrick's face— "Emmett McKittrick and"—hurrying along the defense table to Pellegrino, she launched the accusatory finger in his face—"Mario Pellegrino, to the *victim* of the kidnapping, Charles Newton, and the investigating detective, Lieutenant Cahill. Their defense is all smoke and mirrors, ladies and gentlemen, a magician's trick to divert your attention from the irrefutable fact that the murder weapon that took the lives of Hiram Goldenstein, Gerald Doherty, and Chiang Yu was recovered in a locked vault at Emmett McKittrick's house, opened by a judge outside the police presence, and that weapon registered to Mario Pellegrino's deceased brother. That is not theory or conjecture, ladies and gentlemen; that is hard, incontrovertible, physical evidence. The State asks that you find Emmett McKittrick and Mario Pellegrino guilty on all counts."

Cox and Belkind huddled together comparing notes as Dina returned to her seat. Cox stood and sauntered toward the jury, head bowed low in profound thought and both hands shoved deep in his pockets.

"Ladies and gentlemen of the jury, like the prosecutor's office, the defense is also grateful for your time and patience. Ironically, we agree with the prosecutor; the fact that the murder weapon was found in Mr. McKittrick's locked safe is irrefutable. The question you must ask yourselves is when was it put there and by whom? You've heard Kerri Cahill, who has lived in Emmett McKittrick's home for eighteen months, testify on the stand that she is in love with Devlin Cahill. Could she have put the gun in there? Are any of you familiar with the term yegg? A yegg is simply a slang term for a *safecracker*, and we all know what safecrackers do; they crack safes."

I leaned over and whispered in Charlie's ear, "I think this guy's smarter than *you*! I'm going to ask him when this is all over what racecar drivers do. I've been curious about that for a long, long time."

Cox continued, "And do you know who some of the best safecrackers in the business are? Police officers." Cox fake-laughed on cue. "No, no, no, I'm not saying police officers are burglarizing safes," he explained, "but pursuant to their duties in law enforcement, some police officers are assigned the responsibility of doing follow-up investigations into bank robberies, and such officers are highly trained in the latest techniques for cracking safes. Could one of Devlin Cahill's colleagues have opened the safe for him?" Cox stopped pacing and let the question hang in the air for the jurors to consider before he went on. "Devlin Cahill, the felon out on bail, is a violent man. To quote Ms. Bernichio, that is *irrefutable*. Emmett McKittrick, on the other hand, has no history of violence. And famed author Charlie Newton, what do we know about him? He's a gifted writer. Many gifted and talented celebrities have a dark side."

Cox walked to the center of the jurors' box and placed both hands on the rail. "This is a complex matter and your job is cut out for you. Please carefully consider all possibilities when you deliberate. If there are any doubts in your mind, any doubts whatsoever, you must return with a verdict of not guilty. Again, thank you for your time and your careful consideration." Cox returned to his seat.

Dina Bernichio rose, smiled wryly, and shook her head as she passed the defense table. Still smiling and shaking her head, she stood before the jury and began her concluding argument.

"Ladies and gentlemen, more smoke and mirrors. This is a case of common sense and reasonableness. Did Kerri Cahill crack the safe and plant the gun? Hmmm. Did Lt. Cahill, or one of his unknown and unnamed mysterious colleagues, crack the safe and plant the gun, a gun that happened to be registered to Mario Pellegrino's brother? Hmmm. Or, did Santa Claus plant the gun? Hmmm. Another viable theory, if you believe in Santa Claus. The State does not refute Lt. Cahill's disciplinary record, but we do object to him being depicted as a violent man. Police work is a violent business, evidenced by the fact Lt. Cahill has been shot, not once, but twice protecting the public.

Consider his record in light of the years he's been on the job, and the number and types of people with whom he deals on a daily basis. What do we know about Charlie Newton? We know if anything in Charlie Newton's history indicated any involvement with the deceased victims prior to their demise, the defense certainly would have brought it out at trial instead of alluding to it during closing arguments. Here's the State's case in a nutshell: three men are dead, and the murder weapon, which belonged to Mario Pelligrino's deceased brother, was found in the locked safe in Emmett McKittrick's home. The State once again asks that you return a verdict of guilty on all counts."

Judge Karlovich gave the jury instructions before beginning their deliberations, and the court recessed. The bailiff led the jurors from the courtroom; spectators spilled out into the corridor, and the judge retired to chambers.

Waiting for a jury to return with a verdict is the hardest part of a trial. All it would take is one holdout for a not-guilty verdict; McKittrick and Pellegrino would walk, and my ass would be fried. The State's Attorney's Office would proceed with its prosecution against me, and the Department would take immediate steps to fire me. The bitter irony was, like McKittrick and Pellegrino, my fate rested in the hands of the same jury. Charlie and I approached the prosecutor's table as Dina gathered up her paperwork.

"What do you think?" Charlie asked.

Dina shrugged. "I think it went well," then, voicing my concerns, added, "but you never know about juries."

"What do we do now, Ms. Bernichio?" Charlie asked.

"We wait, Mr. Newton. We wait."

CHAPTER 64

July 18, 2014
Friday
1200 hours

ASA Bernichio declined Charlie's ulterior offer to grab a breaded steak sandwich with us at Ricobene's. She said she was going to hang around the criminal courts building for a while and catch up on some paperwork. She'd call us when and if the jury was returning with a verdict this afternoon.

For the first time in my life, I couldn't finish the breaded steak sandwich. Granted, it's the size of a football with mozzarella cheese on it, but I had never failed before. Charlie froze in mock surprise, with his mouth agape and his sandwich stalled in mid-air, when he saw me drop mine back into the basket.

"Devlin lad, you are upset about this, aren't you?" he asked, putting down his sandwich and dabbing the red sauce from the corners of his mouth with a brown paper napkin.

"Yes, I am. The last few months on suspension have been hell, but I've believed at the end of all this drama that I'd get my job back. McKittrick and Pellegrino would be convicted, and I'd be back in homicide. I don't feel as sure now as I did then. Cox may have scored some points with a couple of jurors during his closing argument. Civilians tend to believe that Hollywood bullshit; the police always turn out to be the real bad guys."

Charlie stared at me. "Devlin, let's consider the worse case scenario." The tone of his voice was stern, and he didn't call me lad. This was one of those rare occasions when Charlie was being serious. "Let's say McKittrick and Pellegrino do beat the case, which I don't think they will; that doesn't necessarily mean the State's Attorney's Office and the CPD is going to go after you. I don't see what the outcome of this trial has to do with anything. I think if they wanted to jam you, they would have done so months ago."

"Trust me. I've been doing this shit for almost a quarter of a century now, and I've seen them in action before. I know how they operate. If McKittrick beats this case, he'll be testifying against me at my trial. Even if he refuses to cooperate in the prosecution, which I think is unlikely, and the State's Attorney's Office is forced to drop the charges against me, the police department will still fire me, and I fear that more than going to jail. I need this conviction."

Charlie wrapped his big paws around the sandwich and resumed eating. "If I were you, Devlin lad, I wouldn't start worrying yet. The jury hasn't returned a NG, so your consternation may be for naught. In Southside patois: Quit worrying, bitch!" Charlie said and then asked, "How long do you think the jury will be out?"

"Sometimes it's two hours, sometimes two days. The longer they're out, the worse it is for us."

Charlie finished his Italian breaded steak sandwich; mine lay there uneaten in the basket, minus three bites.

A mortal sin. I prayed word didn't leak to my paisans from 69th Street. I'd lose standing. No call from Dina Bernichio. Things were not shaping up to be a great day.

Charlie and I picked up our heels trotting across 26th Street to avoid being run over by a Connie's Pizza mini delivery truck. "Fucker," I yelled as the mini truck whizzed by us. "They got a lot of balls driving by Ricobene's, don't they?" I said.

"I thought it was a drive-by," Charlie replied.

"Don't worry, when Connie's does a drive-by, they hit you in the face with a pizza; tastes good and doesn't hurt."

The Vette was parked in the unpaved lot across the street under the overpass next to an enormous concrete pylon. I was trying to squeeze in the car without damaging the door when a gust of wind kicked up out of nowhere and blew enough dirt in my eyes to plant a garden.

"Are you crying?" Charlie asked.

"No, but you will be if you don't shut up, you insufferable prick."

Charlie started the car. "Where to?"

"I don't want to drive all the way home in case Dina calls. We'd have to turn around and drive right back, and I'm afraid we wouldn't make it in time. Let's go back to the criminal courts building."

"And do what?" Charlie asked.

"You already asked that, and Dina already answered it for you. We wait."

CHAPTER 65

July 18, 2014
Friday
1830 hours

The early evening sun was sinking in the west and hung over the criminal courts building like a red rubber ball. The last vestiges of light reflected off the front doors and mirrored our images as we climbed the stairs to the entrance.

The deputy sheriff on duty relaxed by the metal detector reading a book. He casually waved us by. The corridors, always bustling during regular court hours, were silent and vacant, save an elderly gentleman in blue khakis mopping the floors at the far end of the hallway. A strong disinfectant smell permeated the air.

"Should we go to Dina's office to wait?" Charlie asked.

I pushed the illuminated up arrow for the elevator. "No, she said she wanted to catch up on some work. She'll find us, or we'll find her, when it's time."

The elevator whooshed to a stop on the ground floor, the doors slid open, and Charlie and I entered. We got off on the fourth floor and re-entered the courtroom. I proceeded toward a chair in the witness room while

Charlie stood motionless in the doorway, his eyes spanning the room.

"What are you doing, Charlie?"

"I'm trying to arrange sleeping accommodations. I'm much taller than you, so I think it's only fair I should get the conference table."

I glanced at my Seiko. It was after seven o'clock. The jury had been out six hours. Not good.

"Do you plan on annoying me for the next several hours?" I asked.

"What else can I do?"

"Write a book or do more butt crunches, but leave me alone."

"Remember, Devlin lad, I saved your life."

Leaning back in the chair, I propped my feet upon the conference table and closed my eyes. Lacing my fingers behind my head, I sighed, "How could I ever forget? I'm beginning to wish Giaccone had put a second bullet through my forehead. You're a pain far worse than death."

The next couple hours crawled by and were torturous. Charlie rambled on about his paradigm for economic recovery in minute detail—tax neutrality and incentives, rate of increase for gross domestic products, and I don't know what else he was saying. I tuned him out like white noise. I had no doubt the Mensa mush could do it, though I didn't understand a word he said. I would have preferred to pass the time watching reruns of the Pee Wee Herman Show. It was 10:15 PM when I looked at my watch again.

I snuffed my cigar out on the floor and tossed the evidence out the window. "We may as well call it a night, Charlie. They're not coming back now."

Charlie flicked off the light as we left the room. We were fumbling our way around in the darkness, using the wooden benches as a guide, when my phone rang. I looked at the caller ID. It was Dina Bernichio.

"Where are you?" she asked.

"We're leaving the witness room," I said.

"Stay there; the jury's coming back. They've reached a verdict."

CHAPTER 66

July 18, 2014
Friday
2235 hours

The courtroom was as quiet as 6:00 AM Mass at St. Christina's on a Tuesday morning. Cox and Belkind sat chatting idly with each other at the defense table. A few spectators shuffled in, presumably friends or family of McKittrick or Pellegrino. Dina Bernichio tousled her pixie shag and brought it back to life, then spritzed her wrists and neck with Bottega Veneta eau de parfum and smoothed her linen skirt. She looked and smelled as fresh as when we arrived sixteen hours earlier. Charlie didn't look the worse for wear, either. I thought there was almost an angelic aura about him, then realized it was the fluorescent light overhead shining off his shaved pate. I don't know what I looked like, but I felt like death taking a shit.

The judge's chamber door opened. Seismic tremors reverberated across the floor as Judge Karlovich plodded to the bench and plopped his mass in the chair. Flushed meaty cheeks, like Old Man Winter, expelled hurricane-force winds across the room. He took several deep breaths and dabbed the perspiration from his forehead with a hankie.

"The County should put a Richter scale or Doppler radar in here for the safety of those present," I said.

"That's what happens if you don't do your butt crunches everyday, Devlin lad," Charlie replied.

"If this guy did butt crunches, he could crack bowling balls between the cheeks of his ass."

After catching his breath, the judge instructed the sheriff to bring out the prisoners. McKittrick and Pellegrino leered at Charlie and me as they made their way to the defense table. I smiled and gave them the finger.

Judge Karlovich told the sheriff to bring the jurors out.

I studied the faces of the jurors as the sheriff herded them into the jury box, trying to get a feeling for which way they were going to go. When I was a young policeman, a defense attorney told me to watch the jurors' faces when they were coming back with a decision. He said, "If the jurors avoid eye contact with my client, wave bye-bye to him." Over the years, having sat through many trials, I found that to be true.

One of the young, white, female jurors snapped a quick glance at Pellegrino, only a flicker, but not a good sign. I was relieved when the elderly black woman, who looked like a schoolmarm and had smiled at me when I was on the stand, gave me a fleeting glimpse. I thought I recognized the faintest of smiles cross her lips, but it could have been optimism on my part. This was a hard jury to read.

After all the jurors were seated, Judge Karlovich asked, "Ladies and gentlemen of the jury, have you reached a verdict?"

The jury foreman, an older white guy dressed in business attire, responded, "Yes, Your Honor, we have."

The bailiff retrieved the written verdict from the jury foreman and delivered it to the judge. Judge Karlovich adjusted his glasses on his nose and read silently.

C'mon, read the goddamn thing already, I thought. I felt like I was standing before the Rose Room in my Michael Jackson dream. I tried to appear relaxed and confident, but I was trembling inside and my breathing was shallow. As bad as it was for me, it must have been immeasurably worse for McKittrick and Pellegrino. I could almost empathize with the mutts.

Judge Karlovich spoke, and the room fell dead silent.

"We, the jury, find the defendant, Mario Pellegrino, guilty on three counts of murder and one count of Aggravated Kidnapping."

Pellegrino remained still and expressionless.

The judge continued, "We, the jury, find the defendant, Emmett McKittrick, guilty on three counts of Conspiracy to Commit Murder, one count of kidnapping, and three counts of murder."

Emmett McKittrick covered his face with both hands and shook his head in disbelief.

Words cannot express the sense of relief that washed over me. I was exonerated. Liberated. My thoughts went to Kerri. I wanted to celebrate my victory, my elation, with her, and then realized it was no celebration for Kerri. Her life with Emmett McKittrick had been good until fate reared its ugly head. Life had pulled the carpet out from underneath her feet once again. She was alone. What did

Kerri ever do to anyone to deserve this? My emotions ran the gamut, and my triumph darkened and turned hollow. I could beg her on my knees to come back home, remind her that she testified under oath that she still loved me and I could prosecute her for perjury if she denied it. She'd laugh, but she wouldn't return, not as long as I was a copper. The Irish suffer from at least one of the seven deadly sins, pride. If they ever incorporate pigheadedness as the eighth deadly sin, then the Irish have two. Kerri is Irish to the bone. As am I.

When I emerged from my reverie, Charlie was embracing Dina and giving her a prolonged kiss on the cheek. I broke up the clinch before he started disrobing.

"Do you plan on ending your expression of gratitude any time soon?" I asked Charlie.

He locked eyes with Dina and smiled. "For now."

Charlie was quiet and introspective for the first few minutes on the ride home. We had the windows down, the night air was crisp and refreshing, and Garland Green was singing *Jealous Kinda Fella* on the blues station.

"What's wrong, Devlin lad?" Charlie asked, "I thought you'd be giddy after the verdict."

"I've been thinking about Kerri. After McKittrick's conviction, and her testimony, she won't be staying in that lovely home in Beverly. She doesn't have a job, and has no place to go."

"How about your place?" Charlie asked, "Your, being plural, meaning you and Kerri's house."

"Kerri would live in a cardboard box under the overpass before she'd come back home," I said.

"Far be it from me to comment on the ludicrousness of your relationship, but you love her and she loves you. Algebraically, this seems like an easy equation to solve. D plus K equals DK."

"How about D minus C equals D?"

Charlie grinned. "Outstanding, Devlin lad, I've been under the impression all this time you were mathematically challenged." Charlie lowered the volume on the radio. "Seriously, why don't you and Kerri sit down and try to iron this out? Find a common ground. It doesn't make any sense for you two to be apart when you love each other."

"We've tried, Charlie. Many times. When I got shot the first time, Kerri collapsed in the emergency room. It was worse when I went back to work in a few weeks. She was an emotional train wreck. I'd call home during the tour to assure her I was all right. She'd pick up the phone on the first ring, and I could hear the fear in her voice. Calling home to allay her fears had the opposite effect. When the phone rang, she expected a notification I was dead. She only sees the glass as half empty."

"The problem, as I see it, Devlin lad, is your egregious selfishness. You could easily transfer into a less hazardous unit. You'd still be a police lieutenant, still have your badge and your gun, still get the same paycheck, and you'd have Kerri, but you aren't willing to make any concessions."

"And what would I do? Investigate broken windows or stolen bicycles for the rest of my career?"

"Broken windows or broken hearts, Devlin lad—they both shatter."

Charlie was right, of course. The ball was in my court,

always had been. All things considered, it didn't seem like much of a concession on my part to become a housecat for my remaining years on the job. I've had enough excitement for ten men anyway. Besides, getting shot isn't fun. I don't like it. I stuck my head out the window and filled my lungs with night air.

"Well?" Charlie asked.

"Well, what?"

"Your thoughts on transferring to a less dangerous unit?"

"Your thoughts on writing children's books?" I asked.

• • •

Charlie dropped me off in front of my house and said he was spending the night in his suite at the Congress. I watched the Corvette's taillights until they disappeared from sight.

I entered the garage and started the Beamer. I didn't want Kerri to have to learn about McKittrick's conviction in the newspapers, nor did I think notifying her by phone was in good taste. Or maybe I didn't care one way or the other how she got the news, and I was simply looking for an excuse to see her?

CHAPTER 67

July 19, 2014
Saturday
0015 hours

I felt uncomfortable as I pulled up the drive of the McKittrick estate on Longwood Drive. Hours earlier, I sent the guy who owns it to prison for the rest of his life. The house was dark. I knocked on the door much more quietly than I did the last time I was there to rearrange McKittrick's face to look like a Picasso painting. Kerri didn't answer, so I knocked louder and then rang the bell. Still no answer. No lights on inside the house. I traipsed to the garage in the rear of the house and peered through a windowpane. McKittrick's black Benz was parked in there, but Kerri's gray Lexus was gone. I drove down to the foot of the drive and waited several hours for her to return, but she never showed.

I didn't get back home to Mount Greenwood until the wee hours of the morning. The streets were deserted, and all the houses were dark. It was the most peaceful time of the day.

When I entered the house, I saw the message indicator blinking on the phone. One message.

"Devlin, I booked a flight on Aer Lingus. By the time you hear this, I'll be well on my way to Dublin. I've gone back to my parents' to live. It was selfish of me to ever ask you to leave your job. We may never see each other again, but no matter where I'm at or what I do, I'll always love you and you'll always own the biggest piece of my heart."

I slumped down onto the sofa and buried my face in my hands. And I cried. Once the floodgates opened, I couldn't stop crying, nor did I try. Kerri was gone. I drove her away. Charlie was right; the ball had been in my court all along, and I fumbled miserably. The finality of it all pierced me to the core. Kerri was gone, and she wouldn't be coming back. I never felt so alone in the world in all my life.

I stayed up all night, drinking coffee, smoking cigars and crying like a bitch. I would have gotten drunk but I was afraid if my inhibitions diminished in my present state of mind, I might wind up sucking the business end of my Browning, which would only hurt Kerri worse. Even when she was with McKittrick, I always felt she was near and she was happy. I could live with that. I could see her smile and her eyes dancing, and I could hear her laughter. I love her laughter most of all. A verse from *When Irish Eyes Are Smiling* kept repeating itself over and over in my head, like a scratched record; "*In the lilt of Irish laughter, you can hear the angels sing.*" That was Kerri. She made the angels sing. D minus K equals D. I hate algebra.

I was in the oval office on my knees retching when the phone rang early that morning, so I couldn't answer. I played back the message a few minutes later; it was Bill

Sherwood from the Crime Lab. He left a number and asked me to call him back, so I dialed his number.

"You heard about the convictions, no doubt?" I asked.

"Yeah, I called Dina Bernichio, and she gave me the news," Sherwood replied. "Something strange has come up, Devlin. I didn't tell ASA Bernichio, and I don't want to discuss it on the phone. Can we meet?"

"I'm under the weather right now, Bill. Would you like to come over here to discuss it?" I asked.

"I'll be there within the half hour."

I sprayed a half-bottle of Febreeze around and de-puked the house.

CHAPTER 68

July 19, 2014
Saturday
0800 hours

I heard Bill Sherwood's unmarked squad car pull into my driveway within the half hour. I've known Bill my entire career; we were rookies together in the Deuce. He was a great street copper and an even greater lab tech, but our relationship has always been strictly professional. He never called me at home or dropped in for coffee, so I knew this visit was important. I went out onto the front porch to greet him. The old man from across the street hobbled behind his black Pomeranian, Annie. He waved to me and called out, "How's Kerri doing today?" I'd lost track of the number of times I've told him over the last two years that Kerri doesn't live here anymore, but the old guy's in the early stages of dementia.

"Fine, Anthony. Kerri's doing fine."

Bill smiled at me as he neared the stairs. "Looks like you had a rough night, Devlin."

"Too much celebrating," I said. "C'mon in."

Bill followed me into the living room.

"Take a seat. I just made a pot of fresh coffee," I said.

"Thanks, Devlin, but I'll pass on the coffee. I've had my fill already this morning." He eased into the recliner.

"Well, what 'strange thing has come up' that brings you to the Cahill Castle this lovely morn?"

Bill reached inside his sport jacket, removed a piece of paper, and then handed it to me.

He spoke as I began reading the ATF report. "This was on my desk this morning when I got to work. As a matter of procedure, I had ATF run an e-trace on the weapon recovered from McKittrick's safe. They do a history on the gun, from the time it was manufactured until the time it comes into custody."

As I was perusing the report, I asked, "So?"

"So, the DEA hit Pellegrino's brother, Paul, with a narcotics search warrant a year before the murders in Avalon Trails. The weapon recovered from McKittrick's house was seized in that raid. Pellegrino's brother died in the motorcycle accident before his trial, and the weapon was ordered destroyed by a federal judge. According to the ATF Tracing Center in Martinsburg, West Virginia, your murder weapon doesn't exist. It was burned six months ago."

"What?" I exclaimed. "How can that be?"

Bill Sherwood shrugged and shook his head. "I have no idea. I've never heard of such a thing before."

"Could the ATF have run the wrong serial number?" I asked.

"No, that's the gun. If the report had landed on my desk one day earlier while the trial was still in progress, I would have been obligated to notify ASA Bernichio, and you may not have had cause to celebrate last night. I hate to piss on your parade, Devlin, but I thought you should know."

"I appreciate it. Thank you."

Bill stood and I showed him to the door. I watched as he pulled from my driveway, and then I went back inside the house.

I poured another cup of coffee and lit up a panetela. I stood leaning against the kitchen counter and staring at an empty wall in deep thought, completely befuddled. What the hell is going on here? I couldn't come up with a single plausible explanation for how this could happen. Bill Sherwood's words echoed in my ear: *Your murder weapon doesn't exist.*

CHAPTER 69

July 21, 2014
Monday
0745 hours

I don't recall most of the weekend. I remember locking the door and unplugging the phone Saturday morning after Sherwood left and then crying and vomiting intermittently, until I decided somewhere in the early afternoon on Saturday to break my two years of abstinence and raid the liquor cabinet. Judging from the number of empty Jack Daniels' bottles, the party must have lasted well into Sunday. I shouldn't have unplugged the phone; Kerri might have called.

I'd call Dina Bernichio and tell her about the ATF report before it reached her through normal channels, unless Bill Sheridan already had, but not yet. I wanted to make a few inquiries of my own first. I didn't know how the ATF report would affect the convictions of McKittrick and Pellegrino, but it would surely give them a basis for appeal. I'd let the State's Attorney's Office worry about that. My worrying was almost done. McKittrick and Pellegrino were in jail. Kerri was safe; Charlie was out of the woods, and I should be reinstated soon.

I felt better after I showered and shaved and put on a fresh suit, though my eyes were still red and swollen. I'd blame it on alcohol. I planned on spending the day kissing asses. I would go meet with the Special Prosecutor from the State's Attorney's Office first to see if his office planned on dropping charges against me, then I'd take a ride to the IPRA Office to ensure they were aware of McKittrick and Pellegrino's convictions. It would be better if I approached them with a copy of the court transcript in my hand, but I wanted to expedite things. I needed to get back to work more than a heart needs blood.

• • •

An hour later, I took the elevator to the fourteenth floor office of the Special Prosecutor, Chester Carrothers, in the annex building at 26th & California.

Chester was a tall, thin black man, clean-shaven with short-cropped hair, and impeccably dressed in a gray pinstripe and heavily starched white shirt. All he needed was a bow tie, and he could stand on the corner handing out *The Final Call.*

I anticipated a ration of shit from him, but I was pleasantly surprised when he turned out to be cordial and professional. He smiled, shook my hand, congratulated me on the convictions of McKittrick and Pellegrino, and then promised he'd take the matter before the judge later that day and notify the court of the State's Attorney's intention to decline prosecution. One major hurdle out of the way.

• • •

I decided to stop at headquarters on 35th Street to thank Chief Daniels on my way up north to the IPRA offices at Chicago & Ashland. I ran into Curt Scheer, the Bomb and Arson Investigator, in the parking lot.

"Cur-teese the po-leese," I said, and we shook hands.

"What brings you down here, Devlin?"

"I'm on my way to Goldblatt's to blow an IPRA Investigator so I can get back to work and thought I'd stop to say hello to the chief en route."

"Goldblatt's?"

"Yeah, that's where the IPRA offices are at now. I guess you haven't stepped in shit for awhile?"

Curt chuckled. "Not lately, ain't much trouble I can get into in Bomb and Arson, unless I accidentally blow up the building."

"Speaking of Bomb and Arson, anything new on Charlie Newton's car bombing?" I asked.

"We've made some progress," Curt replied, and then asked, "Are you sure you didn't bomb him?"

The question surprised me, but I played along. "I'm sure—though I'd like to sometimes. Why do you ask?"

"Sophisticated VBIED, the kind the Irish Republican Army makes."

My brows raised and my eyes widened. "You think the IRA planted the bomb?" I asked incredulously.

"I have no idea who tried to bomb him," Curt laughed. "I gathered some bomb components and fragments from the scene and submitted the technical information to a couple of national databases. They're the ones that said it looked like an IRA bomb because there were two holes drilled in the end cap, instead of the usual one, which they've only seen before in IRA bombs. But, although the IRA may have perfected car bombs, they teach terrorists all over the world how to make them. Could have been ISIS terrorists for all I know."

"Or some mutt from Taylor Street?"

Curt shrugged. "Whoever it was, they knew their bombs. The bomb was designed to kill one or two people with minimal damage to the car and minimum noise. The car jockey on the first floor didn't even hear it go off. An inexperienced bomber would have put enough explosives in there to wipe out a city block, but there weren't enough explosives in Newton's car to make a good firecracker."

"How about the surveillance cameras?" I asked.

"Two or three parking spaces on each level are out of the camera's range. Unfortunately, Charlie Newton was parked in one of them."

"That figures," I said. "Let me know if you find out anything else, will you?

"You'll be the first to know, Devlin."

Curt and I bid our farewells in the parking lot, and I went up to the fourth floor office of Chief Daniels. The Chief wasn't in so I left a message with his secretary that the State's Attorney's Office dropped the charges against me.

About a half hour later, I entered the IPRA Offices in the annex of the old Goldblatt's Building, a former retail giant, on the fourth floor. I asked to speak to a supervisor; moments later, a skeleton in an ill-fitting blue suit appeared, looking like Vincent Van Gogh with ears, which he sorely needed to secure a pair of wire-rimmed glasses to his head.

"I'm Boris Baranovsky, the IPRA supervisor, how can I help you, sir?"

Boris *fucking* Baranovsky? I fought the urge not to laugh or say, "Where are Natasha and Bullwinkle?" I checked my rapier wit and said, "I'm Lt. Cahill. I've been on indefinite suspension for some time now, and I wanted to inform your office that the complainant in this matter was convicted the other day on three counts of murder. The State's Attorney's Office is dismissing charges against me. I hope both recent developments will have some bearing on IPRA's findings. I'd like to get back to work as soon as possible."

Boris Badenough strolled over to a computer and typed something. He returned a moment later and said, "Investigator Gallagher is handling your complaint register investigation, Lieutenant. It would be best if you talked to him directly."

I followed Boris to a cubicle in the center of the room. Oh no, I thought when Investigator Gallagher swiveled around in his chair. I can't catch a break. It was the same IPRA investigator who came to my house with the Deputy and pizza face from the Bureau of Internal Assholes and later showed up at the hospital when I was shot. Does IPRA only have one investigator? Or am I lucky enough to pull this guy's number out of the hat three times in a row?

Investigator Gallagher glared at me with black, contemptuous eyes and furrowed brows, waiting for me to speak. Whoever spoke first lost. Mind games. I conceded and repeated what I told his supervisor.

"Oh, so now you want a favor?" he smirked. "You want me to expedite my findings to accommodate you?"

He had a pinched face and beady black eyes like a rat, now twinkling smugly with delight and self-satisfaction.

"No, I don't want a favor," I said. "I want you to do your fucking job, you peter puffer."

I think it would be accurate to say the meeting with the Special Prosecutor went better. All wasn't lost, though; maybe Boris would light a fire under Gallagher to close the investigation in the interest of time and efficiency.

I looked least forward to my last pilgrimage to the FBI Headquarters on Roosevelt Road. Didn't know if I should even bother. The G wouldn't tell me anything. As I was cruising west on tree-lined Roosevelt Road past the FBI Building, I got the urge to jump the median in the middle of the street and turn around; go get a steak sandwich at Ricobene's instead. I didn't have the business cards the agents who came to my house gave me, and I hadn't been cordial to them, so I couldn't expect them to treat me any better. But, since I was already there, I thought I'd give it a roll. I parked the car and went in.

I explained to the receptionist that I lost the two agents' business cards and didn't remember their names.

"Do you remember what they looked like?" she asked.

This is stupid, I thought. Waste of my time.

"Dickheads. Two dickheads with short haircuts and wingtip shoes. Anybody around here fit that description?" I asked.

She was still reeling when I left the building. Maybe I could impose upon John Willick to find something out for me.

Habit pointed me toward the Bene's to grab a steak

sandwich, but my stomach was upset, so I decided instead to drop by Area Central to see if any progress had been made on the Schwartzman homicide. If they still considered me the prime suspect, they wouldn't be forthcoming either, but it was worth a shot.

Donovan and Barcomb were sitting at the long rectangular table outside the Commanding Officer's office typing reports when I entered through the back door. They both rose to shake my hand.

"Congratulations on the convictions, Lieu," Donovan said.

"Congratulations to you guys. Charlie Newton could be sitting in the shithouse right now, instead of McKittrick and Pellegrino, if you didn't give us a little leeway."

"Just doing our job," Barcomb said.

"Everybody does their job; some do it better than others, though," I said. "I appreciate all you did for us."

"What brings you back to beautiful Area Central?" Barcomb asked.

"Have you heard anything on the Schwartzman homicide?" I asked.

"No, I know it's still open, but I haven't heard anything new on it," Barcomb replied. "You know our lieutenant, why don't you ask him? He's in his office."

I frowned, "Yeah, I know him, but he's one of those officious types: scowl on his face all the time like he's got a cucumber stuck up his ass."

Barcomb and Donovan laughed. "He's uptight, but he's not a bad guy."

Lt. Thomas Hayes, my counterpart at Area Central,

wasn't a bad guy. I knew that. But he wouldn't have been my choice to run a homicide unit. He was never a detective; spent his entire career in patrol. No doubt he could process a DUI better than I could, but dead people don't drive cars or have to blow breathalyzers, so his talents were wasted.

I knocked on his door. He glanced up from whatever he was reading and motioned for me to enter, with a look on his face like his mother-in-law was coming to visit.

"Hi, Tom, how are you?" I asked.

"Devlin," he acknowledged soberly with a brief nod. Not the warmest reception I've ever received but not the worst either.

"I stopped by to see if there have been any developments on the Schwartzman homicide?"

"No," Hayes said: succinct, to the point, with no superfluous bullshit.

"Suspects?" I asked.

"Yes."

"Tom, let me be frank, my patience is wearing thin and I'm starting to get pissed off, and I'm not a nice man when I'm pissed off. I'm tired of being treated like a leper. When I ask you a question, I expect the courtesy of more than a one-word response."

Hayes sighed, tossed his glasses on the desk, and said, "Yes, Devlin, we have one suspect. I'm talking to him now, and I don't think it's appropriate for me to discuss the case with you."

"That's all you had to say, you anal retentive asshole." I stormed out of his office and slammed the door behind me.

Donovan and Barcomb chuckled outside the office. "How did that go, Lieu?"

"Great!" I said, still red faced. Hayes watched me through the glass. I pointed at him, in overly demonstrative fashion, and told Barcomb and Donovan, "That man will make a great policeman someday." They stepped out of Hayes's line of vision to laugh. I'm sure they would have liked to say the same thing to him a thousand times but lacked the rank to get away with it.

I passed on the Bene's and opted to stop at Walgreen's to grab a bottle of Maalox for lunch instead.

CHAPTER 70

July 21, 2014
Monday
1405 hours

Upon entering the house, toting my Maalox in a plastic bag, I glanced at the phone to see if the message indicator was blinking. It wasn't. I hoped Kerri had called to let me know she arrived okay or maybe left a number where I could reach her. Her parents' phone number was in her directory, and her directory was with her. I didn't even know the town where her parents lived, some rural area outside of Dublin. I never met them but managed to alienate her old man the first, and only, time I ever spoke with him on the phone. He was a gruff old buzzard and had one of those thick brogues that made him sound like he had a mouthful of shit when he talked. Obviously, Kerri inherited her charm from her mother. The miserable curmudgeon asked me what nationality I was, and I said Irish. That was it. That's all I said. You would have thought I rammed a shillelagh up his ass. He called me a DP, narrowback, "fookin" Yankee and hung up on me. I said, "Happy St. Patrick's Day to you, too, sir," into a dead phone. Kerri laughed and said he and I would get along famously. I don't think so.

If Kerri calls, I'm going to ask her to come back to Chicago. I'll pay her alimony or maintenance or whatever they call it these days, and she can have this house. That's all it is to me now, a house. It hasn't been a home since she left. Besides, what single, macho, heterosexual male has salmon-colored carpeting? This is not a man cave.

I filled a wine glass with Maalox and went to sit out on the patio. The grass was on the ragged side, and the flowerbed wasn't looking too healthy either, but the warmth of the sun penetrated my tired body, and the sweet nectar from the lilac bushes and a trellis of roses swept across the yard on the faintest of breezes. I gulped down the Maalox, lit a cigar, and lay back in the chaise lounge. My red, swollen eyes burned and pulsated when I closed them. They became heavy after a moment, and I drifted off into a twilight state. Somewhere in the far distance, I heard Michael Jackson singing, *"I don't understand the way you think, saying that she's yours, not mine, sending roses and your silly dreams, are really just a waste of time, the girl is mine."* I ran after him, and when I caught up to him and spun him around, it wasn't the face of Michael Jackson. It was Emmett McKittrick. My nerve endings twitched and convulsed like from an electric shock, and I bolted upright in the chaise, the cigar still lit and stuck between my fingers.

"No, you're wrong, Emmett," I said, giving voice to my thoughts, "the girl is mine. The doggone girl is mine."

CHAPTER 71

July 22, 2014
Tuesday
0810 hours

My body ached, my eyes were on fire, and my throat was raw from vomiting. I hadn't slept again, but my stomach knew alcohol wasn't the answer. I didn't know what to do with myself; I couldn't eat and I couldn't sleep, I didn't have anyone to talk to and I had no place to go, but I knew I had to stay busy to keep my mind off of Kerri, so I did housework. Several hours later, the house was spotless and I was exhausted. An immaculate house and salmon-colored carpeting; maybe I am gay?

At 4:15 PM, the phone rang. I hurried to pick it up before the answering machine took the call, hoping it was Kerri. It was Charlie.

"Devlin lad, good fortune has once again smiled upon me. My Corvette was totaled twenty minutes ago. Shattered like a champagne bottle at a ship's christening."

"Are you okay?" I asked.

"I'm talking to you, aren't I?"

"What happened?"

"An inept motorist rear-ended me on Interstate 94."

"I'm glad your driving ninety-five miles per hour and weaving in and out of traffic didn't have anything to do with it. Where are you now?"

"The state trooper investigating the accident was kind enough to give me a ride to the Congress Plaza."

"Do you want me to pick you up and take you to a car rental place to get another car—if anyone will lease you another car?"

"Thank you, but no. I'm leaving for Jamaica Thursday and I've decided not to rent another car. I have a few revisions and some editing I want to get done on my manuscript before I leave, so I'm going to lock myself in my room for the next several days and work."

"Sounds grueling, locking yourself in a $500-a-day suite with room service. Are you sure you'll be okay?"

"I'm a survivor, Devlin lad."

I stacked my Clint Eastwood DVDs on the cherry wood coffee table and went through them. I turned on the TV and slipped *Million Dollar Baby* into the Blu-ray, a morose choice given my current state of mind. Clint nicknamed his female boxing protégé in the movie Mo Cuishle, which means *my darling* or *my blood* in Gaelic. Though I've seen the movie fifty times, I couldn't bear to watch the ending again. Not today. I lost my Mo Cuishle in the end, too. I hit eject.

CHAPTER 72

July 23, 2014
Wednesday
0730 hours

Sparrows chirped and the fragrant morning dew leaked through the windows. Bright sun obscured the TV screen. When I rose from the sofa, I was surprised to find I felt refreshed, invigorated. The pains and aches were gone. I lit a cigar and strolled over to the picture window to look out upon a placid, serene morn, worthy of a Norman Rockwell illustration. The old man across the street was being dragged down the block by his nine-pound Pom on a pink leash. His seventy-five-year-old neighbor wore a straw sunbonnet and was on her knees working in the front garden.

I sauntered into the kitchen and dumped a carafe of cold water into the Bunn, then sliced open a couple of hamburger buns, buttered them, and popped them into the broiler. Amazing what a good night's sleep, fresh air, sunshine, and a cigar can do for the body and human spirit.

I ate the toasted buns and took my second cup of coffee into the bathroom with me while I took a cold shower. God, I was feeling good.

I didn't have an itinerary for the day, but moping around the house all day wasn't on the agenda. I put on a pair of khaki chinos, pulled a green polo the color of summer grass over my head, and slipped on a pair of calfskin leather boat shoes. All dressed up and no place to go.

I called the Congress Plaza to see if Charlie wanted to meet me someplace for breakfast or lunch, but the front desk informed me Mr. Newton wasn't accepting any calls.

I could drive to Donna's Café Chicago in the South Loop for breakfast, or I could drive around until lunchtime and hit the Bene's. I decided on Donna's. I was in a good mood, and Donna always gave me a good shot of laughter in the arm. Donna's it was.

I was heading toward the door leading to the garage when the phone rang; still hoping Kerri would call, I jogged to the phone. It was Chief Daniels on the other end.

"Devlin, good news. I talked to IPRA, and you've been reinstated. You can pick up your badge and ID at personnel."

I tried not to let the excitement show in my voice. "That is great news, Chief. I've been waiting for months to hear those words."

"I thought you would be."

"Do I still have Area South?" I asked.

"I haven't been told otherwise."

"I'm surprised they closed their investigation, though, with the federal investigation still pending."

"There is no federal investigation pending. Somehow, you must have managed to garner a friend at the FBI Office. They closed their investigation, too."

It was over. Done. Finis. Charlie was no longer a suspect in a triple murder; the feds, the state, and the police department were no longer investigating me, though I was still under the umbrella of suspicion for the Schwartzman homicide, which reminded me that Art Kiese had never contacted me.

This was indeed starting out to be a beautiful day. I'd go to personnel and pick up my badge and ID on the way to Donna's. I hooked the hip-grip on my five-shot onto my waistband and was out the door. I was beginning to feel like a policeman again already.

I backed the Beamer out of the garage, dropped the top, and sped off up Central Park at Charlie-Newton speed.

Forty-five minutes later, I was standing in the personnel office at Police Headquarters. A police officer handed me the badge, and I stared at it like a long-lost friend. Funny, I thought, how a piece of tin can mean so much to someone. I slipped it into the back pocket of my chinos and left the office.

• • •

Donna saw me enter the Café Chicago and met me at the front door. "Do I have to hide you in the back room again, or can you sit out here with the law-abiding folks?"

"You do remember I was your boss, don't you?" I asked.

"Hmmm, hmm, but I'm the boss up in here, cracker. Do you need a menu?"

"No, give me ham and eggs and grits, and don't spit in my grits."

"Then yo' ass better change that attitude."

Donna came back a few minutes later, a few extra slices of ham on the plate and an additional egg or two. She sat down at the table with me.

"Seriously, Devlin, how's everything going?"

"Couldn't be better, Donna," I said, and I brought her up to date on everything. She said she had other customers she had to take care of, leaned across the table and kissed me on the cheek. "By the way, them grits taste funny to you?"

"Bye, bitch."

• • •

I decided to take a ride up north to the IPRA Offices and tell Gallagher I was sorry. I was kind of rough on him.

I entered the fourth floor offices and walked to a cubicle in the center of the room.

"Investigator Gallagher," I said.

Gallagher spun around in his swivel chair and eyed me suspiciously.

"I came to apologize to you," I said, "for everything. I'm sorry I called you names and gave you a rough time. I know it's no excuse, but police lieutenants are humans, too, and sometimes when humans are under extreme pressure, they don't respond appropriately. I hope you will accept my apology." I held out my hand.

"You understand, Lieutenant, there was a finding of non-sustained against you for the altercation you had with Emmett McKittrick, but the Schwartzman investigation is still open and pending?"

"I'm aware of that, but the Schwartzman investigation

wasn't preventing me from coming back to work. Now, that I'm back to work, thanks to you, maybe I'll be able to clear it. In any event, I want to thank you for expediting your findings. I'm sorry I called you names."

My hand was still hanging out there in the air. Gallagher's eyes were dark brown, not black. His features softened, and he smiled, then extended his hand.

"That's okay, Lieutenant, I understand. I've been under the gun a few times myself."

We shook hands, and as I walked away, Gallagher called out to me, "Lieutenant."

I stopped and turned around. He was laughing. "Where did you ever come up with peter puffer?"

We were both laughing when I left the building. Turned out he wasn't such a bad guy after all.

• • •

The day was young. Where to go? What to do? I called the Scum Times and asked if Art Kiese had ever come back to work. They told me he hadn't, so I decided I'd take a ride back to Presidential Towers.

I was able to flash a badge to the security officer this time, which made the inquiry more officious.

"I was here a while back and left a card with you for Mr. Kiese to call me. Do you know if he ever got that message?" I asked.

"I don't know for sure, officer, but I don't think he did. I used to see Mr. Kiese almost every day at the end of my tour, but I haven't seen him in months. You may want to check with one of our rental agents and see if he even still lives here. He may have moved. They come and go all the time.'"

I thanked him for his help and checked with the rental office on the way out. The rental agent told me Kiese still lived there and was up to date on his rent.

When I got back into my car, I called the office on my Blackberry. Sgt. Abels answered.

"Congratulations, Devlin. We read about your court victory, and everybody's looking forward to your return. The place isn't the same without you. We miss your wit and charm."

"Thanks, dickwad, but I'm still not out of harm's way. I told the editor of the Scum Times if he cut me some slack I'd clear this Schwartzman case. He held up his end of the bargain, and I want to hold up mine."

"What do you need?"

"I'm trying to track down one of Schwartzman's friends, a guy named Art Kiese. A few months ago, I asked Barcomb and Donovan to run him for an address. They came back with two guys named Art Kiese; one guy was seventy years old and the other guy was thirty-five. The younger guy is the one I'm interested in. He lives in Presidential Towers, but he hasn't been seen there in months, nor has he returned to work. This is starting to smell. Could you run the name again for me and get me an address on the older Kiese? He lives somewhere on the north side. Maybe it's his old man?"

"No problem. I'll call you back in a few minutes."

• • •

I pulled out of the parking lot and started heading in that general direction on I-94. A few minutes later, Sgt. Abels called me back.

"Arthur Kiese, DOB 1944, 5000 West Balmoral. Do you need anything else?" Sgt. Abels asked.

"No, that should do it," I said. "I'll stop by the office when I'm done here."

• • •

I pulled up in front of a large white house on a double lot with a white picket fence around it. A large black Doberman pranced anxiously by the gate as a scraggly, geeky-looking guy, carrying an armful of groceries, approached the house. Looked like a Network Systems Analyst to me if I ever saw one. When I stepped out of my car, he dropped the groceries on the ground and flipped over the fence, running for the front doorway, with the dog running playfully by his side. I pulled my gun and ordered him to stop as I flipped over the fence after him. Flashbacks of John Giaccone turning and shooting me went through my head. I was tired of being used for a silhouette target. If this guy as much as turned his head toward me, I'd put a hole in his skull you could drive an L train through.

I caught him as he reached the front door. Fortunately, the Dobie had the heart of a Poodle and ran around to the back of the house. Scraggly man crouched down and put his arms over his face and began screaming, "Don't kill me; please don't kill me."

I stared at him like he was insane. "I'm not going to

kill you, dickwad; stop screaming before somebody calls the police."

A few seconds later, he lowered his arms from his face.

"Stand up," I ordered him. "What in the name of Christ is wrong with you?"

Kiese stood up warily. "You're Cahill, right?"

"Yes, you're Art Kiese, right?"

Kiese was still visibly shaken. He blinked and licked his lips.

"Can we go inside and talk?" I asked.

Kiese didn't respond. I could read in his eyes that he was afraid to go into the house with me alone.

"If I wanted to kill you, I would have killed you when you took off running. The last guy that did that turned around and shot me."

Reluctantly, he opened the front door, and I followed him across a glossy dark hardwood floor into the parlor where he motioned for me to be seated on one of the matching floral-patterned love seats opposite each other. A magnificent Rococo-style rosewood and burl Steinway baby grand piano, with intricately carved serpentine legs, was nestled in the oriel of the room, and a large oil painting of a distinguished-looking elderly gentleman with white hair and penetrating blue eyes hung over the mantel of a white brick fireplace.

"Beautiful home," I commented.

"Thank you, it's my father's," Kiese replied, pointing over his shoulder at the painting.

I nodded toward the baby grand, "Do you play?"

"No, my mother was the musician. She passed away several years ago."

"Art, I'm guessing you think I killed Eric, too, and that's why you've been running from me?"

"I haven't been running from you; I didn't even know you knew I existed."

"Why haven't you been back to work, then, or back to your apartment in Presidential Towers?" I asked.

"I haven't been back to work because I'm not going back to work. They gave me a paid leave, and I'm going to milk it as long as I can. As far as going back to my apartment, my father is in the hospital dying of pancreatic cancer, and I've been staying here to take care of the house and Percival."

"Percival? I asked.

"Yeah, the Dobe, my mother named him."

"If I don't learn anything else here today, I know why the dog ran away. Sheer embarrassment."

Kiese smiled.

"I'm sorry if I scared you. That wasn't my intention, but why the hell did you run?"

"Honestly, I don't know. I recognized you from your photo in the newspaper, and I got scared and ran."

"I know a lot of people believe I killed Eric, and I'm trying to clear my name and solve his murder. I'm told you were his best friend. and I was hoping there was something he may have said, or told you, that could help the investigation."

"How do I know you didn't kill him?" Kiese asked.

"You don't know, neither does anyone else, except me and the guy who killed him. What can I possibly say or do to convince you, other than find his murderer?"

Kiese collected himself, glanced down at several computer magazines on the coffee table. and nervously began aligning them with his fingertips. We sat in silence for several seconds as I waited for him to speak, but he continued rearranging the magazine display.

"Did Eric have any enemies that you know of, besides me, of course?"

Kiese shook his head.

"When was the last time you saw or talked to him?" I asked.

"I talked to him on the phone a few hours before he was murdered."

"What did he say?"

Kiese looked at me for the first time and sighed.

"He said he was going to go meet you."

CHAPTER 73

July 23, 2014
Wednesday
1545 hours

"He said he was going to meet me?" I asked skeptically.

"That's what he said."

"Why would Schwartzman go to meet me? We didn't like each other."

"I don't know. Eric rambled when he was excited. He said something about a friend of his, a foreign correspondent, who gave him information on a drug cartel and a defunct airline, and then he said he was going to meet with you."

I studied Kiese's expressionless face as he continued to push the magazines around. He was scared but telling the truth.

"Art, I promise you, I wasn't supposed to meet Schwartzman that night, or any other night. The last time I saw or spoke to him was that morning of the triple homicide."

"Maybe he said he wanted to meet with you, I'm not sure."

"I don't work in Narcotics; why would he want to meet me to talk about a drug cartel?" I asked.

"I have no idea. I can only tell you what he told me."

"Did he give you the name of his friend who is the foreign correspondent?"

"No. He said the guy was a foreign correspondent in China and he was locked up by the Chinese government."

"For what?" I asked.

"He didn't say."

"What about the drug cartel?"

"I believe he said they are called the Cocaine Importers Association."

"Are they here or in China?"

"He didn't say."

"What does a defunct airlines have to do with any of this shit?"

"He didn't say."

"Did he mention the name of the airlines?" I asked.

"I thought he said American Airlines, but I'm not sure."

"American Airlines isn't defunct."

Kiese shrugged.

"Is there anything else you can tell me?"

For the first time since we sat down, Kiese lifted his gaze from the magazines and looked me in the face, then sighed.

"It's true, I probably was Eric's best friend, and I guess it would be fair to say that I was also his worst friend, because I was his only friend. He was a nice guy, but we weren't that close to be honest with you. You had to take everything

Eric said with a grain of salt. Most people couldn't listen to his bullshit. He thought he was overqualified to be doing local news, and he wanted to be an investigative reporter in the worst way, like Bob Woodward and Carl Bernstein, so he added yeast to everything he said or wrote."

"I can attest to that," I said.

"I don't want to talk bad about the guy, he's dead, but I don't want to see you spin your wheels trying to track down his friend, the foreign correspondent, who may not exist. Like I said, Eric didn't have friends."

"Thanks for being so candid, Art. Schwartzman may not have had friends, but he certainly had enemies, at least one."

CHAPTER 74

July 24, 2014
Thursday
1000 hours

Thursday arrived, Charlie's departure date. No telling when I'd see him again; Charlie drifts in and out of one's life. I called him at the Congress.

He perked up when he heard my voice. "Devlin lad, call to say goodbye?"

"No, I called to give you a ride to O'Hare."

"Thoughtful, but not necessary. I'll grab a cab."

"I insist. I want to make sure you get out of Shitcago without getting involved in any more murders, and besides, it's the city's gas."

"Since you put it that way, can you pick me up in front of the Congress in about two hours?"

The conversation last night with Kiese haunted me. It didn't make any sense. I called the Narcotics Section before leaving to pick up Charlie.

"Is Sgt. Martin working?" I asked.

A moment later, Tom Martin, my ex-partner, picked up the phone.

"Tom, have you ever hear of a drug cartel called the Cocaine Importers Association?" I asked.

He began laughing. "I certainly have."

"What can you tell me about them?"

"Nothing you don't already know," he said.

"I don't know shit about them."

"You're getting slow on the upswing, Devlin. I don't think they're called the Cocaine Importers *Association*; they're called the Cocaine Importers *Agency*—C.I.A."

My mind raced. I don't remember saying goodbye or hanging up the phone. I went to the computer and looked up defunct airlines. Minutes later, I learned an airlines called Air America was a CIA front, which had reportedly ceased operations in 1976. I called Art Kiese and asked him if the airline Schwartzman had told him about could have been Air America, not American Airlines. He said he was sure that was the name of the airline.

What the hell was I into? Pieces of the puzzle were all starting to fall into place, but I still didn't have a clear view of the whole picture. Homicide victim, Chiang Yu, from the Province of Yunnan; homicide victim, Hiram Goldenstein, laundering Chinese dope money through the Mercantile Exchange; Schwartzman's story to Kiese about receiving information from a foreign correspondent in China and the CIA and Air America. Did Schwartzman finally uncover his big story about the CIA's complicity in the importation of drugs into this country, and it got him killed? CIA involvement would explain the murder weapon in federal custody mysteriously reappearing after it was supposedly destroyed.

• • •

Two hours later, I was parked in the taxi lane in front of the Congress. A First District squad car rolled up on me, recognized the vehicle as an unmarked police vehicle, gave an acknowledged wave and cruised by. A minute later, Charlie exited the Congress. I popped the trunk, and he loaded all his worldly belongings into it: a leather suitcase, a drab olive duffel bag, and a laptop.

It began drizzling as I pulled away. By the time I got to the entrance of the Eisenhower Expressway, the skies opened up. The rain pounding on the car was deafening. I turned the wipers and the defrosters on high and cranked up the volume on the police radio. Taillights of vehicles in front of us were barely visible as we inched forward.

"Not that I haven't enjoyed your company, Devlin lad, but there's a tall, dark woman in a white bikini waiting for me in Jamaica with two ice-cold Red Stripes. I'm looking forward to seeing her."

I leaned over the steering wheel and strained to see out the windshield.

"Sure you can't come?" Charlie asked.

"Us guys who have real jobs can't take off on a whim, Hemingway. More bad guys to catch—more dancers."

"Dancers?"

"Private joke," I said.

The storm put a stranglehold on northbound traffic. Red brake lights loomed up in front of me. Distance was hard to judge, and I kept hitting the brakes harder than necessary. I lit up a cigar to help me focus.

"Are you going to smoke that in this car with the windows rolled up?" Charlie asked.

"Roll your window down if it bothers you. I thought you'd be used to it by now."

Thirty minutes elapsed without conversation. Charlie let me concentrate on the road, but I was concentrating on something else. We crawled toward the last tollbooth on I-294 before the O'Hare Airport exit.

Charlie broke the silence. "I'm glad our adventure came to a successful conclusion, aren't you?"

"I'm not so sure it did," I said.

"Why would you say that with McKittrick and Pellegrino behind bars?"

"Several things about the case bother me."

"Such as?"

"Such as, do you remember the first time we met twelve years ago?"

"Like it was yesterday," Charlie replied.

"I remember thinking at the time I would have made you for anything but a novelist, and I'm rarely wrong about these things. Intuition and a good left hook are my gifts."

Charlie started to say something, but I interrupted him. "Let me finish. We only have a few minutes before we get to O'Hare." I took a shot at the ashtray from half-court with my cigar and missed. "My intuition told me that night when I had you stand by the door of the interrogation room that when Pellegrino said he had never seen you before, he was telling the truth. I dismissed the idea, though, because if he was telling the truth, that meant you were lying."

"So you think I was lying?" Charlie asked.

I didn't respond to the question.

"Did you ever meet my friend, Dominic Vimarco?" I asked.

Charlie thought about it a moment and then said, "I don't believe so."

"Dominic was the CPD's range instructor for years. He has a wall full of trophies and plaques for competition shooting. I asked him a couple of days ago if he could put five bullets in the 10-ring from seventy feet away at night with a snub nose. Do you know what he said?"

"No idea."

"He said he wished he could. He'd be one of the best marksman in the country."

"Really?"

"Yeah, *really*. That started me thinking about my visit from John Willick, the FBI agent. Even the FBI was dumbfounded that the U.S. Attorney's Office didn't prosecute you, or the two guys on the plane, on that narcotic's seizure in the '80s. And, of course, there was your trip to Laos. You've conferred with me on every manuscript you've ever written but failed to mention to me any manuscript set in Laos. Strange."

"Not so strange, Devlin lad. It wasn't a police- related manuscript. Why would I mention it to you?"

"Maybe not, but it still strikes me as odd," I said. "By the way, did you ever write that manuscript? I'd like to read it sometime."

"Not yet, but I'll get around to it someday. Perhaps after I get this manuscript published."

I changed the subject abruptly. "Do you remember the night we abducted Kerri?"

Charlie chortled, "Of course I do; I don't have Alzheimer's."

"I directed you to the block she lived on that night, but I didn't tell you which house she lived in. You pulled up right in front of her house like you'd been there before."

"I assumed it was the one with the three police cruisers parked in front of it."

"That would have been a logical assumption, other than the fact we couldn't see out the car windows that night with the driving sleet."

"Maybe you couldn't from your vantage point in the passenger seat, but I could from the driver's seat."

I continued, "Then there's the car bomb. Sophisticated, designed to cause minimum damage with minimum noise, it goes off prematurely, and you don't get a scratch. How lucky for you."

"Would you have been happier if I lost a hand or an arm?" Charlie asked.

"I don't think there was much chance of that happening, Charlie. It was also strange you happened to park the car in one of only two parking spaces out of the surveillance camera's range."

"I took whatever parking space was available."

"Do you know what bothers me the most?" I asked.

"Trust me, Devlin lad, I have no idea."

"The murder weapon."

"Why does that bother you?"

"A couple of reasons. The gun was in the custody of the federal government and ordered destroyed, but it somehow turns up in McKittrick's safe several months later, and how stupid would an attorney have to be to hold on to a gun used in a triple homicide? If it were me, I'd put as much distance between me and that gun as possible and go buy another one for a couple hundred bucks if I felt I needed protection. I'm sure McKittrick's financial situation allowed him to do that."

"How else would the gun get into McKittrick's safe?"

"As his attorney pointed out in closing arguments, someone well trained and skilled in safecracking could defeat the locking mechanism. He'd have to be smart, like a member of Mensa."

"So what's your theory, Devlin lad?"

"Homicide investigations are like puzzles. Individual pieces of the puzzle may seem insignificant when they stand alone, but when you put them all together, they form a picture. Everything seems to keep coming back to the government. The U.S. Attorney's Office declined to prosecute you on a prosecutable case; you're in Laos, presumably doing research for a book, where coincidentally one of our victims is from; a gun is missing from federal custody; a sophisticated bomb is planted in your car but nobody is hurt and you're parked in one of two spaces that's out of the camera's view; and there's a novelist with no military or police training who ranks as a world-class marksman. That's when it occurred to me what a wonderful cover it would be for a spook, a CIA operative, to pose as a novelist. He could travel in and out of every country in the world under the pretext of doing research for a book. Nobody would give a second look at a guy who's been on the bestseller's list twice. What do you think about my theory?"

"Great plot for a book. Would you mind if I borrowed it for my next novel?"

"Be my guest."

The rain let up and Charlie powered down his window, hung his head out, and inhaled deeply. "I love the petrichor of a summer morn, Devlin lad."

My cell phone rang, and I answered it. "Thank you, John, I appreciate the information."

I volunteered, "That was John Willick."

"How's John doing these days?" Charlie asked facetiously.

"He's fine. I called him before I left the house to pick you up."

"You and John are friends now, are you?" Charlie asked.

"In a manner of speaking," I said. "Have you ever heard of Air America?"

"Not that I can recall," Charlie replied.

"It was a front run by the CIA, supposedly ceased operation in 1976," I said.

"Ol' John is a wealth of information, isn't he?"

"Actually, I got that information off of the Internet last night. I called John this morning to ask him if he could find out the name of the airline you were suspected of being onboard in the '80s."

"Let me guess—Air America."

"Chalk up another right answer for the Mensa guy," I said.

"Did you know, Devlin, that CIA agents are required to keep their identities and their assignments secret, even from their own families?" Charlie asked. "And even if they're killed in the line of duty, their names are not posted on the Memorial Wall at Langley. They're simply represented by a star."

"You seem to know a lot about it," I said.

"No secret. The CIA conducts public tours of their facility, you know? It's open to the general public."

"Do they show tourists the white residue in the cargo areas of Air America?"

"You're letting your imagination play tricks on you, Devlin," Charlie said with a hollow smile.

"I can understand why a CIA agent couldn't, or wouldn't, divulge his identity, but, if I were to ask my friend, Charlie Newton, to deny he's a CIA agent, what would he say?"

"He'd say, we're at the International terminal, Devlin lad. I'd love to continue this conversation, it's intriguing, but I must go before the ice melts in the cooler with my two Red Stripes. I'll send you a copy of the manuscript when I'm done with it."

Charlie took all of his worldly possessions out of the trunk, slung the strap of his canvas duffel bag over his shoulder, and said, "Last chance. Sure you don't want to come?"

"No, thanks. I booked a flight on Aer Lingus."

"Good for you. You're not as dense as I thought," Charlie said. "Any more questions?"

"One," I said, nodding toward his shoulder, "Where was that duffel bag when you were abducted? It wasn't in your room because I searched it myself, and it wasn't in your rental car the police seized. Did Pellegrino and

Giaccone allow you pack a bag before they abducted you?"

Charlie smirked brazenly, like he beat me in a game of chess, and then mouthed the words, "Must have left it at Pete and Beth's."

I watched him as he strode toward the International terminal doors.

"Charlie," I called out, "What's the name of your next book?"

He stopped, turned around, and smiled back at me. "*Dead Men*, Devlin lad … *Dead Men*."

The End

ABOUT THE AUTHOR

 Author Dennis Banahan is a retired Chicago Police Lieutenant who, after a colorful thirty-year career, retired as one of the department's most highly decorated officers. He was a homicide detective from 1973-1981, and then transferred into the Narcotics Section, where he worked with the US Department of Justice's Drug Enforcement Agency Task Force. He was promoted to lieutenant in 1991 and headed both the Tactical and Gang Units at the time of his retirement, after which he wrote his first novel, *Threshold of Pain*.

Made in the USA
Lexington, KY
22 March 2018